SEAWEED ON ICE

Stanley Evans

TouchWood
Editions

TouchWood Editions
www.touchwoodeditions.com

Library and Archives Canada Cataloguing in Publication
Evans, Stan, 1931–
Seaweed on ice / Stanley Evans.—1st ed.

ISBN-13: 978-1-894898-51-5
ISBN-10: 1-894898-51-6

I. Title.
PS8559.V36S39 2006   C813.54   C2006-904952-1

Edited by Rhonda Batchelor
Proofread by Jonathan Dore
Book design by R-House Design
Cover design by Jacqui Thomas
Front-cover photo by Gremlin/iStockphoto

We gratefully acknowledge the financial support for our publishing activities
from the Government of Canada through the Canada Book Fund, Canada
Council for the Arts, and the province of British Columbia through the
British Columbia Arts Council and the Book Publishing Tax Credit.

2 3 4 5 13 12 11 10

PRINTED IN CANADA

to Helena and Olivia

CHAPTER ONE

My troubles started after a young sea lion hauled itself onto the beach below the Warrior Reserve. Old Mary Cooke told us that in a previous life the sea lion had been a beaver. Now he was a lost soul who didn't quite know how to be a sea lion and was too stubborn to learn. He was no good for anything, except barking—he shone at that. His barking kept the whole reserve awake. After a week, we were really fed up.

Then Chief Alphonse had a dream about a one-legged dwarf. When Chief Alphonse yelled at his dream dwarf it turned into a sea lion. Old Mary Cooke said it was a dream from the unknown world. Chief Alphonse took a spirit stick from his medicine bag, made some medicine over it with his hands and told his dream to the sea lion. The sea lion stopped barking, waddled into the ocean, and that was the last we saw of it.

I was looking forward to balancing my sleep deficit, but that night howling winds and a cold snap hit Vancouver Island, freezing beaver ponds and driving deer down from the northern peaks. Driftwood being pounded onto the shore outside my cabin brought me awake before dawn. Above the tumult, I heard revving engines—hunters were leaving the reserve in SUVs. Our tribe was getting things ready for Winter Ceremonial; fresh game was needed.

I got out of bed, threw a couple of logs into my wood stove and opened the damper.

My phone rang. It was Moran, sounding ticked. "Get over to the gym, Silas. I need you right away."

"You mean right away immediately? Or right away when it's daylight?"

"Right away immediately. Isaac is missing. He hasn't been home the last two nights."

"Call 911."

"What's the matter with you?" Moran asked bitterly. "Are you too busy to help your old friends now?"

"Take it easy. I'll be there as soon as I can," I promised.

I opened the faucet to fill my coffee pot. Nothing. The pipes had frozen. Outside, my rain barrel was covered with ice—I had to bust a hole to get water. Inside again, I heated it to wash, shave and make coffee. After that I spent 15 minutes scraping ice off my car's windows before I could drive it downtown. A wrecker was winching a car out of a ditch near Catherine Street. I slowed down after seeing that, and parked in my usual spot behind Swans Hotel.

Moran's Gymnasium occupies the top floor of a two-storey heritage building. Once, when Victoria was young, the place was probably a ship chandler's or a gold-rush outfitter's or an opium den. Now the bottom floor was rented to a woman who sold second-hand ladies' fashions. I entered the building through a side door and climbed a steep flight of stairs to the gymnasium.

Walking into Moran's is like stepping into the 1950s—except seedier. Moran didn't believe in opening windows, so a couple of ceiling fans were blending the odours of sweat, liniment, long-dead cigars and coffee into a mix potent enough to kill canaries. Old boxing posters covered the gym's exposed-brick walls. Bare light bulbs cast inadequate rays over weight-training machines and punching bags. Despite the weather and the early hour, two hopefuls were already hammering each other in the boxing ring. A couple of old pugs sat on folding chairs, checking the *Racing News*. Three young gym rats were there too, fooling around with speed bags. Tony the masseur had a half-naked man stretched out on his leather-covered table. Tony glanced up from pummelling his client's muscular back. "Chrissake, it's Silas Seaweed. You here for a workout?"

"I'm looking for Moran."

"Moran's around here someplace," Tony said. "Help yourself to coffee."

I was splashing coffee into a mug when the washroom door banged open. Moran appeared, zipping up his fly. He looked angry as usual, but I didn't take it personally—Moran had spent his whole life concealing all emotions except cynicism and rage. As always, the old scrapper wore a wrinkled grey suit, white shirt, red necktie and a black fedora. He looked rather likeable, in spite of two cauliflower ears and meaty red lips.

Moran came over, planted his feet like a boxer and said belligerently, "You took your own sweet time getting here."

"What's the hurry?"

"It's like I told you on the phone. I ain't seen Isaac Schwartz in two days."

I couldn't understand why Moran was so upset about it. "Isaac's a grown man, not a kid. Maybe he took a day off."

Moran's eyebrows came together in a scowl. "He don't get days off. He's my *resident* janitor. Isaac's slept in this gym every night for 20 years."

I'd tasted the coffee and was now dumping it in the sink. "What'd you make this out of, acorns?"

Moran wasn't listening. He hunched his shoulders and said, "Day before yesterday, Isaac swept the gym and emptied the garbage cans. After lunch he went out, and that's the last I've seen of him." He reached into his pocket for a cylinder of Rolaids, peeled back the silver wrap and popped a tablet into his mouth. He offered one to me, but I shook my head.

Moran burped. "Goddammit," he said. He looked miserable.

"Okay," I said. "Let's take a look at Isaac's room."

Moran opened a door next to the locker room and switched on the light. I'd known Isaac Schwartz for years, but this was the first time I'd seen how he lived. His home was a windowless fleapit, about 12 feet by 10, with as much charm as a welding shop. An unframed picture of the Banff Springs Hotel was taped above an iron bed. There was a chest of drawers, a wooden table, a kitchen chair. The room was lined with books. Cartons full of books jammed the space beneath the bed. Shirer's *Rise and Fall of the Third Reich* and Reitlinger's *Final Solution: The Attempt to Exterminate the Jews of Europe* lay on Isaac's table, along with miscellaneous cutlery, odd cups and plates, a jar of Robertson's marmalade. Isaac's bed was the only neat object in the room; it looked as if a soldier had just readied it for inspection. The top blanket was stretched tight and folded with a sharp crease where it covered the pillow. I pulled the blanket aside, exposing musty flannel sheets and a mouse-coloured pillow flecked with spots of blood. A damp greyish blotch discoloured the centre of the bottom sheet. This glimpse into the secrets of male desolation was too much for Moran. He cleared his throat noisily, shuffled his feet and turned his eyes away.

I lowered my face toward the stained sheet and sniffed. "Did Isaac bring women in here?" I asked.

Moran flushed with embarrassment. "What kinda question's that?"

"I'm asking you. Did Isaac bring women in?"

My question disturbed Moran's tough-guy pose. "Hell no," he said, evading my eyes. "Isaac Schwartz never picked up a girl in his life."

"The hell he didn't," I said. "How old are you?"

Moran's mouth opened in surprise. "What?"

"I asked how old you are. About 70?"

My abrupt questions were getting to him. Moran mumbled, "I'm 76."

"Isaac was probably older than you. I guess he was in his 80s."

"So what?"

I smiled. "You think Isaac was past it, Moran? Couldn't get it up?"

Moran's head sagged under the weight of his embarrassment. "Jesus," he said, still blushing, "Maybe Isaac *could* get it up. But so what? It makes no difference. I know he never brought no women into my gym."

"Why not? Give a man a prescription for Viagra and there's no telling what he'll do."

Moran's lips tightened. "Well, even if he did, he wouldn't tell *me* about it. The guy's been with me for 20 years but I hardly know him. He sweeps the floor, locks up at night and that's that. He's kind of a loner. Isaac's only real friend is Nimrod."

"Yeah, Nimrod," I said. "Nimrod was quite a handful, in his heyday."

"You got that right," Moran replied, finally agreeing with something I said. "But Nimrod's no fun neither. Not since he found Jesus and went on the wagon. I ain't seen him lately either, come to think of it."

Isaac's table had a single drawer. I opened it. The drawer was cluttered with old keys, nuts and bolts, a hairbrush, a pair of opera glasses, a shoe horn and an ancient Webley .38 eight-shot revolver. I lifted the gun and sighted down its empty barrel. The gun was rusty and hadn't been fired in years. I put the Webley on the table and shoved more junk around in the drawer until I found a cigar box at the back. It was full of old letters and photographs. One photograph showed a stern-faced old man with a huge walrus moustache, sitting in a bamboo chair. The photographer's trademark was embossed in the lower left-hand corner: "Mueller, Bad Harzburg, 1883." The reverse side was blank. It occurred to me that in the whole world there was probably nobody, apart from Isaac Schwartz, who could now identify this long-deceased man. There were a few family snapshots, one of which showed a young couple accompanied by two small children dressed in sailor suits. The letters were written in a heavy, undecipherable Gothic script. A Canadian Immigration ID card attested that Schwartz, Isaac Jacob, a German, had arrived in Quebec City from Bremen aboard the steamer *Samaria* on April 23, 1948.

I showed the ID card to Moran. He sighed. "The poor guy should have stayed in Germany. He never had much fun in Canada."

"Jews weren't having much fun in Europe back then either."

Two faint black parallel lines scuffed the linoleum floor between Isaac's bed and the door. With Moran trailing me, I followed the lines until they faded out a few feet beyond Isaac's room. We went through the gym and down the steps. Here and there I saw faint black smudges and traces of the same parallel lines. At the bottom of the stairs a narrow corridor led to a rear emergency exit. Moran opened the door. Nothing. The only thing worth looking at was a dumpster, but it had just been emptied. I told Moran I'd report Isaac's absence to Missing Persons.

We shook hands and I left the gym. For a few minutes I just stood on the sidewalk. In Victoria's grey December light, the Sooke

Hills rose up indistinctly, their forested shoulders mantled with clouds. Icy breezes picked up a sheet of discarded newspaper and blew it skyward. I followed it with my eyes as it flapped and twisted in the air before falling to the ground beside the grassy banks of the Gorge waterway.

Archaeologists had discovered the remains of an ancient house down there and had started excavations. It was still early, but two people were hard at work near the water's edge, shovelling dirt onto sifter screens—shaking out ancient bones and harpoon points. Those things had belonged to my ancestors, so I went over to see what was going on. The diggers turned out to be a couple of greasy long-haired guys dressed in black coats and combat boots—teen-aged devil worshippers, to judge by the upside-down crosses hanging from their necks. They saw me coming and ran off, screeching and flapping their arms like bats. I let them go.

CHAPTER TWO

I'm a Coast Salish Native, born on the Warrior Reserve. Once, I was a member of Victoria's detective squad. Now I'm a neighbourhood cop stationed on the ground floor of a grimy brick palace. My bathroom with attached one-room office corresponds with my diminished status. There's a tiny cast-iron fireplace with a brass surround, a battered coal scuttle that I use as a wastebasket, an oak desk and a vinyl swivel chair. There's also a hat tree, two metal filing cabinets, a floor safe and a couple of chairs for visitors. Except for missing-kid bulletins and a print of Queen Victoria in her widow's weeds, the beige walls are unadorned.

Neighbourhood cops spend their days lubricating a city's delicate machinery. They're supposed to be visible and accessible, so I opened my curtains and smiled at passersby as I listened to my voice mail. Somebody wanted me to mediate a husband–wife donnybrook. Somebody else reported that a wolf had been sighted loping across the Bay Street bridge. A merchant had left an irate message about the serial shoplifters who kept looting his store.

Detective Inspector Bernie Tapp came in to use the toilet. Bernie is a tough-looking cop, a little under six feet tall. People take one look at his lean muscular shape and figure he's a lumberjack or a longshoreman. Bernie is only about 50, but that day he looked haggard and gloomy. I like him, and from time to time, I suspect, Bernie reciprocates my sentiments.

I was pitching scrunched-up balls of junk mail into the cold fireplace when Bernie came out of the bathroom. He nodded at me, then glanced out the window and said, "Aleister Crowley."

Bernie had spotted a couple of goths and was studying them. They were women, about 18, dressed in black and wearing combat boots, their heads tilted self-consciously high. When they reached the corner of Store Street they turned left and went out of view.

"Aleister's a boy's name," I said.

Bernie's face twitched a little. "Aleister Crowley was a Satanist," he said. "A magician and practitioner of the black arts. The guy who inspired L. Ron Hubbard. Those two are a couple of Crowley's latter-day admirers."

"Sounds like you've been boning up on the subject."

"I've talked to some of those jokers," Bernie said, folding his arms and drumming his fingers against his sleeves. "They hold black masses at midnight, get their thrills making pentacles, drinking chicken blood. Practising sex magic."

I felt my mouth making an involuntary O. "Sounds like fun. Where do I sign up?"

"I expect there's a long waiting list."

"Feel like breakfast?"

Bernie nodded. As I locked up, pale sun was pushing the greyness from the sky, a gradual yellow light painted the street. A man with a rhinestone nose stud, dressed in a Santa Claus outfit, was stationed outside Swans, rattling a few coins in a bucket. Shoppers scurried past him with bowed heads. I pointed toward the wreckage of the old Jamieson Foundry. The foundry dated from the same era as my office. Back then, Victoria had been home port to sealing schooners and coastal steamers. In those days Jamieson's had employed scores of men. But a quarter-century had passed since the last ingots had been poured, and for years the Jamieson building had stood empty. Vagrants used it as a flop. Two nights previously somebody had torched the place.

"I found a full-grown cougar inside Jamieson's once," Bernie said. "I'll never forget those big yellow eyes, staring at me from the dark. I thought it was a prowler and shouted: 'Come on out with your hands up.'"

"A live cougar? In downtown Victoria?"

"It was alive until I shot it. I couldn't get over how big that cougar's feet were. As big as my hands. That was a bad winter, too."

Lights flickered inside the foundry's dark recesses. An arson investigator, wearing rubber boots and a long yellow raincoat, waved a flashlight across bits of charred rubble.

"Soon there won't be any pioneer buildings left in this town," I mused.

Bernie shook his head. "I dunno. I'm tired of looking at old red bricks and rusty corrugated iron. Gimme modern. Gimme cedar and glass any time."

Police and ambulance sirens began to wail. Two patrol cars raced across the Johnson Street bridge and Dopplered past us, going north. Bernie's cellphone started to bleep.

"There goes my breakfast," he grumbled after listening to the call. "It's gonna be one helluva day, I can tell."

"What's up?"

"That was Bulloch. According to him, my monthly report is late."

"No more promotions for you then, pal."

"I put it on his desk yesterday," Bernie said, with weary resignation. "He's probably filed it under T, for toilet paper."

LOU'S CAFÉ IS almost next door to my office. As usual, it was crowded. Graveyard-shift workers from the Esquimalt dockyards were having breakfast before going home to sleep the day away. Clerks from nearby government offices were watching Lou's wall clock. In half an hour they'd be doing exactly the same thing at work. I helped myself to coffee. Lou looked up from flipping pancakes on his grill. "Hey, Silas. You look hungry."

"How about corned-beef hash and eggs with whole wheat toast?"

"Coming right up, pal."

I headed for my usual booth by the window, but Sammy Lofthouse had beaten me to it. I heard his penetrating voice first, then barks of laughter as he applauded one of his own jokes. Chantal Dupree was sitting across the table from him, her eyes full of mischief.

Chantal was a sidewalk entrepreneur who went into business when cops started arresting johns instead of prostitutes. Lofthouse was her lawyer, a short, fat man who resembled an overweight chimpanzee, although bald, red-faced, cigar-smoking chimpanzees must be rare if they exist at all. In motion or while speaking, Lofthouse moved his long arms as if swinging from branch to branch.

When she saw me, Chantal parted her glossy red lips in a welcoming smile. She was wearing low-slung corduroy pants and a silk shirt that revealed a bare midriff. Her hair was pulled back into a tight ponytail. She shuffled sideways along the bench to let me sit beside her.

Lofthouse leaned across the table, winking and leering at Chantal as he said, "Hey, Seaweed. You hear the one about the guy had the ecstasy franchise for Rollin' Stones tours?"

I shook my head, tuned Lofthouse out and brooded about Isaac Schwartz. My nose and my brain told me there had been a woman in Isaac's bed; my instincts told me something else.

When I came back to reality, Lofthouse was concluding his joke. "So Mick said, 'Don't stick it in there, yer silly cow. Yer supposed to stick 'em in yer mouth.'"

Overcome with hilarity, Lofthouse banged a hand on the table and wiped away tears of mirth with a white handkerchief. Still chuckling, he said, "So, Seaweed. I hear you've been travelling."

"True. I was in Reno."

"What's the big attraction?" Lofthouse asked sarcastically. "Reno's just a bunch of blue rinses trolling for husbands. Stop wasting your money; try Club Med."

"Right now I'm saving up for a trip to my podiatrist," I said.

"I go down to Ixtapa, or Turks and Caicos, get my oil changed," Lofthouse went on. "Club Med's wall-to-wall with gorgeous secretaries from Houston and Vancouver. They meet a gentleman like me, a man with a law degree, lots of fancy moves, and they think they've died, gone to heaven."

Chantal smiled indulgently. Lofthouse glanced at the I've-got-it-made Rolex strapped to his hairy wrist and said, "Jeez, you guys are holding me up. I'm due in court." He spread his hands on the table and pushed himself to his feet. Without another word he waddled out of the café, simian arms swinging. Soon he'd be performing in the Blanshard Street courthouse, his barrister's gown flapping, white necktie askew, doing a song-and-dance routine for one of British Columbia's Supreme Court judges.

I looked at Chantal over the rim of my cup and said, "You're up early."

"For a change. The weather kept the customers home last night, so I went to bed by myself. Now I got to do some Christmas shopping."

Lou arrived with my breakfast. The restaurateur was short, pudgy and dour. He had been born in what used to be called Yugoslavia. Quick to anger, Lou was by temperament more suited to guerrilla fighting than hamburger flipping. "I hear Isaac Schwartz is missing," he said as he put down my plate.

News had travelled fast. "Who told you that?"

"Moran." Lou crossed himself and added, "Poor guy. I always felt sorry for Isaac."

I noted the past tense but let it go. "Why?" I asked.

"I dunno. He always had a sad-sack look about him," Lou said as he hurried away.

Chantal dragged a huge handbag from the seat beside her and began to repair her makeup. Staring intently into a pocket mirror, she applied a fresh glossy red layer to her pouting lips. Satisfied, she dug her fingers into my thigh and rubbed a leg against me. It was just a professional reflex. I stood up to let her out of the booth. She grabbed a faux-fur coat from a hook, slung it across her shoulders and walked toward the door, wiggling her hips and drawing interested glances from a workman in coveralls and steel-toed boots. She paused by his table, gave him a heavy-lidded smile and said hello. Within a minute she was sitting beside him. I heard her say, "You heard about the guy had the Rolling Stones ecstasy franchise?"

A flurry of hailstones rattled against the café windows, melting almost the instant they landed. I cleared a little circle on the fogged-up glass with a paper napkin. Across the street, two men were mixing it up in Swans parking lot. Lofthouse was one. The other was a hulking, barrel-bellied Native man wearing a navy pea jacket and a black toque. He grabbed Lofthouse by the throat and pushed him roughly against a white Cadillac. When he released his grip, Lofthouse slid to the ground.

I've seen worse violence in kindergarten playgrounds and decided to stay out of it. Lofthouse picked himself up and leaned against the Caddy, gulping air. The Native shook his fist under Lofthouse's nose before stomping away. Lofthouse unlocked the Caddy and slumped into the driver's seat. Minutes passed before he drove off.

I was spreading marmalade on what was left of my toast when Bernie Tapp came into the café. "I thought you'd still be here," he said. "Let's go. There's a chopper waiting for us at Ogden Point."

He wasn't asking, he was telling. I left a 10-dollar bill on the table and followed him outside.

Winds solid enough to lean on were hammering the city when Bernie aimed his unmarked Interceptor along Wharf Street. A nor'wester rippled the dark waters of the Inner Harbour and a flurry of snowflakes appeared, suddenly white against the grey sky. Bernie was driving too fast. "Slow down," I told him. "The streets are covered with black ice."

"Black ice is an urban myth. Ice is white."

"Ice comes in all kinds of colours. Black *and* white. Yellow."

"Yellow, maybe. I'm telling you, there's a whole myth industry, cranking these yarns out for a gullible public."

"Don't talk to me about myths," I said. "I'm Coast Salish, remember?"

"That's why I'm taking you to Mowaht Park." Bernie took one hand off the steering wheel, produced a single wooden kitchen match from his pockets, struck it with a thumbnail and lit his pipe. It was two-handed driving weather. Bernie didn't seem worried, but I was. To divert myself, I started thinking about Mowaht Park.

The Mowaht is a 10,000-hectare chunk of undeveloped real estate situated on the remoter shores of southern Vancouver Island. Its closest boundary is more than 20 miles from Victoria. Over a hundred years ago the property was gazetted as a park. Back then, responsibility for policing and administering the park was assigned to the City of Victoria. It's been that way ever since. For more than a century, the Coast Salish Nation has been arguing with Ottawa about who actually owns it.

The police helicopter was warmed up and waiting for us at the Ogden Point heliport. Bernie and I were airborne five minutes after we reached it.

CHAPTER THREE

Mowaht Sound is a pear-shaped saltwater inlet with a narrow mouth, about 10 miles across at its widest point and 30 miles long. After a 10-minute chopper ride, Tree Island rose up ahead. An ocean-going freighter was moored to a pier alongside a sawmill. Dozens of anchored log booms floated along the sound like links in a chain. The helicopter pilot altered course slightly. Far away, mice were scampering across a snowy ridge. The pilot handed me his binoculars. When I put the binoculars to my eyes the mice became a herd of deer, led by a stag with an immense rack.

Bernie took the binoculars. After eyeing the surroundings, he pointed. The chopper pilot nodded and did a flyby along the banks of the sound to check for landing sites. Minutes later we put down on the muddy shore. "The guy who phoned us, Ted Meyer, he's supposed to be waiting here someplace," Bernie yelled above the noise of the engine.

The pilot stayed put with the chopper as Bernie and I started walking. An oily swell was washing snow off shelves of sedge, and a flock of Canada geese and a dozen white swans were dining on eelgrass in the shallows. Three damp, bedraggled raccoons feasted on clams. At our approach the mother raccoon looked up, nose twitching, then loped unhurriedly into the bush with a clam in her mouth. Two kits scurried along behind her.

We tramped along the mud banks for half a mile or so and finally two figures materialized from beneath the trees where they had been sheltering. They were wearing sou'westers and yellow oilskins over rubber waders. A runty middle-aged man with protruding eyes and a nose covered in burst capillaries looked us up and down. "We seen you land with the 'copter. I'm Ted Meyer. This here's my boy, Albert."

Albert was a skinny teenager with a slack jaw and a perpetual half grin. He let his father do all the talking.

"I'm Detective Inspector Tapp, Victoria PD," Bernie said. "This is Sergeant Seaweed."

"It took you long enough to get here," Meyer snapped. "We're about froze to death, waiting."

"That right?" Bernie said harshly. "If you'd given us better directions or signalled from the beach, you wouldn't have had to wait so long."

Taking the rebuff in his stride, Meyer pointed along the shore. "He's at Johnny Creek, up there a ways. Albert never seen a dead person before, so he was pretty leery when we found him." Meyer smirked at his son. "Ain't that right, son? Scared, weren't you?"

Albert blushed and nodded.

"But the dead guy, he was getting ready to drift away on the tide," Meyer continued. "What did I do? I made Albert help me move him. Between us, we pulled him outta the water. We had to go all the way to a payphone by the mill to call you guys. Wasted half a day on this deal already."

Bernie smiled nastily. "You were sure he was dead?"

Meyer's jaw dropped. "'Course he was dead," he shot back. "Crabs had chewed his eyes out, for one thing."

Bernie suddenly changed tack. "What were you two doing out on the water in this weather?"

Meyer's negligible chin jutted. "Me and Albert don't take no notice of weather."

It was a cockeyed answer; Bernie kept smiling.

Meyer shrugged. "Anyways. When we spotted him first, this dead person, there was some guy messing with him." Meyer licked his lips. "He was an Indian guy, dressed funny."

"Indian?" Bernie asked innocently. "You saw a South Asian male?"

"No," Meyer said, tipping his head toward me. "An Indian same as him."

"Did you recognize him?"

"No. Never seen him before. If I saw him again I'd know, though. I sure would. Anybody would. He was wearing a cone-shaped grass hat and a kind of grass cloak. When he seen us coming, he took off into the bush. He was moving pretty good, wasn't he, Albert?"

Albert nodded again.

"Fine," Bernie said. "Let's go see the body. Lead the way, Mr. Meyer."

Meyer looked at our footwear. Bernie was wearing walking shoes with mesh uppers; I had on leather boots. Meyer said hesitantly, "I hope youse are ready to get wetter'n you are already."

He turned his face into the weather and set off. The rest of us followed behind, in single file. The mud banks grew wider and became a viscous grey muck that buried our feet and sucked at our ankles. The adjacent forest was a dense and almost impenetrable mass of trees behind a screed of driftwood and other flotsam. Barnacle-encrusted arbutus trees and cedars leaned over the mud. In many places we had to duck branches or splash through shallow water to get around obstructions.

The mouth of Johnny Creek was in a cove scattered with rocky outcrops. Fat harbour seals had hauled themselves out of the water and lay dozing on an islet a hundred yards out. The sleek animals raised shiny dark heads, showed us their whiskery faces and went back to sleep.

The creek had carved a deep, wide channel across the beach to where a blue heron was fishing. Miffed by our presence the heron took to the air, squawking, and flew off. The four of us stood on a large smooth rock, taking a breather. I gazed down into the water. Gardens of kelp undulated in swells. Ten feet below the surface, dogfish and rock cod drifted across dense mats of starfish and clamshells. Crabs and bullheads, trapped in rocky tide pools, darted amid beds of blue mussels and red sea anemones.

"That's it," Meyer said, pointing ahead to where his aluminum boat lay aground on the beach. But when we reached it, Meyer stared around in consternation. "This is where we left him," he said uncertainly. "He was lying right here."

There was no dead man there now. The rising tide was flooding the footprints and depressions made earlier when the Meyers had dragged something heavy. Beneath the trees, the Meyers' footprints were clearly distinguishable. Additional tracks had been made by others and led to a trail through the bush.

"He was right there," Meyer insisted. "We jammed him up on them rocks, my boy and me. That Indian must've moved him."

Bernie hunched his shoulders and let them fall. After thinking things over he turned his back on the water and headed along the trail. I followed him up a steep bank. Tangles of blackberry, Oregon grape and salal bushes fought for space between firs and cedars. Underfoot, slippery boulders lay barely visible beneath vines, exposed tree roots and ferns. Alongside us, Johnny Creek rushed toward the sea. Away from the shore, the ground inclined steadily upward. Trees were coated with thick green moss, and orange-coloured mushrooms sprouted from rotting deadfalls. The trail—covered with shod and unshod footprints—was as easy to follow as a railroad track.

I heard Bernie panting ahead of me. "Wait a minute," I called.

He stopped walking and looked back at me.

"We've lost the Meyers," I said.

Bernie scowled. "We'll give 'em a minute to catch up."

"I doubt we'll see either of them till we go back to the beach."

His scowl deepened.

I said, "Summertime, this is a great place for picking berries, but most people would rather go 10 rounds with Mike Tyson than come up here."

"Why?"

"It's supposed to be haunted."

"You're yanking my chain, pal."

"People see bog apparitions—otherwise known as will-o'-the-wisps. In Coast Salish mythology, bog apparitions are exceedingly evil spirits. It's believed those who see them will soon die."

Bernie spat on the ground and said, "Yeah, right."

We resumed our walk and plodded together around an old beaver meadow, half swamp and half grass, to reach a spot where long ago somebody had built a cabin. Ten feet square, it was built in the traditional Coast Salish way, with split cedar. Wall planks were stacked between heavy vertical posts. Wide roofing planks could be pried apart to let daylight in or smoke out. Instead of a door, a woven cedarbark mat hung over a low opening in the east-facing wall. Beetles and ants were busily converting the cabin's ancient wood into elemental soil. The roof sagged, and the walls were rotten where they touched the ground. The whole ramshackle building was leaning precariously; soon it would collapse like a house of cards. A few more years, and hardly a trace of it would remain.

"My father brought me here once, when I was a kid," I told Bernie.

"We're going inside."

"Me first," I said.

I hailed the house. The only reply was a woodsy echo, so I got down on all fours, pushed the rotting cedarbark mat aside and crawled in. My head brushed against something in the darkness, and I heard a sound, like pebbles rattling inside a wooden box.

Grey light seeped into the cabin through holes and chinks. It was unfurnished, apart from a foot-high sleeping platform against the back wall. The sweet smell of balsam rose from a mattress of feathery boughs. When my eyes had adjusted to the dimness I saw that the rattling had been created by a string of dried deer hoofs dangling across the entrance. Bernie, crawling inside after me, set them rattling again.

A naked, eyeless corpse lay on the platform. His head had been shaved and his sparse grey hair had been rolled into a ball and placed between his thighs. His face and body were painted with lines, circles and ellipses of fantastic design. His clothing was bundled beside him. One shoe had a missing heel.

"Moran called me from the gym early this morning," I said. "Told me Isaac Schwartz was missing. I checked it out, but I never got around to calling Missing Persons."

"Well, he's not missing anymore," Bernie said. "But what does all this mean? Why would somebody shave his head, paint the body like this?"

"I don't know. It's off kilter. That ball of hair should be hanging in a tree, outside."

"What about those deer hoof things?"

"Noisemakers. Put up in the doorway when somebody dies to stop evil spirits from entering. Traditionally, when a Native man died his body was prepared by women inside his house and placed facing the door. It was also customary to cover the dead man's head with a wooden hat, paint his face black and give away his treasure. Mourning usually lasted four days. After that, depending on his status, his body was either cremated or disposed of some other way."

"Buried, you mean?"

"Sometimes. Sometimes corpses were put into canoes or into little houses standing on posts above the ground. Sometimes they were left up in trees."

"Yeah, *Native* corpses, not Jewish ones," Bernie said sourly. "You're talking past tense, I hope. Surely this kind of stuff doesn't happen anymore."

"Correct. White folks hated to see human remains dangling from trees and made us put a stop to it."

Bernie studied the body again. "What this says to me is that it was some kind of ritual murder. Was he killed by a Native?"

"I have no idea," I said.

"Who built this place?"

"Chief Mishtop. He died years ago."

"What was a chief doing up here, anyway? It sure isn't the Hilton."

"Mowaht Mountain is a holy place. Mishtop used to ascend the mountain at daybreak and beseech Sun Father to bless our people."

"Didn't chiefs go in for human sacrifice in the old days?"

"Forget it."

Outside the cabin, Bernie stretched out the kinks that stooping in the cabin had put in his back. "Meyer said he'd seen a Native guy, dressed funny. Couldn't have been one of your bog apparitions, could it?"

"How about this for a theory?" I said. "Somebody murdered Isaac in his room last night and hauled his body down the gymnasium's stairs. I could see the marks left on Moran's floors. One heel was torn off. Isaac was brought here and dumped into Mowaht Sound. His body was in the water long enough to be found by crabs before it washed ashore."

"Sounds possible," Bernie admitted, "but how does a Native guy fit into this?"

The moon was faintly visible in the daylight sky. I pointed to it and said, "On Native calendars, that's called Snow-Coming Moon. It's the time of year when spirits finish travelling around the world and return to their masters. It's the time of year when qualified Coast Salish youngsters go out into the world in search of personal spirits."

Bernie's expression was unreadable.

"During Spirit Quest," I went on, "searchers dress traditionally and are forbidden to eat. It's quite common, even normal, for spirit questers to become delirious. It's just possible that a spirit quester came across Isaac's body by accident. If he was delirious he might have heard voices telling him to move it."

Bernie used his cellphone to call headquarters and request that a canine unit and a forensic identification team be brought out. We traipsed back to the beach without speaking. The Meyers were waiting for us. White plastic bleach bottles bobbed up and down in the waves without drifting.

"Are those your crab buoys?" I asked Meyer.

He gave me a blank look. "What?"

"You were checking those crab traps when you found the dead man, I suppose?"

"Me, crabbing?" Meyer retorted indignantly. "No chance. Crabbing's illegal unless you've got a licence."

Bernie was sitting on a rock. He had taken his shoes off and was wringing water out of his socks. His feet were blue with cold.

I turned away and wandered along the beach to the north, looking at herons, mallards and buffleheads, but thinking about my ancestors and the places to which—if you believe Coast Salish stories—the souls of our ancestors sometimes return. I heard footsteps slopping along behind me. It was young Albert Meyer. I said hello, but instead of replying he stared down at his feet. "You can stop worrying," I said. "I'm not with Fisheries. I won't be reporting you and your dad for crabbing."

Albert raised his eyes as high as my chest. "It's not that, it's just …"

"What?"

"My dad. I guess his eyes ain't so good," he said, breaking off.

Albert was the kind of kid directors want for movies like *Angela's Ashes*. Poverty, misery and cruelty were corroding his soul and sapping whatever pluck he'd been born with, but he still retained a vestige of unconquered spirit. "My dad told you there was only one person messing with the dead person, but he was wrong," Albert said, glancing back nervously for fear of being overheard. "There were two people there. One was kind of tall. Tall as you are. The other was small—a young guy, or a girl maybe. I only spotted them for a second or two."

"Another Native?"

"I dunno. Like I said, I didn't get a good look."

I patted his shoulder. "Okay, this is a great help."

"You won't say anything to my dad, will you?" Albert went on. "It's just … sometimes he gets mad at me."

I was still thinking about father–son relationships an hour later when I heard helicopter blades slicing the air. This time it was a twin-rotor Buffalo. Faces peered out its windows as it descended noisily to the beach. Forensics had arrived, along with two German shepherd dogs. Once disembarked, they floundered across the mud to receive Bernie's instructions.

Before turning his attention to them, Bernie cast a sidelong look at me and said, "Bog apparitions, spirit questers and a Salish chief who died a long time ago. Silas, this case is right up your alley."

I nodded.

"Right," he said. "Let's keep each other posted."

With that, he led the bunny-suited forensics gang toward the cabin, briefing them as they went.

I flew back to Victoria in the police chopper.

CHAPTER FOUR

S ammy Lofthouse showed up at my office about five o'clock that afternoon, chomping the usual unlit cigar. He collapsed into a chair. Snowflakes, melting on his black overcoat, dripped onto the linoleum.

"Jesus, Seaweed," Lofthouse complained. "Swans' parking lot is jammed. I had to park three blocks away."

"That's what you need. Exercise. Stay away from steak houses. Spend more time working out, it'll strengthen your heart."

"What are you?" he snarled. "My medical adviser?"

He looked exhausted and tense. A network of fine wrinkles ringed his eyes. I opened a drawer and brought out two plastic cups and a bottle of Seagram's VO that I'd confiscated from an underage mall rat. I poured two fingers into each cup and slid one across the desk to Lofthouse, who emptied it in one draught.

"Hit me with some more of that," he said. "I'm a thirsty guy."

"Having a rough day?"

"Please," he said. "Just fucking pour me another."

I topped him up and settled back in my chair.

Lofthouse produced a gold Zippo. Ignoring the No Smoking sign pasted beside my door, he lit a cigar, breathed smoke over me and settled down to pant. He was wearing a signet ring set with a chunk of ice big enough to cool a jug of lemonade. While I admired his jewellery, he scowled at Queen Victoria, who was frowning down at *him* from her picture frame.

Lofthouse looked and sounded more like a hoodlum than a successful lawyer. He shaved twice a week and liked to socialize with tough guys, speak their language. His clients were hard-core criminal losers. Lofthouse had tangled with the Law Society more than once because of his unethical practices.

On the street outside, angry drivers were honking car horns. I got up and looked out the window. The Johnson Street bridge had been raised to let a tugboat pass from Point Hope to Victoria's Inner Harbour. Road traffic to and from Vic West was temporarily stalled.

Lofthouse wagged a finger. "You're listening to the death rattle of civilization. One of these days, there'll be a traffic snarl that can't be fixed. It'll be bumper-to-bumper from coast to coast. People will die in their cars."

He was waiting for me to speak, but I rolled Seagrams around my tongue and kept quiet.

Finally he came out with it. "I need you to help me with something."

"That's what I figured."

"One of my clients needs protection. Old woman named Mavis Tranter. Mrs. Tranter's nephew is about to be disinherited and kicked off her property. The guy's a nut and could be dangerous."

Lofthouse's cigar had gone out. He produced the Zippo again. "Here's the deal," he said. "When I've got my breath back, we'll go meet her."

I scowled to let him know his words were beginning to annoy me. "Sounds serious. You'd better clear it with my boss."

"That'd be Chief Inspector Bulloch?"

"Not anymore. Oatmeal Savage owns my ass now."

"At least it's not Bulloch. Jesus. Any other organization, Bulloch's the guy they'd send out for coffee." Lofthouse moderated his tone and added, "I want you to defuse a threatening situation. Is that asking too much?"

"Probably."

Lofthouse blew smoke at the ceiling and said, "Mrs. Tranter asked me to prepare a new will—"

"Hold it a minute," I interrupted. "Tell me about the guy who roughed you up this morning."

"Who said somebody roughed me up?"

I looked him in the eye. He blinked as if a wind had just blown sand into his face. "Okay. The guy's called Lennie. Lennie Jim, a half-baked hick who thinks I owe him something."

"Such as?"

"I'm Lennie's lawyer," Lofthouse said. "He's a head case, a complete fucking yo-yo, been in and out of the joint since juvie hall. He pulled a convenience-store heist a while back. The whole episode was captured on video. The dumb fucker wasn't even wearing a mask, so what could I do? Lennie's sore at me because he was sent down."

Lofthouse inserted a pinky into his ear and twirled it around while he sulked. "Forget Lennie. That was just a business thing. Can we talk about Mrs. Tranter?"

"I'd like to know some more about Lennie first."

"Please, you're wasting your time. In a year, maybe less, Lennie will be phoning me from the city lockup. I should have a hundred clients like him. They're worth a coupla large a year to me, each one of 'em."

"What's a large?"

"A thousand bucks. Christ, don't you watch *The Sopranos* on TV?"

"No. I get all the fantasy I can handle listening to guys like you."

Lofthouse relaxed and started to laugh.

"All right," I said. "Tell me about Mrs. Tranter."

"Mrs. Tranter has no kin except for one nephew, Richard Hendrix. Originally, Hendrix was Mrs. Tranter's sole beneficiary. Now she wants a new will. She's cutting him off without a nickel."

"So what? It's her money, she can do what she wants."

"But what makes this interesting is that Mrs. Tranter's new beneficiary is somebody she just met. A stranger."

Something else occurred to me. "You specialize in criminal law," I said. "Isn't estate work outside your line?"

"I'm a lawyer," he snapped. "If there's a buck in it, I'll do it."

Then he remembered his manners. With a shrug he added, "But you're right, it's not my usual gig. Anyway, Mrs. Tranter phoned me. Said I'd been recommended. I'm curious, so I make an appointment, go see her. She lives in an old house off Bay Street. The house is a dump, but it's sitting on a nice big chunk of subdivisible land."

"You said Mrs. Tranter wants a *new* will. Who prepared the old one?"

"Derek Battle."

Derek Battle was the senior partner in a prestigious, long-established firm. Lofthouse must have guessed my thoughts, because he added, "You're wondering why she didn't ask Battle to make the changes? Simple. She thinks Battle might try to influence her."

"And should he?"

"Hey, Seaweed!" said Lofthouse irritably. "What Battle would or wouldn't do is irrelevant. We're talking about my client's perceptions."

"Is Mrs. Tranter mentally competent?"

"She's nearly blind, a recluse. But she's still sharp, got all her marbles. As you said, it's *her* will, she can do what she wants. Just the same, it's a screwy deal. " Lofthouse paused. He frowned, flexed his long arms, inspected his cigar and added soberly, "Let me tell you something. People make weird wills all the time. They leave their money to cats and fucking canaries. Compared to some I've seen, Mrs. Tranter's will is sane and reasonable."

"Have you spoken to Derek Battle about this?" I asked.

"Don't be ridiculous."

"Tell me about the nephew then. Richard Hendrix."

"Another fucking yo-yo. He's been living in a shed on Mrs. Tranter's property. The old woman was pretty generous with him till he got hold of her chequebook and started dipping into her account. She didn't notice anything amiss at first, being blind and all. By the time she realized what was going on, Hendrix had stolen thousands."

The recitation of these perfidies brought Lofthouse's simmering temper to the boil again. "Hendrix is an eco-freak," he added sharply. "He spends his time hugging trees and protecting owls, when he isn't sponging off his aunt."

"That's irrelevant. *Nice* people hug trees and love owls."

Lofthouse opened his mouth to say something, thought better of it and made a visible effort to relax. "Richard Hendrix does more than hug trees," he said. "He specializes in tree spiking—driving long steel nails into old-growth timber. If a logger's power saw happens to touch a spike, his cutting chain can break and rip somebody's head off. Hendrix is a menace."

"So who's Mrs. Tranter's new beneficiary?"

"Her name is Ellen Lemieux. As I said, Mrs. Tranter is legally blind—she can actually see a little bit using special glasses. She has photophobia, a disease that makes it hard for her to tolerate light. Anyway, she was out shopping one day. This girl, Ellen Lemieux, notices the old lady stranded at a crosswalk and helps her across the road. Then helps her shop for groceries. One thing leads to another. Mrs. Tranter's grateful. She invites Miss Lemieux around for coffee. The two women become friendly. In the meantime, Mrs. Tranter is having problems with her nephew."

"Apart from stealing, what else does Hendrix do?"

"Not much. He's never held a regular job, been sponging off people for years. Hasn't even got the moxie to cut the grass or help around the house. Mrs. Tranter is just sick of him. One day she woke up and realized that she didn't want her money to support him when she was gone. Then Miss Lemieux came into the picture."

"Tranter's estate. How much money are we talking?"

"She has a few thousand in the bank and a small pension that dies with her. Her big asset is all that real estate."

"How is Miss Lemieux reacting to this windfall?"

Lofthouse smiled. "This is the interesting bit. Ellen, Miss Lemieux, has no idea what's going on. She's going to be one very surprised young woman when Mrs. Tranter dies."

That *was* interesting. "What's my part in all this?"

"Tranter sent Hendrix a letter telling him she'd found out he'd been writing cheques on her account. She told him to stay away from her and from her property. She also let him know that he was disinherited."

"Was that wise?"

"No. Richard Hendrix is gonna be mad as hell. I expect fireworks. My idea is to head off problems before they begin. I *could* hire a security cop, but Hendrix's kind of a tough monkey. I think we need a real cop." Lofthouse smirked. "You may have to lean on Hendrix a bit, big fella. But hey, you're good at that."

I thought it over. This matter was taking place inside my bailiwick and had potential for criminal violence. Violence is the sort of thing neighbourhood cops are supposed to forestall. I picked up the two empty plastic cups, carried them to the bathroom and washed them in the sink, then put them back in my drawer along with what was left of the whisky. Sitting down again, I said, "Have you met Ellen Lemieux?"

He hesitated. "Yeah. Accidentally on purpose, if you know what I mean. She works at a farmers' market. I went there one day just to have a look at her. Pretty cute. I didn't speak to her, obviously."

"Okay, spell it out. Just what exactly do you expect me to do?"

"Come with me and you'll find out," he said, standing up and bustling toward the door but stealing a look from the corner of his eye to see that I was following.

I was pretty sure I was letting myself in for something I'd regret, but my curiosity was aroused. I was just locking the office door when my phone started ringing. Lofthouse was already outside. "Hang on a minute," I called.

Lofthouse had an agenda and was sticking to it like a gecko sticks to a ceiling. "Forget the goddam phone, Seaweed," he said. "Let's go!"

MAVIS TRANTER'S PROPERTY was surrounded by dilapidated picket fences and overgrown laurel hedges. Fifty years ago, people had been proud to live in this part of Victoria. Now the area was zoned industrial and was a wasteland of rundown houses, car-wreckers' yards, scrap merchants, machine shops and bottle depots. Street lights were few.

Lofthouse nosed his Cadillac up to the curb behind a Budget rental truck. The earlier snow had turned to freezing rain, and we dashed to Mrs. Tranter's front veranda.

The house had a stone foundation, but the encircling veranda was barely supported by decaying wooden posts. It was obvious that the house had been beautiful once, with elaborate brick chimneys and a steep slate roof. Half visible in the gloom were wide bracketed eaves and little balconies flanking stained-glass windows. The grounds were as neglected as the house. Clumps of rank grass stretched between untended fruit trees and shrubs.

Lofthouse twisted a bell switch beside the front door. Tinny peals echoed inside the house. After a minute the door opened. Mavis Tranter was barely visible in the unlighted vestibule. She was a stooped, tiny old woman wearing a fur coat buttoned up to her neck, and she moved with a shuffling, stiff-kneed, heel-dragging gait. Her fluffy white hair contrasted sharply with the dark lenses of her eyeglasses. She said without ceremony, "Come in, but mind your feet. You'll find it rather dark. My eyes cannot tolerate much light." She pointed with her white cane to a hat rack and added assertively, "Hang your things there."

We did as we were told, then followed her down a dim corridor to a shadowy living room as grim as a Dickens orphanage. A small electric table lamp with a one-candlepower light bulb glowed dimly on a sideboard. The dying embers of a log fire cast negligible beams from the fireplace. Mrs. Tranter sat down in an armchair and motioned for us to sit too. Her own chair was positioned to the side of the fire, where she could enjoy its feeble warmth without having to look at it. The half-panelled room was cluttered with old—and what I then incorrectly judged to be valuable—oak furniture. Bookcases covered one entire wall but contained few books except Agatha Christie mysteries and similarly dated paperbacks. On one wall hung a small Turkish rug; on another, a dark and hideous painting of a ruined monastery.

Mrs. Tranter shook her white head and appraised us from behind her dark glasses. "Excuse the condition of the house," she said. "I have few visitors."

She spoke carefully enunciated English. I noticed that beneath her fur coat she was wearing a blue cotton dress printed with tropical flowers.

Lofthouse said, "Mrs. Tranter, this is Sergeant Seaweed of the Victoria police."

"Of course it is," she snapped, in a display of idiot peevishness. She turned toward me, but her gaze missed mine by a couple of feet. She said, "I suppose you know all about it, officer?"

"Mr. Lofthouse told me that you've changed your will, and that you're worried about your nephew—"

"In that case you know nothing," she barked. "I haven't changed anything yet."

"I've got your new will right here, ready to be signed," said Lofthouse breezily, seemingly unaffected by Mrs. Tranter's strange animus. He opened his briefcase and shuffled through it, but in the poorly lit room couldn't find what he was looking for. Muttering to himself, he moved the briefcase closer to the lamp.

Mrs. Tranter peered toward Lofthouse and said, "My nephew telephoned from Tofino. He's hitchhiking back here tomorrow. If he's lucky catching rides he should arrive by mid-afternoon." She put her head back and cackled with amusement.

"Hendrix lives in a shed in the back yard," Lofthouse started to say.

"*Lived* in the shed," Mrs. Tranter snapped, with a ring of malicious triumph. "Past tense. That arrangement is over. Richard cheated me and must face the consequences." Her face swung in my direction as she added, "When he arrives tomorrow, officer, tell him to clear his things out of my shed. After that, he's to stay away from me."

"Mrs. Tranter is quite within her rights," Lofthouse told me. "Hendrix has no legal tenancy because he's never paid rent. He has performed no services in lieu of rent. Mrs. Tranter, therefore, has no obligation to him whatsoever."

"Yes. I don't want him mooning about the place, upsetting me with his foolishness," she said. "I've had enough of Richard's shenanigans. It's time he made his own way in the world."

I looked squarely at Mrs. Tranter and she seemed to return my gaze from behind her dark glasses. I wondered what she could see. Perhaps vague shapes, hardly more. The lenses seemed utterly black in this weak light.

"Mr. Lofthouse has suggested that I be absent when Richard returns," she said. "He thinks I should move out of this house for a day or two. Give Richard a chance to collect his things and calm down."

I was already sick of the pair of them. "Ejecting tenants isn't police work. We have enough to do as it is," I said. "I'm afraid you'll have to make other arrangements."

"I'm a taxpayer!" Mrs. Tranter exclaimed. "Surely I'm entitled to help from the police!"

"Let me be blunt," I said. "From what I've been told, you've goaded Mr. Hendrix unnecessarily. If you are seriously worried, hire a security guard. I'm a city policeman. We're not paid to sort out personal family problems."

My words met with deep silence. Mrs. Tranter's hands began to pick nervously at the fur of her coat.

"Besides," I added, "Mr. Hendrix is likely to hang around indefinitely. The city can't station personnel here forever."

"No, no, Sergeant," said Mrs. Tranter in a conciliatory tone. "I know my nephew. Richard will fume and fuss at first, but he hasn't the guts to stick with anything long. Not even anger. He'll come to his senses soon enough."

The doorbell rang, and Lofthouse stood up. "I'm expecting my clerk to join us. That'll be her." As he went to answer the door, I heard him stumble in the dim hallway.

Mrs. Tranter leaned forward. "Does plain speaking offend you, officer?"

"Policemen are not easily shocked."

"You think I'm being unnecessarily cruel," she said.

I didn't answer.

"Richard abused my hospitality. He robbed me. He's lazy and good-for-nothing because my sister, Richard's mother, spoiled him when he was growing up. He arrived on my doorstep unannounced and penniless. I made the mistake of letting him move into my garden shed." A self-pitying whine crept into her voice. "I'm all alone in the world now. My husband is dead. My sister is dead. They're all gone except me. Richard's the only family I have left. I'd hoped he'd be good company for my old age, but he's just a money-grubbing nuisance."

I still kept quiet.

We heard the front door close. Lofthouse re-entered the room with his clerk, Grace Sleight. Damp tufts of greying hair protruded from beneath her blue beret. I had often seen her chubby, amiable face at the Blanshard Street courthouse, but tonight she seemed preoccupied, even worried. She gave me a weak smile that faded quickly.

"We won't keep you long, Grace," said Lofthouse, taking documents and a pen from his briefcase and moving to Mrs. Tranter's side. He straightened, faced the three of us and stated formally, "Mrs. Tranter will be signing her last will and testament, and two witnesses will watch the signing. Is that clearly understood?"

Grace and I nodded.

"Here's your new will, ma'am. If you'll just initial here first, please," he said, placing the deed on the side table at Mrs. Tranter's elbow. She had difficulty finding the right place. We watched Lofthouse guide her hand so that she could initial each page and scribble her signature at the end. Grace and I appended our signatures last.

Lofthouse said dismissively, "Thanks for stopping by, Grace. That'll do. I'll see you tomorrow."

I looked at Lofthouse and Mrs. Tranter in turn and said, "Unless there's anything else, I'll be on my way, too." I turned to Grace and said, "Which way are you heading, Grace?"

"James Bay."

"Can I hitch a ride to Swans?"

"Of course."

Lofthouse looked at me warily. "We're still hoping you'll help us out, Silas."

"Before I go, could I speak to you privately, Sam?" I said.

Lofthouse stared at me uncomprehendingly for a moment. Then his lips twitched. "Ah, certainly."

Grace and I wished Mrs. Tranter goodnight but got no response. Lofthouse followed us down the hall, clutching his briefcase against his chest as if he couldn't bear to be parted from it. At the front door, he fumbled for a light switch and clicked it on.

I poked his chest with my finger and said, "This deal stinks. If you're really worried about your client's safety, hire rent-a-cops. Keep me out of it."

Exasperated, Lofthouse banged his forehead with the ball of his hand. "All right, all right! You've sure got a hard-on. What are you so pissed about?"

"You're trying to drag me into a private fight. We both know, among other things, that when Derek Battle finds out you've nicked one of his clients, he'll raise hell."

"That's *my* problem. If Battle messes with me I'll hammer the bastard into the ground." Lofthouse smiled grimly and added, "Play ball with me, Silas, and I'll steer money your way. You know, for personal expenses."

Disgusted, I put on my coat and followed Grace out into the cold.

It was just after seven o'clock when Grace dropped me off outside Swans pub. I hadn't eaten much since breakfast, and the bit of whisky I'd had with Lofthouse earlier burned in my stomach. After a hot beef sandwich and a pint of India Pale Ale, I paid up, collected my car and drove home.

ALONG THE FIRST half-mile of its length, Victoria West is bisected by railroad tracks. These tracks separate the rich—who live in luxurious waterfront condos—from the majority of Vic West's inhabitants, many of whom live in tract housing and small apartment buildings. Farther along Esquimalt Road, past the dockyards, pubs and mini-malls, is the Warrior Indian Reserve, partially concealed from the highway by a small forest of Garry oaks.

My home on the reserve is a two-room beach cabin that I built with my own hands. I don't have a hot water heater, so I make do with cold water unless I light my wood stove. My outhouse is a one-holer beneath a big cedar. But I do have electricity. One wall is covered with bookshelves, racks for my blues records and an outdated stereo system. When I look out my front windows, I have grandstand views of the Olympic Mountains, rising from the sea on the U.S. side of the Strait of Juan de Fuca. From my bedroom, I can see black and white killer whales. They're inanimate, though: painted on the walls of the Warrior longhouse. That longhouse—in fact, every house visible—has a moss-covered roof and is surrounded by trees.

As tired as I was when I got home, I changed into running gear and went out. I warmed up with a fast walk along the reserve's unpaved roads, then crossed onto pavement and started jogging toward Victoria. The rain and snow had stopped for the time being. I took it easy at first, conscious for the first 10 minutes of my heavy breathing and cold hands. My right knee ached. Then the old miracle happened and I was out of my body. Suddenly I wasn't gasping anymore.

I forgot my aching knee and my hands were warm. I detoured across the Bay Street bridge. Deadman Island's dark mass rose up on my left. Long ago that small island had been a Coast Salish cemetery; I'd grown up listening to stories about its ghostly occupants.

I headed north. Strings of Christmas lights twinkled on houses here and there. In one yard a plywood Santa cracked his whip over grinning plywood reindeer. Before I knew it, I had jogged to Mavis Tranter's house. I skirted the property until I found the shed where Richard Hendrix lived. I was about to try the door when a large dog howled somewhere nearby. I heard faint crunching sounds as a palpable entity approached. I remembered that a wolf had been sighted in this area. A spirit quester? Then my peripheral vision picked up something. Slowly I turned my head to the right. My mouth went dry. The skin on the back of my neck crawled as a dark shape materialized from behind the shed. I shivered, even as drops of perspiration pricked my body.

The shape moved toward me, then stopped. I could smell it—it stank the way wet dogs smell after rolling in something rotten. I recalled old stories about Ghost People—long-dead humans with the power to assume the animal shapes. Wolves and bears who hunt for souls in the night. Heart thudding, I moved slowly backwards the way I had come and out onto the street. The shape, whatever it was, made no attempt to follow me as I headed home.

CHAPTER FIVE

After fixing myself bacon and eggs for breakfast, I walked up to the band office. I wanted to ask Chief Alphonse something, but he was, as always, busy wrestling with the seemingly endless problems besetting Canada's Native elders. Maureen, his secretary, asked me to come back in half an hour. I went down to the beach and sat on a drift log. Waves rolled in, broke their backs and sighed back out to sea again.

The basis of the Coast Salish class system involves names and titles. Ultimately, the status of an Indian band depends upon the status of its chief. At present, we Warriors were riding high. Chief Alphonse had been only 30 years old when he inherited noble rank, but his career toward Warrior chiefdom had begun before his first birthday, when his first name was bestowed.

Upon inheriting a chiefly name, a Warrior has the right—and the duty—to perform a particular dance. Alphonse now owned several names, each of which had involved giving one or more potlatches and dancing feasts, where vast amounts of money and property were distributed among Coast Salish people. Chiefdom, therefore, implies the right to perform certain dances. It also implies the possession of wealth and a readiness to share it.

In ancient times, an uninitiated class of people existed who were given no names at all. These unfortunates—for the most part slaves and their descendants—had the same rights as stones or pieces of wood. They were forbidden under pain of death from participating in—or even witnessing—important ceremonials.

The progression of names from low to high goes along with the progression of dances leading to Winter Ceremonial. The Coast Salish world is turned upside down at Winter Ceremonial. It is the time when supernatural beings prey upon humans. It is the time of year when personal spirits return to their owners after travelling around the world. It is the time of year when a Coast Salish cop might encounter the ghost of a giant wolf.

Beach pebbles crunched underfoot. It was Maureen. In her soft voice she said, "Sorry, Silas, the chief has run into a snag. He's gonna be tied up for a while. Is there anything I can do?"

"What do you know about ghost wolves?"

"Not much. Why?"

"I was hoping Chief Alphonse could tell me something."

"Old Mary Cooke probably knows all about 'em," Maureen said. "If you have time, I'm sure she'd like to see you. But she isn't well, so try not to tire her out."

OLD MARY COOKE lived on the reserve in a decrepit house surrounded by junk—dead refrigerators, baby strollers, a fibreglass canoe with a hole in it and a gas mower that had died years earlier in a patch of weeds. She was in her kitchen, sitting on an old sofa, looking like a pile of second-hand clothes in her floppy black hat and layers of skirts and coats. Her eyes were closed, but I said hello in a soft voice and sat down beside her.

"I'm a black caterpillar," she said, opening her eyes. "It's pretty near time for me to die, change into a black moth. Fly back to the Unknown World."

Mary was about a hundred years old, so her prophecy was undeniably true. Death was a prospect she faced with total equanimity—or so I imagined. She was holding something in her hand. When she opened it, I saw an abalone shell. I asked her what she knew about ghost wolves.

"The last time I was in the Unknown World I was a young girl," she said. "Me and another young girl were diving for abalones when we saw wolves running along the beach. They all ran away except for one old wolf who was half blind and slow, just like I am now. The other girl felt sorry for that old wolf, but I laughed at him. Threw stones to drive him off, told him he was stupid and useless.

"When me and the other girl had filled our baskets with abalones we started back home. We'd been diving in cold water for hours. The other girl was ill because she'd been shot with sickness arrows. It was a hot day, but with sickness in her, she had the shakes and kept dropping her basket. I wouldn't stop and help so she got left behind on her own."

"That seems strange," I said. "Why not help her?"

"I dunno," Mary replied. "Maybe I was scared because it was turning dark. Then that girl got lost in a forest of trees with feet that kept moving and blocking her way. Animals with human faces howled down from branches. She roamed about in terror till she came to this bunch of dry ferns and lay herself down and cried herself to sleep.

"Next morning when this girl woke up, she saw something in the fog. She thought it was a wolf, standing on two hind legs. The girl was scared till wind blew the fog away and she realized it wasn't a wolf. It was a handsome young man, roasting abalones on a campfire. There was enough abalone to feed 'em both so they ate hearty. By the time this girl had eaten she was feeling pretty good. That sickness power had worn right off. She told this man who she was. He wouldn't tell her who he was, but he did offer to show her the way home. He waited for her to pack the empty shells into her basket. Then they started walking away through the strange woods. Animals with human faces were still howling down from the trees, but she wasn't scared anymore." Mary held her abalone shell up close to one cloudy eye and studied it a moment before resuming her story.

"She followed the handsome man along till they reached a lake surrounded by pit houses. One pit house had smoke coming out of a hole in its roof. The man wanted her to go inside, but she looked closer and saw the pit house was a den full of wolves. She tried to run away, but the man suddenly turned fierce. Grabbed her and took her inside the pit house. When the girl took a second look round, she saw the house was full of people, not wolves. The people were friendly, but the handsome man turned back into the tired old wolf she'd seen when she was diving for abalones. He wanted the girl to be his wife because that girl hadn't laughed at him. "

Mary stopped talking and fingered the shell some more. "What happened then?" I prompted.

"The girl wanted to go home. But the funny thing was, the longer the girl stayed with the wolf, the more she liked him. They got married and he put wolf power into her—you know, the same way a man puts children into a woman if he loves her.

"And all this time the girl's uncles were searching for her. About a year went by till they found her in that wolf den and killed the wolves. One of the uncles cut the wolf's head off and skinned him. The uncles decorated the wolf skin with abalone shells and put the skin on her back.

"From then on, that girl had wolf power." Mary sighed deeply and added, "I've been dreaming about that girl lately, can't stop thinking about her. Sometimes, I think she's watching me."

Mary put the abalone shell she'd been holding into my hands.

"You can have this now, Silas," she said. "Hang it round your neck on a string or put it in your medicine bag. I won't be needing it no more."

I DROVE INTO town, parked behind Swans and sat for a minute with the heater on, thinking about the strange story Old Mary Cooke had just told me. Rain mixed with hailstones slammed my car's roof like the beats of a crazed drummer. I decided to make a run for it.

As soon as I was inside my office, the phone rang. It was Bernie. "What's a whaling shrine?" he asked, not bothering with hello.

"No idea. Why?"

"There's a rumour on the street that someone's planning to steal one."

"Tell me more."

"What's to tell? It's just a rumour." And with that he hung up.

I brought Richard Hendrix's name up on my computer. He'd been busted a couple of times for minor trespasses. I thought for a bit, then went to the public library on Blanshard Street and checked back issues of the *Canadian News Index*. There was nothing under Richard Hendrix. Further digging led me to a file on The Wilderness Preservation Committee, an environmental action group headed by Felicity Exeter.

Mrs. Exeter was a local celebrity, a rich and somewhat reclusive woman who divided her time between protecting British Columbia's trees and gallery hopping in New York City. A few years previously, the Wilderness Preservation Committee, commonly known as the WPC, had confronted logging crews at the Carmanah forest watershed. Ten activists, including Felicity Exeter and Richard Hendrix, chained themselves across a road to prevent loggers from hacking down 500-year-old trees. The standoff ended when RCMP officers cut the chains, charged the activists with public mischief and jailed them overnight. At subsequent trials the activists were each fined

$500 or given 30 days. Mrs. Exeter paid everybody's fines and they all went home, except for one old granny who opted to martyr herself. She served her prison sentence writing letters to newspapers.

Richard Hendrix's name reappeared in a story written for a west-coast weekly. His activities as a tree spiker were described and there was a photograph of the grinning, bearded activist driving a railroad spike into a tree. Asked if he ever worried his activities would injure innocent loggers and sawmill operators, he was quoted as saying, "Tree spiking discourages the rape of old-growth forest. If a few workers get hurt, that's too bad. They're cannon fodder in a big war. Sometimes people suffer, but that's the price we pay for freedom. We've got to stop these timber companies before every forest on the coast has been clear-cut. I'll use any means necessary to stop the destruction of public lands for corporate profit. Maybe we should be worrying more about disappearing wildlife, and less about disappearing lumberjacks."

The reporter then interviewed a couple of unnamed loggers. Both declared that if they came across Richard Hendrix vandalizing trees in their territory, there'd be a chainsaw massacre.

A WINTRY SUN reddened the southern sky and set fire to the banks of cumulus poised over the city as I walked back to my office. I was waiting to cross Pandora Street traffic when a large black sedan with tinted windows pulled up at the curb beside me. A uniform got out of the front passenger seat and opened the rear door.

A deep voice boomed, "Get in."

I peered into the the car's dim interior. The man who had just spoken was Chief Inspector Jack "Oatmeal" Savage. Sitting beside him was Detective Chief Inspector Bulloch. Savage leaned forward and pulled down a jump seat folded against the partition. I got into the car and sat facing them. The uniform returned to his seat in the front. I expected the car to start moving, but it stayed put.

DCI Bulloch was a large, thickset man with a dull, impenetrable gaze and a nose that looked as if it had been flattened by a two-by-four in some prehistoric punch-up.

"Having another busy day, Seaweed?" he barked.

"About normal I would say, sir," I returned politely.

"Yeah, normal if you're a retiree." Bulloch stabbed a manicured finger at his wristwatch. "It's nearly noon and you're just showing up at your office?"

"I've been busy with—"

"Shut the hell up!" Bulloch yelled. "Did I ask you a question?"

"Yes sir. You asked me if I was having …"

"I said shut it! Are you deaf?"

This time I kept quiet.

"You've been screwing up again," Bulloch said. "Dissing lawyers, insulting taxpayers. Just remind me, Seaweed. How old are you?"

"Nearly 40, sir."

"Hear that?" Bulloch said to Savage. "Nearly 40."

"Is that right?" Savage said, with a glance at his watch. "Looks a lot older."

"I was an inspector at 30," Bulloch said smugly.

Savage shook his head and said, not unkindly, "What are we going to do with you, Silas? Sending you to charm school won't work; you're too old."

"Old dogs, new tricks," Bulloch muttered.

I looked at Savage and said, "Sorry, sir, I'm lost. Would you mind telling me where we're going with this?"

"You are going to march your sorry ass over to Mrs. Tranter's house. Now. Render every possible assistance to that distressed taxpayer. Understand?"

"Yes sir."

Savage leaned forward and rapped on the glass of the partition.

The uniform appeared and opened the door again. There wasn't enough headroom for an inside salute, so I backed out and saluted from the sidewalk as their car drew away. Evidently, Lofthouse packed more clout in this town than I'd realized. But orders are orders.

WHEN I REACHED Mrs. Tranter's house, the Budget rental truck was parked outside again, but it departed when I pulled in behind it. The house was locked and seemingly unoccupied, although I noticed fresh muddy footprints on the path leading to the front door. I prowled around the veranda and tried to peer through the windows. Every curtain was tightly drawn. Somewhere, loose metal sheets slammed in the wind.

Seen in daylight, Richard Hendrix's shed was a decaying ruin, about 12 feet by 20, with board-and-batten siding and two inadequate four-pane windows. It appeared to be slowly sinking into the ground because of the untended grass and weeds growing up around it. A thick mat of moss and wet leaves covered its roof. The door was unlocked. I went in and walked right through a dense mesh of cobwebs strung across the opening. A rusty airtight wood stove stood in one corner of the shed, near an iron cot with a foam mattress. Well-stocked bookcases made of cement blocks and planks covered two walls. There was a two-ring Coleman camp stove on the table. A stained porcelain sink was fitted with a single cold-water faucet. An iron pipe suspended from the ceiling served as Hendrix's coat rack. More clothing dangled from nails. Worn hiking boots and dirty sneakers lay untidily beside the door. The shed was damp, and it stank of mould and sweaty clothes.

I left the door open to air the place out, collected an armful of alder logs from Hendrix's woodpile and got a fire going in the stove. As the shed slowly warmed I foraged until I found a gasoline lantern—which I managed to light after a struggle—and put it on the table. The lantern's fierce white radiance revealed more cobwebs, dust and decay. I took a book at random from a shelf. It was the Left Book edition of Orwell's *Road to Wigan Pier*. The book was ruined by dampness, its pages frogged and almost unreadable.

Outside, gusts of wind buffeted the trees, and branches made soft rustlings as they swept across the roof. I was glad to be indoors instead of pounding pavement. "Oatmeal" Savage or not, though, I wasn't planning to spend more than a couple of hours interfering in Mrs. Tranter's private affairs.

Several pictures, which I didn't notice until I lit the lamp, were pinned beneath a shelf. Some were newspaper clippings, others casual snaps. They had been taken at environmentalist rallies, logging-camp blockades and sit-ins outside British Columbia's legislative buildings. Two pictures showed Hendrix standing beside WPC's founder, Felicity Exeter. They made an incongruous pair. Both were in their late 30s, but Felicity was glamorous and beautiful while Hendrix was big and scruffy-looking, with a mop of curly black hair and a full beard.

Suddenly, a car door slammed and an engine backfired like a machine gun. This was followed immediately by the sound of spinning tires as a car raced away. I hurried outside to see what was happening and found a large white envelope pinned to Mrs. Tranter's front door. The enclosed note read:

Seaweed: Sorry I can't meet you, a case is running overtime at the courthouse. Please handle Hendrix yourself if I'm late and serve him with this notice. I'll join you a.s.a.p.

The signature was illegible, but it was obviously Lofthouse's. The envelope also contained a sealed enclosure addressed to Richard Hendrix.

I went back to the shed, left the door open and positioned myself where I could see Mrs. Tranter's house. The stove was heating up the shed nicely. I must have dozed off for a while. I woke up when I heard another car slow down, stop briefly in front of the house, then drive off again.

A hulking, bearded man came into view on the path at the side of the property. It was Hendrix.

He was heading toward the front door until he noticed the smoke rising from his shed. His features darkened as he stormed toward me. He flung the shed door open wider still. I was wearing my uniform, but this didn't impress him much; he looked hot enough to melt. Framed by the threshold, he barked, "Who are you? How did you get in here?"

"Mr. Hendrix, I'm Sergeant Seaweed, Victoria Police Department. I've been waiting for you, sir."

Hendrix was about my height, maybe 20 pounds heavier. The extra weight was flab, not muscle, and he moved clumsily on splayed feet. In ragged jeans and muddy down-at-heel boots, he looked as dilapidated as the shed, but with his bushy beard and great size he seemed threatening. He wore a wide-brimmed black hat and an unbuttoned Australian bushman's canvas overcoat.

"I don't care who you are. This is private property. Get the hell out!" he snarled, jerking a thumb over his shoulder.

I stood up, taking my time about it, then offered him Lofthouse's letter. What happened next was insane. Enraged, and ignoring the letter, Hendrix lurched forward, drew back his right arm and threw a punch at my head. Hampered by his heavy coat, his movements were clumsy. I swayed sideways, and as Hendrix's right arm swung past I grabbed his elbow and gave it a push in the direction it was already moving. That put him off balance, and he started to spin. He ended up behind me, so I stamped my heel down hard on his toes.

He collapsed with a yell. I planted my foot on his neck, pinning him to the floor, and pretended to be cool, as if my pulse wasn't pounding and shoving large men around was just habit with me. "We're doing this all wrong. I came here to talk," I said.

"Jesus Christ," he moaned. "I can't breathe!"

I took my foot away and he sat up, breathing heavily through his mouth. I dropped Lofthouse's note beside him and said, "Better read that before you try anything else."

Hendrix glared up at me from beneath the brim of his cap, then grabbed the note, hauled himself to his feet and hobbled to the lamp. As the import of Lofthouse's letter sank in, Hendrix's bottom lip, thrust forward in an infantile pout, slowly tightened and his brows drew together. "You know about this?" he said, shaking the letter. "My aunt's cut me off, told me to clear out." He'd worked himself into another rage: his bloodshot eyes were unfocused and his lips had a white ring around them. "I'll kill her, the bitch! All the things I've done for that ungrateful cow—I'll kill her!"

He staggered toward me and pointed a quivering finger. "Where's my aunt? Where is she?"

"It's time you wised up," I advised him. "Did something for yourself for a change, instead of being a full-time professional parasite."

"After I punch your head in!"

"You must be a slow learner, Hendrix."

Hendrix drew back his fist, but this time thought better of swinging at me. "I'm not finished with you," he said. "I've got your name, and I'm not gonna forget it." He waved the note under my nose. "It says here I have to get my gear out and that I have to stay away from my aunt. You knew all about it, didn't you?"

"Grow up. I didn't create this situation. You did."

Hendrix licked his lips. "You know what she did to me? You know she took me out of her will?"

I didn't say anything.

"That bitch! That four-eyed, dirty old bitch!" Words failed him. He groaned with impotent rage, fists clenched, and for a full minute just stood there staring forward sightlessly and mouthing incomprehensible threats and insults. The gist of it was that if he could get his hands around his aunt's neck, he'd squeeze the life out of her and do the same for anyone who tried to stop him. At that moment, Hendrix meant every word.

"Face it," I said finally. "Your aunt is afraid of you. That's why I'm here. Take my advice. Find a room somewhere else and take it easy. Tomorrow you might feel different about things. Given time, maybe you can patch things up with her."

Hendrix looked at the letter in his hand and slowly came out of his trance. "This lawyer guy," he said. "He's enclosed a cheque for a coupla hundred bucks. He says I get to keep the money if I renounce all claims against the estate."

I shrugged. Any quitclaim Hendrix signed under these circumstances would probably be overturned on appeal to the courts, but I wasn't about to tell him that.

Hendrix grinned craftily. "They're trying to trick me, cheat me out of what's rightfully mine. She's my aunt, my own mother's sister. I'm the only family she's got. I got every right to inherit family money, and no smartass lawyer's gonna screw me out of it."

"This has gone far enough. It's time to move on," I said. "My car's outside. I'll drive you downtown if you want"

"Fuck you! I got my own ways of dealing with problems. Just tell me where I can get my hands on the bitch."

"Stop with the b.s., Hendrix. I'm tired of listening to it."

His face, half-shadow in the light of the lamp, was like a wooden mask. "What b.s.? I mean every word. Just watch me. Now get out of my way."

We stood face to face, six feet apart. "Find a friend, Richard," I said firmly. "Talk and think things over. Your aunt may feel differently toward you in a couple of months. The world hasn't come to an end."

"Nobody messes with me and gets away with it," he said, as if he hadn't heard me. He added darkly, "It's been tried before."

I blocked his way for a moment, wondering whether to handcuff him and take him to the lockup. But I decided against it. Mrs. Tranter was safely out of the way.

I stepped aside. Hendrix hobbled across the unkempt garden and was gone.

CHAPTER SIX

I waited in the shed for a while in case Hendrix returned, then called Lofthouse's office on my cell. Grace Sleight told me her boss was in conference and couldn't be disturbed.

"Grace," I said, "I've just spent an unhappy half-hour with Richard Hendrix. The guy is very upset about being kicked out of his house and cut from Mrs. Tranter's will. You'd better disturb Sammy's conference and warn him to keep Mrs. Tranter well hidden. Tell Sammy to keep his own head covered, too. Hendrix is acting crazy."

Grace gave a low moan. "Oh Lord. Sammy isn't here. I think I just blew it."

"What do you mean?"

"A man just phoned, asking for Sammy. Maybe it was Hendrix. He said he had important information that Sammy needed immediately."

"You told him where Sammy was?"

"I did. It was stupid, but I told him," she wailed unhappily. "You know Sammy. He works with rats and squealers. We get mysterious calls all the time."

"Where's Sammy now?"

"At the Red Barn Hotel with Mrs. Tranter. Room 311."

"Call your boss right now. Warn him that Hendrix might be

headed his way. If it *was* Hendrix on the phone, there'll be big trouble. Hurry, Grace!"

I dashed to my car and raced down the rain-swept streets, gunning my little coupe through the yellow light at Hillside and Douglas. By the time I crossed Finlayson Street, red and blue lights were flashing in my rear-view mirror. A siren whooped as the police cruiser followed me into the Red Barn's courtyard. I skidded to a stop outside the main entrance and left my car blocking the doors. Ignoring a doorman's shouts, I headed inside. Startled patrons scattered as I raced through the lobby and took the stairs three at a time to the third floor. Somebody was chasing me now, yelling for me to stop.

The door to room 311 was locked. I was hammering on it when a gasping hotel clerk caught up with me. I hammered the door again as the clerk grabbed my arm.

"Sir! Sir! You can't—" he began.

"Emergency!" I shouted. "Open this door!"

The clerk was trying to explain hotel policy when the stairwell door opened and a uniform appeared. It was Harry Biedel, a longtime constable I'd known for years. Biedel, who had not realized whose car he was tailing, was now trying to catch his breath. "What the hell's going on, Silas?" he puffed.

"No time to explain, Harry. We need this door open, now!"

We were ready to smash down the door with our shoulders when the clerk hurriedly produced a master key and unlocked it.

"After you, Silas," Biedel said. "This better be good."

The room was a standard unit with a Formica dressing table and chest of drawers. The double bed was flanked by night tables with oversized lamps. Mrs. Tranter's dark glasses lay on a coffee table. The TV was on—a black man rapping about sex and violence was competing with the sound of running water. A wet stain was growing on the carpet outside the bathroom door. I pushed inside and saw Mrs. Tranter, draped over the edge of the tub with her head partially submerged. One of her shoes was off and lay near the sink. She had on the blue dress patterned with tropical flowers. The hem of a nylon undergarment showed. Instead of diminishing her, death somehow seemed to have increased her. She looked larger dead than she had alive.

IN THE HOTEL courtyard, medics were placing Mrs. Tranter's body in an ambulance. My little coupe was flanked by police cruisers. Harry Biedel and other uniforms were helping the hotel staff control traffic. Wide-eyed rubbernecks speculated among themselves.

An identification team was dusting for fingerprints and making sketches in the room. Cameras clicked as photographs were taken from every possible angle. Dr. Flower, the duty medical officer, had pronounced Mrs. Tranter officially dead and was now typing notes into a laptop.

CDI Bulloch was tied up at a social function in Saanich, but Bernie, in charge of the initial investigation, arrived promptly. He was unshaven, with dark circles under his eyes. When he saw me and realized that I had encroached on Bulloch's turf again, he gave his head a pitying shake.

In the victim's handbag, detectives found an address book, a bottle of aspirin, a bottle of eye drops, a Pharmacare card and 15 dollars in cash.

"Can you confirm that the dead woman is Mrs. Tranter?" Bernie asked.

I hesitated. "I only saw her once, for a short time in a dark room, and she was wearing dark glasses."

Bernie and I watched from the window as the ambulance pulled away and headed for the morgue. I'd already described every detail of my encounter with Richard Hendrix once. Now Bernie asked me to do it again.

Dr. Flower approached. "Got a minute, Bernie?" he asked.

Bernie left my side and the two men exchanged a few quiet words. As the doctor turned to leave, I said, "By the way, Doc. Were DNA samples taken from Isaac Schwartz's bedding?"

"DNA, yes. We did collect some, actually," Dr. Flower said. "It's quite interesting. Somebody—two somebodies, in fact—had sex in that bed. Isaac Schwartz wasn't one of them."

At this, Bernie's mouth dropped open and stayed open for at least 10 seconds. Dr. Flower just smiled and went out.

"Does Flower think Mrs. Tranter drowned in that tub?" I asked.

"Possibly. There were signs of bruising around her neck. He thinks she was throttled first, then had her head shoved under the water. He'll know for sure after the autopsy."

"So what do you think, Bernie?"

"I think a person or persons unknown killed an elderly woman," Bernie replied wearily.

"I think it's very peculiar that two elderly people have been murdered in the same week," I said.

That thought had already occurred to Bernie.

"Another thing," I continued. "I don't understand why Sammy Lofthouse isn't here. According to his secretary, Lofthouse arranged to meet Mrs. Tranter in this very room."

"Uh-huh," Bernie mumbled.

"Sammy might have arrived late, I suppose. Maybe he saw all the activity in the parking lot and decided to pass. Now he'll probably be at home, trembling in his boots. Wondering where Richard Hendrix is."

"Wrong," Bernie said. "Lofthouse is over at the morgue."

His words startled me. "You don't mean …"

"No, Silas, Lofthouse isn't dead. I talked to him on the phone a little while ago, after you told me about your meeting with Hendrix. It seems that when Lofthouse left the courthouse today, he went to Bartholomew's. Had a few drinks and consorted with fellow lawyers."

"You had me going, Bernie," I said. "For a minute there, I thought Lofthouse was dead as well."

"The company he keeps, that could easily happen. Anyway, I told him to head for the morgue and wait for Tranter's body to arrive. To be ready to identify it."

"Do you need me for anything else?" I asked. It had been a long day.

Bernie sat down, leaned back and clasped his hands behind his head. "Tell me something, Silas, 'cause it's been bugging me. Remember when we were on the beach at Mowaht the other morning? What that guy Meyer told us? He said he and his boy saw an old Native messing around with Isaac's body."

"That's what he told us. And Bernie, sorry, it slipped my mind till now. The kid—Albert—told me he saw *two* people."

"Natives?"

"Maybe. He thought a man and a woman. Maybe a man and a young boy."

"Exactly. This is my question for you. How did they carry Isaac's body up to that cabin? You saw what conditions were like. They were terrible. It was all I could do to walk up that bank myself, and I wasn't packing a dead body."

"That's been bothering me too."

We were both silent for a minute, thinking about it. Then Bernie drew us back to the business at hand. "Come by the station tomorrow," he said. "We'll get your statement typed."

"Sure thing," I said. I turned to go.

"Hey, pal," said Bernie.

I stopped at the door, one hand on the knob.

"My advice to you is, keep your house securely locked tonight," Bernie said, with a grin that stretched from ear to ear. "The hands that wrapped themselves around Mrs. Tranter's neck are big enough to stretch around yours, too."

"His hands might be big enough," I said, grinning back. "The question is, are his balls big enough?"

INSTEAD OF GOING straight home, I detoured to Mrs. Tranter's neighbourhood and parked around the corner from her house. I entered her yard and stood motionless in the dark, thinking about the ghost wolf, dog or whatever it was I had encountered there before. This time, all was silent.

I waited for a minute beside a cedar hedge, then slowly moved farther into the yard. Neglected fruit trees and tall shrubs provided plenty of cover. The dark bulk of Hendrix's shed, and the adjacent outhouse and woodpile, was almost invisible in the night—a deeper shade of black in a dark, dripping world. Then I smelled something. Nearby, somebody was smoking—Virginia tobacco. After 30 seconds or so, a tiny golden glow briefly illuminated the face of a man as he inhaled deeply from a cigarette. He was standing under the eaves of the shed, less than 20 feet away. The cigarette fell to the ground and was tramped down by the man's boot. Then the smoker moved away from the shelter of the eaves and walked slowly toward the house.

It was a uniformed constable.

Well, well. Bernie had had the place staked out in case Hendrix came back. Whether a noisy smoker would catch Hendrix napping was another matter.

I waited for the constable to reach the house and step onto the veranda before I stole away home.

CHAPTER SEVEN

I was finishing a morning workout on Moran's heavy bag, leaning into it with my shoulder and gasping as I delivered short right-hand punches. Blinking perspiration from my eyes, I changed shoulders and punched with my left hand.

Tony shook his head at my obvious fatigue. "Now you believe me, what I've been telling you? That jogging you do, it's no good by itself. You gotta work on your upper body more."

Pushing my limits, I did a left-right combination that sent the bag swinging away and allowed my arms to fall. When the bag came back I sidestepped, but it grazed me going by.

Tony grunted. "There you go. I'm looking at a has-been. A guy what can't even duck a bag. Better stretch out on my table, champ— I'll give you a rub down."

I held my arms out for Tony to unlace the 16-ounce gloves and said, "Any time I start feeling good about myself, I come here and get straightened out."

Tony smiled. He tied the laces together and hung the gloves on a wall hook, and I stretched out face down on the leather bench.

"Okay, champ," Tony said, pouring baby oil on my back. "What you want?"

"I want a body like Arnold Schwarzenegger," I said, smothering groans as Tony's strong fingers dug into my neck and shoulders.

"No you don't," Tony said with conviction. "What you want is Arnold's brains. Or maybe his bank account. What you want is a body like Joe Louis, or Muhammad Ali. You ever watch those reruns on TV? The great fights?"

"I saw Ali beat Foreman on a rerun a while back."

"Well, take a closer look at them guys' bodies the next time. Check out them shoulders, abdomens. Them arm muscles. Compared to Arnold, good boxers got no definition at all—they're almost flabby. But let me tell you, they've got more than straight power. What they got is *staying* power, the kind that carries a boxer for 15 rounds."

I closed my eyes and gritted my teeth as Tony hammered my calf muscles. Then I heard Moran's voice.

"When Tony stops beating the tar outta you, Silas, I want to talk to you."

I opened one eye. Moran was already walking away in his wrinkled suit, chomping an unlit cigar. I tried to relax. Now Tony had started to squeeze the flesh along my spine between his thumb and forefinger.

"What the hell are you doing to me, Tony?"

"Getting rid of calcium deposits. You've got a lot of crystals building up; I can feel 'em in there."

"Are you trying to pop them through my skin, like orange pips?"

"Just relax, Silas. Tell me how you're doing on this Tranter murder, the one in the paper."

"I'm not officially involved. The detective squad's taking care of it."

"Have they found the guy they're looking for, that Henpix?"

"*Hendrix*. His name is Richard Hendrix. And that reminds me: has Sammy Lofthouse been in here lately?"

Tony's massage got even rougher when he heard Lofthouse's name. "That sleazebag? I'm surprised Lofthouse has the nerve to show his face anywhere in this town. It's about time somebody fixed that hustlin' little prick."

"I thought he was one of your best customers."

"Not anymore."

"What did Lofthouse ever do to you?"

"To me, nothing. But he conned my nephew, Teddy. Conned him outta thousands," Tony said, forgetting my massage as he vented his irritation. "Teddy's my sister's boy. He gets into a bit of mischief one time and hires Lofthouse. That bastard was no help at all. All he did was take a vacuum cleaner to Teddy's bank account."

"How did he manage that?"

"Lofthouse said he'd fix it. Talked Teddy into copping a plea, promised he'd get probation instead of jail. Cost Terry a bundle. I think he gave Lofthouse five thousand bucks. That was three years ago, and Teddy's still breaking rocks at William Head."

I had to laugh. "Breaking rocks! Are you kidding? William Head's a holiday camp. Club Fed for hoodlums. Waterfront views from every window. They've got tattoo parlours in there now. Instead of cells, murderers get private cabins with kitchens. If Teddy doesn't like the Head, tell him to try Kent Prison."

I heard myself getting hostile—something Chief Alphonse was always warning me against—so I changed direction and said, "All this dough Lofthouse got from your nephew. How did the kid earn it? Flipping hamburgers at McDonald's?"

I rolled onto my back. The mirth came back into Tony's face as he massaged my feet. Tony avoided the question. We both knew how Teddy had earned Lofthouse's fee—hustling while out on bail.

"Well, there you go," I said.

Tony was pulling individual toes now, wiggling them between his thumb and forefinger. He said, "This hurts, right? Hurts, but feels good at the same time. You know anything else works like that?"

"Charity," I said. "Giving money to Pastor McNaught so he can feed guys who sleep under bridges."

"Right. I see those bloodsucking evangelists on the tube Sundays and think I'm a sucker. But then I get to thinking about it some more and I feel better."

Tony finished my feet and slapped my stomach with the flat of his hand. "That'll do you, champ," he said. "Hit the showers."

MORAN WAS WAITING for me at the poker table, drinking coffee and chomping that poor cigar as if he hated it. The old warhorse shoved a cardboard box across the table at me and said, "This is some more of Isaac's stuff. I found it in a locker."

The box contained more old photographs and receipts, as well as a bundle of letters in yellowing envelopes, tied together with a red ribbon. I opened one envelope and pulled out the letter. It was written with a broad-nibbed pen, in German; the only thing I could decipher was the date: January 15, 1939.

The photographs were mostly family snapshots, similar to the ones we'd found in Isaac's room earlier. They showed stern-faced old men sitting in wicker garden chairs, glaring fiercely at the camera. There were also pictures of a little family—a man who might have been a young Isaac Schwartz with a wife and two small children. More recent pictures of the same people showed an additional child, being held in its mother's arms. Moran sighed when he looked at it.

In addition to photos, there was a 30-year-old BC Tel receipt, another from a dentist and a bundle of miscellaneous papers that included a 1967 bus pass. At the bottom of the box was a small notebook covered with spidery foreign handwriting and a fat envelope containing an illustrated auction catalogue.

"It's funny what people save," Moran said.

"I'll pass this along to Bernie Tapp," I told him.

"Whatever." Moran scowled at his reflection in the wall mirror beside the table. The old scrapper had scar tissue around both eyes—souvenirs of bad cut-men in long-forgotten prizefights. Moran turned away from the mirror and asked, "You coming to the poker game Friday? Usual time."

I pretended to be a hard sell. "I dunno about poker. I keep asking myself, is it sexy enough? Maybe I should take up dancing on Fridays for a change. Maybe I'll get lucky."

Moran, thinking I was serious, gave me a look of incredulity, "No way. You started dancing?"

"Yeah," I lied. "There're regular Friday-night singles dances now."

"Dancing? At your age?"

"What do you mean, my age? Besides, dancing is great exercise."

"Yeah, sure. Dancing and bowling and bingo, they're all good for the heart," Moran said. Disgusted, Moran went over to the electric percolator and poured more coffee, shaking his head and muttering beneath his breath. Over his shoulder he called, "What's the big idea, taking all those samples?"

"What are you talking about?"

"Bernie Tapp and them were here this morning. Took spit samples—saliva—from me and Tony and the others."

"Don't worry about it. They're checking DNA to eliminate you guys as suspects, that's all. It's routine."

AFTER I'D SHOWERED I put my uniform back on, collected the box of Isaac's belongings and, for no particular reason other than to take in the view, went up to stand on the roof of the building.

Icy onshore winds were bringing more dark clouds in from the Pacific. To the west, the Sooke Hills descended in slow waves before disappearing under the Strait of Juan de Fuca. Twenty miles on, the same range of hills re-emerged from beneath the sea, rising up in steep, irregular chunks to create the Olympic Peninsula before finally sinking into the distant Pacific. Closer in, rooftops stretched in every direction. The tide was ebbing. A hundred yards from where I stood, the Gorge Waterway flowed into the Inner Harbour. Several fishboats and a small freighter were under refit at the Point Hope Shipyard. A fringe of white scum bubbled south along the Gorge's muddy shore, where legitimate diggers busily excavated the archaeological site.

I went downstairs to the street and walked to my office. I was letting myself inside when a car door slammed shut nearby. Something made me turn around. A woman had just exited a Land Rover. She moved with long, easy strides and got prettier with every step. She was tall, with streaky blonde hair, and wore an open Burberry raincoat that showed off a shapely figure beneath a turtleneck sweater and tartan skirt. "Sergeant Seaweed?" she smiled.

I nodded.

"I've been waiting for you. My name is Felicity Exeter."

"It's cold. Let's go inside my office," I said. "After you."

I set Isaac's box on my desk and asked, "Would you like coffee? There's a diner next door; I can have some sent 'round."

She shook her head. "Lou's place. I drank a cup there earlier, waiting for you."

"I'm glad you waited," I said. "Please, have a seat."

Here she was, beautiful and rich, another mysterious door of opportunity opening up. She sat down across from my desk and crossed her legs. She smelled very nice. There were no rings on her fingers. "What can I do for you?" I asked.

Perhaps she could read my mind. The tip of her tongue touched her upper lip and the tiniest suggestion of a smile brightened her eyes as she composed her thoughts. "I'm involved with an environmental group, the Wilderness Preservation Committee," she said. "You may have heard about us?"

"The WPC, yes."

"Well, this type of group tends to attract its share of hotheads. People with views so extreme they're really over the edge—*too* radical. Richard Hendrix falls into that category."

She stopped speaking and waited for my reaction. But being Coast Salish means I am patient by definition. It suited me to conceal my emotions and wait.

"Well, Sergeant, do you have anything to say?"

"I can confirm that Mr. Hendrix has a bad temper," I said.

"My—our—group doesn't condone tree spiking, malicious damage to logging equipment or anything like that. Even apart from the moral aspect, mindless sabotage alienates people who might otherwise support us. Richard can't see that. He wants total war against all loggers—" She stopped in mid-sentence and laughed. "I'm sorry, Sergeant, sometimes I get carried away. Am I sounding preachy?"

"Not seriously. But Hendrix is in a lot of trouble. We want to talk to him about a recent murder."

"I know," she said calmly. "Richard and I read about it in today's paper."

I listened without taking my eyes off her face.

"I live on a farm in View Royal," she explained. "There's a barn on my property, a couple of other outbuildings and a guest cottage. The cottage isn't visible from the main house, but yesterday morning before breakfast I went out to check on my sheep and noticed that the cottage curtains were drawn wide. I'd closed them myself a day or two earlier. The next thing I knew, Richard appeared." She laughed nervously. "Seeing him gave me quite a shock. He came right over and admitted he'd spent the night there."

"Has Hendrix used your cottage before?"

"No, but he's been on my property several times. We often hold WPC meetings at my house, and occasionally he's shown up." Her face tightened and she moved restlessly. "I think he knows we don't really want him, that some members don't like him. But Richard seems quite friendless. There isn't much else enlivening his existence, so we tolerate him as best we can."

Her gaze lighted on my desk calendar, and she stared at it as if it contained the answer to some mystery.

"Technically, then, Hendrix was trespassing," I said.

"Trespassing?" she said, coming out of her trance. "That's a bit harsh. I admit that when I first saw Richard I was annoyed and asked him to leave. Then I saw something was wrong. He looked different. Human. For a change he wasn't posturing and showing off like he usually is. He was being genuine. I could tell he was frightened. I invited him into the house and gave him a cup of tea. That's when he told me his story."

"Did he tell you if he killed his aunt?"

"Richard insists he had nothing to do with it. He says he arrived at his aunt's house after hitchhiking to Victoria from Tofino. It seems you were there, waiting for him. The two of you had an argument, and he left in a rage." She hesitated. "Apparently, he beat you up first. Is that true?"

"We exchanged a few pleasantries."

She nodded. "Anyway, Richard said that afterwards he wandered the streets for a bit, wondering what to do. When he heard about Mrs. Tranter's murder he panicked. Then he remembered my cottage. He thought it would be a good place to hole up. He knows I'm away a lot."

"Did he tell you how he found out his aunt had been murdered?"

She thought for a moment before shaking her head.

"Do you believe his story?" I asked.

"I'm sure Richard didn't kill his aunt. Or maybe that's wishful thinking."

"Where is he now?"

"I don't know. He left my place without saying where he was going."

"After reading the paper, you must have known he's wanted by the police."

"Yes. I felt sorry for him. It isn't wrong to want to help people, surely?"

"In this case, yes. You must have known you were breaking the law. Aiding and abetting a wanted man is a serious matter."

She smiled. "Tell me—because I've always wondered—what's the difference between *aiding* and *abetting?*"

"Abetting is the same as inciting."

"Whatever I did," she admitted, "it was probably a bad idea. But beneath all that bluster, Richard really is quite pathetic."

"Do you have a lawyer, Mrs. Exeter?"

"Of course. I thought of calling him before I spoke to you, but I knew he'd advise me to report all this to the police."

"I *am* the police. Detective Chief Inspector Bulloch is the senior officer in charge of this investigation. You should go to police headquarters now and tell Bulloch what you just told me."

"No doubt I *should* tell him. But that's not what I *want* to do."

I started to interrupt, but she held up a hand, smiled and leaned forward. "You've got a reputation for being a maverick. People say you don't always do things by the book."

"Perhaps, but this is a murder investigation. Anything you know about Hendrix is material, and DCI Bulloch needs to hear it from you directly." I gave her a smile. "Will you come quietly? Or do I have to arrest you?"

"I'm one of those tiresome eco-activists, Sergeant Seaweed. I've been arrested several times, so another arrest wouldn't bother me. But I'm not looking for trouble, either. What I'm really hoping is that somehow Richard will be cleared."

"Did Hendrix threaten you in any way?"

"He cut the telephone wires to my house."

"What for?"

"I don't know. He was in a panic, I suppose. After talking with me, he apologized."

"So what, exactly, do *you* want?"

"I want the real killer found, of course, because I'm certain—I just *know* Richard is innocent of this. I'm afraid if he's arrested he'll start grandstanding and dig his own grave. I want him to have a decent chance."

She stood up and looked out the window, gnawing her bottom lip.

I thought about what she'd said. Had Hendrix murdered his aunt? Possibly—but the timing was off. Hendrix didn't have a car or, as far as I knew, a cellphone. To find and kill Mrs. Tranter before I got to the Red Barn Hotel, Hendrix would have had to find a taxi in an area where taxis were scarce. It was technically feasible, but only just. Police inquiries so far had failed to locate any taxi driver who had picked up Hendrix. Mrs. Tranter's murder had received plenty of publicity—every cabby in Victoria knew about the Red Barn killing.

Felicity had her back to the window now and was facing me. I asked again, "You're certain you don't know where Hendrix is?"

"Quite."

I might have been scowling, because she looked away. I still had a hunch that Sammy Lofthouse might have some idea where

Hendrix could have gone to ground. Maybe he could find out something through his network of low-life pals. I decided it was worth another shot, even if Bernie had already asked him about it. Lofthouse might talk to me.

"Excuse me a minute," I said to Felicity. I called Lofthouse's office and asked the receptionist to put me through to him. Grace came on the line instead. When I asked her to let me to talk to Lofthouse directly, she didn't say anything.

"Still there, Grace?"

"I'm here, Silas. But you can't speak to Sammy—he's not in the office."

"This is important, Grace. Where is he?"

"I don't know. He just vanished. I can't find him anywhere." Grace sounded distressed.

"Vanished? Since when?"

"Since viewing Mrs. Tranter's body at the morgue." She paused, then added, "He's never done anything like this before."

"Isn't Sammy married?"

"Was. His ex, Serena, lives in Vancouver. Serena hates Sammy's guts. But there are a couple of little kids, so they keep in touch. I've phoned her, of course, but she says she hasn't spoken to him lately."

"Is your office busy these days?"

"Very busy."

"Who's handling Sammy's cases during this absence?"

"We have a loose arrangement with another firm. They step in if Sammy's sick or on vacation. But our clients don't like it. Sammy has the fastest mouth in town."

I refrained from saying that he was so fast he was downright slow.

"Right now I'm so worried I can't think straight," Grace said.

"Well, let me know if you hear from him, all right?"

Grace promised she would, and I hung up.

Felicity had picked up a highway-safety manual from the top of the filing cabinet and was idly leafing through it while pretending not to listen to my telephone conversation. She felt me watching her and put the manual down. I wanted to say something that would make her smile and erase the two deep lines that had appeared between her eyebrows. But what I said was, "Hendrix has a short fuse. I saw a sample of it the other night. It's possible he killed his aunt during one of his rages. If he killed once, he might kill again. It's supposed to get easier every time. I mention this because your own life could be in danger. Maybe you should keep away from your farm for a few days, to be on the safe side."

"Richard is no threat to me, surely!"

"I know you have a social conscience, but I'm not sure Richard is a suitable object for your concern. He's a liar, and he's violent."

Felicity sat down again. "It was only a little lie, Mr. Seaweed, a touch of male vanity," she said. "I *knew* Richard didn't beat you up. It was obvious from the way he said it. You beat *him* up probably."

"I just stepped on his toes a little."

"I'm impressed. Richard must have been quite a handful. All the same, I'm convinced he wasn't lying about his aunt."

"Why are you bothering yourself with this? We have a good legal system in this country. People don't get railroaded nowadays. If Richard didn't do it, he has little to worry about."

"Come, Mr. Seaweed, is that what you really think?" she said scornfully. "What about the Milgaard case? Sentenced to life for a murder police knew he probably didn't commit. What about those poor saps prosecuted for Satanism in Saskatchewan a year or two back? *Satanism*, in the twenty-first century! Come on!"

As she looked directly at me and continued, I saw that her eyes were not dark blue, as I'd thought, but a dark emerald green.

"Poor Richard. He hasn't a single real friend, not one. He's done a number of things in his unhappy life, none successfully. Now he's alone and miserable. I just want to help a little, show him that *somebody* cares."

"Okay, that's fair enough. Just don't expect much. Hendrix may not be a murderer, but he's pretty unpleasant all the same."

Felicity studied me for a moment, then said, "You're not what I expected, Mr. Seaweed."

I raised my eyebrows.

"Sarah Williams is a friend of mine. I believe you were very helpful to her and her family once. Sarah speaks highly of you." She cocked her head to one side and said, half-smiling, "Well? Won't you help me, too?"

"I'm a lowly neighbourhood cop. Your next step is to see DCI Bulloch. Call your lawyer first is my advice."

She stood up and started for the coat rack, but I beat her to it and held her coat for her to slip into. Her hair brushed my cheek and I inhaled her fragrance again.

She jammed both hands into her coat pockets and looked deep into my eyes. That's when my door banged open and DCI Bulloch strode in. He had trouble written all over him, even before he noticed the cardboard box on my desk and found out what was in it.

I HAD BEEN ordered to wait in Bulloch's outer office. Felicity Exeter and her lawyer had been closeted with Bulloch for nearly an hour. Now they had gone. It was my turn.

Bulloch was lolling in his chair behind the gleaming mahogany desk, his face flushed. In a voice of cold hostility he said, "Just remind me, Seaweed. How long have you been a policeman?"

"About eight years, sir."

"You went to cop college, didn't you?" he said derisively. "You were exposed to the same kind of training as every other officer?"

I wondered if this would be the day I'd lose it with him. Reach across that desk, grab him by the collar and add another bump to his broken, red-veined nose.

"Maybe, because you're Indian, a visible minority, instructors made special allowances?" he went on. "Gave you a pass on the hard courses? Skewed marks in your favour, that sort of thing?"

My fists bunched automatically, so I put my hands in my pockets.

"Evidently, Seaweed, you skipped the chain-of-command lecture. The one that explains that sergeants and constables do whatever the fuck inspectors and chiefs tell them to do. I have told you, not once but a thousand times, that you are *not*, repeat *not*, a *detective* …"

After a few minutes of this sort of thing, Bulloch had worked himself into a panting rage. He poked Isaac's cardboard box with his index finger and pounded his fist on the desk. His chair crashed backwards as he stood up, leaned forward and jabbed the same finger into my chest. "You've gone too far this time, Seaweed. The articles in this box are evidence, and you were holding onto it. Concealing evidence from a senior officer."

Just what Isaac's junk was evidence *of* wasn't clear, but Bulloch's face was completely red so I listened as his tirade continued. "I've got your number," he shouted. "You're a glory hunter, planning to work this case yourself and grab the headlines. Well, we'll see about that."

Bulloch opened the deep bottom drawer of his desk, shoved the box into it and kicked the drawer shut with his boot. "Now get the hell out of my office."

I placed both hands on his desk and leaned in toward him. I was satisfied to see him flinch.

CHAPTER EIGHT

It was time for Isaac's memorial service at the Good Shepherd. The mission's free hot lunch had ended. Homeless men and women shuffled around on the steps outside the building, psyching themselves up for another cold lonely day on the streets. A skinny old Native man was in the Good Shepherd's small chapel, arranging a pair of sawhorses before the altar. It was Nimrod, Isaac Schwartz's friend.

I said, "Ya, hey, Nimrod. Is Pastor McNaught around?"

Nimrod squinted short-sightedly. He didn't recognize me. "Pastor'll be out in a minute," he muttered.

I sat on a chair in the front row and gazed at the wooden cross over the altar. A door opened and four pallbearers entered, carrying Isaac's coffin. They were new to the task and handled the coffin clumsily. When they lowered it to the sawhorses, one pallbearer lost his grip. There was a loud crack as the coffin suddenly tipped. The sawhorses wobbled a bit, but held. Scowling as the embarrassed pallbearers hurried out, Nimrod carefully tested the coffin's stability by pushing it timidly with one hand. Satisfied, he covered the coffin with a purple velvet cloth and spent a few minutes patiently smoothing its folds. After that he came and sat next to me, his narrow shoulders bowed, looking at the floor.

We waited in silence until Moran, Tony and a half-dozen gym regulars arrived. I was expecting Bernie to attend, but he never showed up. Recorded music swelled in volume on the PA system until the Mormon Tabernacle Choir had drowned out the noisy dishwashers working in the kitchen. Then Pastor Joe McNaught entered.

McNaught was a reformed drunk and one-time prizefighter. Now he was bringing muscular Christianity to Victoria's street people. His declared commission was to feed the hungry and bring sinners to the arms of Jesus. He had a bushy beard, and his sparse remaining hair encircled an enormous shining dome. It was a joke on the street that McNaught's clothes were made by Jones Tent and Awning. He had on a long black sleeveless vestment over a black shirt and white clerical collar. He looked like a World Wrestling Federation heavyweight impersonating the Messenger of Doom, but he was nobody's fool.

McNaught and I were the same age. We had been in the fight game together and had fought a couple of times. McNaught had been a dirty, ring-smart boxer. If he could blindside the referee he'd bring his knee up in your groin, stomp your instep; stick a thumb in your eye. I'd quit the swindle early, but McNaught boxed on for years. Long enough to get a broken nose, cauliflower ears and, some people thought, scrambled brains. His fighting weight had been 225 pounds, but I guessed he'd push the scales at over 350 now. Too much booze and too many punches eventually caught up with him, and he spent years on skid row before he found Jesus and dried out. Victoria's established churches had him pegged as a religious fraud. To me, he was the enigma he had always been.

McNaught stood behind his pulpit and opened his mouth to speak, but the chapel door opened again and he delayed his words until a late arrival had taken a seat at the back. Then he pushed a button on his lectern and, to everyone's surprise, a tenor's voice rang out over the PA:

On the Road to Mandalay
Where the flyin'-fishes play,
An' the dawn comes up like thunder
Outer China 'crost the bay ...

Without the least sign of perturbation, McNaught pressed another button. The Rudyard Kipling song ended abruptly and was replaced by the Mormon Choir's version of "Abide with Me."

Smiling as if nothing had happened, McNaught waited for the music to fade, then said, "We are here today to say farewell to our departed brother, Isaac Schwartz. Isaac and myself wrestled with demons together many a time, and I loved him. He led an interesting life."

"Amen," said Nimrod, stirring in the chair beside me.

"Some ancient horrors are best forgotten, some tales best untold, and the grave claims all secrets in the end," said McNaught, squinting at his notes. "But Isaac's history should be remembered.

"Isaac was born in Berlin, Germany. He came to manhood between the great wars and took himself a wife. In time, he fathered three children." McNaught peered at the tiny audience and adjusted his eyeglasses until they were balanced on the tip of his nose. He continued, "Isaac was born into the Jewish faith. Everyone knows the misery that Hitler's regime inflicted on Jews during those terrible years."

McNaught gave us a moment to reflect before continuing. "Prewar Germany was an age of madness and terror. For the 'crime' of being Jewish, Isaac and his family were arrested by the Nazis and transported to concentration camps. Isaac spent five years behind barbed-wire fences, enduring hardships that we, in this tolerant democracy, can hardly imagine. Isaac was beaten and starved and forced to work as a slave. His sufferings were made worse because he did not know what fate had befallen his wife and his children.

Isaac ended up in the concentration camp at Bergen-Belsen. In 1945, more dead than alive, he was liberated by the British Seventh Army. Afterwards, Isaac learned that his whole family had perished."

McNaught blew his nose on a big white handkerchief before continuing. "Isaac came to Canada in the 1940s. He worked as a camp cook in the northern woods. In his spare time he loved to fish."

Nimrod nudged me with his shoulder and muttered, "Isaac wasn't no camp cook. He was a *bullcook*."

McNaught fingered his clerical collar and turned a benevolent eye on Nimrod. "Later," he went on, "Isaac was employed at Moran's Gymnasium, where he was well known and respected by Victoria's sporting fraternity."

McNaught stared at Isaac's coffin. "The final bell has sounded for Isaac Schwartz. Now the Referee is checking his scorecard. I believe that Isaac was a champion who will dwell in the Lord's corner forever."

At the back of the room, somebody coughed. We recited the Lord's Prayer, then the Mormons sang "Amazing Grace." When the music faded there was a minute's silence during which a chair creaked at the rear of the room. I twisted around and saw an elderly woman in a fur coat hurrying out. Nimrod, head bowed, was mumbling a private prayer.

Joe McNaught made the sign of the cross with his hand, smiled at the congregation, and that was that. Isaac's memorial service was over.

I followed Nimrod into McNaught's office for the funeral feast. Moran and the others couldn't stay, so there were only three of us, sitting around a big desk. McNaught, who had a specially reinforced steel chair to sit on, poured three glasses of orange juice and invited us to share a plate of ham and cheese sandwiches.

Nimrod picked up his glass and said shakily, "This is for you,

Isaac." He tipped the juice down his throat and held out his glass for a refill.

I looked at him and said, "Well, how you been, Nimrod?"

"Do I know you?" he asked, peering at me.

"You should. I picked you up for shoplifting at Eaton's, 1997. They had you in that back room. Your pockets were full of ladies' lingerie."

Nimrod focussed his narrowed eyes. "Shit," he said. "It's Silas Seaweed. Sorry, Silas, I don't see nothing since I busted my glasses."

McNaught smiled at me. "Since Brother Nimrod's discovered the Lord, he's given up shoplifting. Now he's my strong right arm in the soup kitchen."

"Maybe," I said, "but has he given up wearing ladies' underwear?"

Nimrod's face reddened for a few seconds, then reverted to its usual mournful expression. Outside, fire and police sirens wailed. Nimrod had downed his second glass of juice and was staring morosely at the wall. McNaught said pointedly, "Nimrod, we've got dirty dishes piled up in the kitchen."

"Fuck the dishes," said Nimrod, not moving. "Where's it get you, busting your ass all the time? Where did it get Isaac?"

I said, "I never saw Isaac bust his ass. All I ever saw him do was lean on a broom at Moran's gym, or roam the streets with a sack, checking garbage cans."

"That Isaac," sighed McNaught, clasping his hands and resting them across his belly. "He loved garbage. Never seen anything like it. Do you think he learned that habit during the war, in the camps?"

"Isaac never had much to say," I said. "Until recently I didn't even know he was Jewish or had been in a concentration camp."

"Isaac was railroaded out of a fortune," said Nimrod as if his keenest interest had been aroused. "Set up by a thieving Englishman. You never heard that story?"

"I never heard more than 10 words at a time out of Isaac," I said.

Nimrod leaned forward. "Let me tell you."

"What about the dishes?" McNaught said. "The lunch dishes need washing."

Nimrod held his empty glass out and said again, "Fuck the dishes."

McNaught winked at me. "I'm trying to wean my brother from swearing in the House of the Lord, but it's hard to break the habits of a lifetime."

"That's right, Pastor Joe. I got a dirty mouth," said Nimrod, unabashed.

"You were going to tell us about Isaac?" I prompted.

Nimrod said, "Before the war, Isaac was a bookkeeper in Berlin. After Hitler took over, things got bad for Jews. But what could Isaac do? Somehow or other, I don't know how these things worked, him and his family got jammed, didn't have no rights, wasn't allowed to travel. Couldn't get travel papers to leave the country."

McNaught's telephone rang. He leaned forward and yanked the plug from its wall socket. His chair creaked as he resettled his enormous frame.

Nimrod continued, "Jews had to wear this Hebrew sign on their sleeves so everybody would know what they was. On the streets they was insulted and spat on. Their Jewish friends was disappearing, one at a time. Every time Isaac's doorbell rang he'd wonder if it was the SS.

"Then Isaac heard about this guy at the British Embassy. This Englishman who could arrange for Jews to get visas outta Germany. If the price was right. The Englishman didn't want money. He was only interested in art. As it happened, Isaac had a big collection of Old Master drawings. I don't know what them things are, but they was supposed to be real valuable. Anyway, Isaac makes a deal with this English guy. Art for visas. The Englishman insists on getting his hands on the Old Master drawings first. Isaac don't have no choice; he hands his drawings over and hopes for the best. That same night, Isaac's door is busted down, and him and his family is arrested. The English guy has gypped him."

"That's quite a yarn," McNaught said.

"How come you know so much about Isaac?" I asked.

Nimrod laced his bony fingers into a steeple and lifted it to the tip of his chin. "Years ago we worked in logging camps together. I was a catskinner in them days. Isaac was a bullcook. I was separated from my old lady. Isaac had no family so neither of us had any place to go when we got time off. Me and Isaac used to stay in camp, maybe go fishing together. Open a few beers and shoot the breeze. After a few drinks Isaac loosened up, talked about Germany and the old days. I heard his story plenty of times, and I never got tired of listening to it, neither."

Nimrod's moist black eyes and red-veined nose stuck out like the coal eyes and carrot nose of a snowman. He settled back into his story. "After his arrest, Isaac was jerked around till he ended up in Bergen-Belsen. Some of the things Isaac went through made me sick just hearing about 'em, but he hung in there. See, Isaac had a dream, that's what saved him. He knew the war would end sometime. Hitler and his gang would get beat. When that happened, Isaac was gonna take himself and his wife and his kids to Canada. They'd have a little farm on the prairies maybe. Somewhere quiet where they'd never go hungry and wouldn't have to worry about no SS knocking at their door. That dream kept Isaac going. But when the war ended, Isaac was the only one of his family still left alive."

Nimrod lifted his head. His voice rising, he said, "Listen. You think a guy who lived through that agony, he'd talk about it when he was sober?"

"What's a bullcook?" McNaught asked, obviously trying to change the subject.

"A *bull*cook's a guy what cleans out bunkhouses and such. A *camp* cook's a guy what cooks meals," Nimrod answered. Then he bowed his head again.

I lifted a hand to Nimrod's shoulder. "I tried to get a conversation going with old Isaac once or twice," I said. "It was like pulling teeth. He was really withdrawn, private."

Nimrod looked up and I added, "You're probably the only person who knew he'd been a bullcook, had a family. Did he ever tell you the name of this traitor? The Englishman who betrayed him?"

Nimrod shook his head. "Nah. Maybe. If he did, I've forgot. I was drinking heavy them days, and I'm not so good with names."

I turned to McNaught, who was gazing at the ceiling with a faraway smile. "Joe. How come you did the service?" I asked. "Isaac was no Christian."

McNaught sat up straighter. "Isaac lost his religion along the way. He came to me years ago. He wasn't worried about salvation, and he liked my style. Told me that when his time came he wanted to have me do a little service, nothing fancy. That's what he got. I'd have been glad to do more. He left all his money to this mission."

"Yeah," Nimrod retorted sarcastically. "All Isaac's money. Fifty bucks and a pair of old socks."

He got to his feet, gripping the back of his chair for support. A skinny little man in a hand-me-down suit he'd probably borrowed for the occasion. He was overdue for a shave, and moisture gleamed in the corners of his eyes. "Well," he said, "I better get back to the kitchen, right? If it snows again the mission's gonna be full of sinners at suppertime."

When Nimrod was gone, McNaught selected his fifth sandwich. "Nimrod was wrong about one thing," he said, his mouth full.

"Isaac didn't die broke. His estate is worth 50 thousand. Maybe a bit more."

I was incredulous. "*How* much did you say?"

"You heard."

"And Isaac left it all to the Good Shepherd Mission?"

"Every cent. I plan to set up a memorial in Isaac's name."

"Where the hell did Isaac get that kind of dough?"

McNaught just looked at me and shoved the rest of the sandwich into his mouth. I could see that even if he *did* know, he had no intention of telling me.

As I stood up to go, I glanced out the room's huge plate-glass window. "Those clouds over the Sooke Hills are full of snow," I said.

"What do you expect, December in Victoria?" McNaught got to his feet. The floorboards complained as he lumbered across the room and stood next to me at the window.

"When I was a kid, it never snowed in Victoria," I said.

McNaught smiled. "That's one nice thing about growing older. You remember what you want to remember. I did my growing up in Vancouver, and it snowed every winter, especially on Grouse Mountain, so we could ski." His grin widened. "Come to think of it, we only had two kinds of weather. Snow every winter, sun every summer, so we could stretch out on Kitsilano Beach and work on our tans. When I was a kid the weather was always perfect."

I looked into McNaught's black eyes and caught a glimpse of some old passion. The ancient ghost of a ring hustler still animated the street preacher. The cocky pride that had kept him butting heads with contenders was still intact. McNaught's agenda wasn't all tied up in religion.

I walked to the door, but then something occurred to me. "A white-haired woman came in late for Isaac's service," I said. "She left before the rest of us. Did you recognize her?"

"Never seen her before," said McNaught. "Just some little old lady in a fur coat."

VICTORIA'S DOWNTOWN LIBRARY is across the street from the city's main courthouse. I walked straight over there after leaving the Good Shepherd. Light snow was dusting the windswept courtyard, where a guitarist wearing fingerless gloves was playing Christmas tunes. Shivering in a thin coat, he stamped his feet in time to the music. People were dropping money into his guitar case, but, alone in icy dreams, he seemed to neither notice nor care. Maybe he warmed up inside the library occasionally; it felt tropical in there.

I told a reference librarian what I was looking for, and she helped me select several books on pre-war Germany. I found out that Britain's ambassador to Germany in 1938 and '39 was a diplomat named Motlow. I assumed that the man who'd betrayed Isaac Schwartz must have been a lesser official. Soon more books surrounded me, including a German equivalent of *Who's Who*. I skimmed through it and many other tomes before hitting pay dirt, almost two hours later, in a memoir written by an Angela Knoeffler.

Mrs. Knoeffler was an Australian woman married to a German engineer. Both were Jews who had spent several pre-war years in Berlin before being interned by the Hitler regime. According to Mrs. Knoeffler, many British politicians and senior diplomats had been naive and inept, incapable of understanding Hitler's dark complexities. Neville Chamberlain and Ambassador Motlow were typical of the Englishmen Hitler had dealings with, leading him to believe that Britain would do little, if anything, to impede Germany's territorial aggressions. In one intriguing chapter, Mrs. Knoeffler reminisced about an amusing diplomatic dinner party hosted in 1938 by Sir Hugh and Lady Baineston, wealthy art collectors, at their big house in Berlin-Dahlem.

It was getting dark when I left the library. The snow had stopped, but a cold rain was falling.

In the window of a newspaper and magazine shop, two-inch headlines framed the front-page photograph of a defiant teenaged murderer: KELLY ELLARD GETS LIFE. I hurried past, musing about the girl who had tortured and then drowned a schoolmate. Attending Isaac's memorial service had dampened my spirits. I wondered what kind of Victoria Kelly would discover when, youth and beauty faded, the prison doors opened for her many years hence.

Turning down Courtney Street, I saw a Budget rental truck double-parked outside Gottlieb's Trading Post. Two men were transferring heavy cardboard boxes from Gottlieb's to the truck. Dressed entirely in black, they were dead ringers for the two I'd scared off the Gorge archaeological dig. They were driving away as I entered the Trading Post.

I knew the place well, and things looked about the same as usual: high-quality carved and painted Indian masks on the walls, along with Hudson's Bay point blankets, beaded shirts and Native paintings and prints. Displayed inside glass cabinets were handmade gold and silver bracelets, rings and brooches, as well as old and, in some cases, extremely valuable baskets, steeple hats and miniature argillite totem poles. Whalebone carvings and scrimshaw work lay on shelves fitted into upended dugout canoes.

Mary Kranmer, a Haida woman who'd worked as Gottlieb's chief buyer for at least 20 years, was behind a polished mahogany counter, making entries in a ledger. Otherwise the store was deserted. When she saw me, Mary closed the ledger and slid it away in a drawer. "Ya hey, Silas," she said, smiling. "What's up?"

"Hi ya, Mary, just passing by," I said. "Somebody told me Gottlieb sold the business. I find that hard to believe."

"I find it hard to believe myself," Mary agreed.

"End of an era. I hope the new owner won't change things much."

Mary's smile faded, and her brow furrowed. "A guy from Vancouver owns it now. Mo Dillon. He's changed things already. Most of the old employees have been sacked. I'm finished at the end of the month. Dillon's bringing in some hotshot sales guy to run the place."

Mo Dillon?

I turned my mental clock back more than 20 years, and slowly the features of a bona fide teenaged badass materialized in my mind. *Mo Dillon!* Could this be the same guy?

The Mo I'd known was kicking the tar out of his stepdad at age 14. Then he'd attacked a truancy officer with a baseball bat. For that one, a soft-headed judge sent Mo to juvie hall for six months. Afterwards, in compliance with the terms of his probation, he had presented himself for instruction to Mr. Barnickle, my Grade 9 homeroom teacher, showing up in greasy jeans and a black Harley T-shirt, with a joint dangling from his mouth.

Mr. Barnickle was easygoing, but Mo was way over the top. Mo's formal education ended that very day, with Mr. Barnickle laid out on the floor in a pool of his own blood and the school principal barricaded inside his office with a broken arm.

That spectacular act of senseless violence cost Mo two years less a day in Wilkinson Road penitentiary. After that he'd dropped out of sight. Had I thought of Mo at all in the intervening years, I'd have assumed he was either dead or doing life in Kingston Prison.

I said to Mary, "Big black-haired guy? Has a long scar across his left cheek?"

Mary nodded. "That's the one. You know him?"

"I used to," I said.

Mary sighed. "This is a very specialized business. Dillon doesn't know the first thing about it. Brian Gottlieb developed excellent relationships with local carvers and artists over the years. Without great craftsmen keeping you supplied, you're sunk. Dillon doesn't get that. I've been ordered to stop giving people advances, for instance. You know how that works: some old carver will come in and tell us he's thinking of doing a Thunderbird mask. If it's somebody we know and trust we'll advance a few bucks on spec. Sometimes it takes months, even years, but sooner or later a beautiful Thunderbird mask gets delivered. Dillon's put the kibosh on all that. 'No more advances,' he says. What's worse, we're supposed to take all our new stuff on consignment."

She shook her head in frustration. "We're losing our best artisans. There's no way they'll give us their stuff on consignment. This place was making good money the way it was. Why change things?"

"Beats me," I said. "So how is Mo treating you? Personally, I mean."

Mary put her head to one side. "All right, I guess. He can be kind of scary at times, but other times, when he puts himself out, he's almost charming."

I found it hard to imagine a charming Mo, but all I said was, "So, Mary. What'll you do next?"

"I dunno, really. Maybe I'll head up to the Queen Charlottes for a bit."

"Sounds like a plan." I motioned toward the door. "I noticed a couple of guys loading a Budget truck outside."

Mary nodded. "Big consignment for a U.S. buyer. Something Mo Dillon set up personally. I don't even know what it was."

CHAPTER NINE

Back at my office, a mountain of paperwork awaited me. My head teeming with thoughts, I plugged in Mr. Coffee and prepared to spend tedious hours writing and filing reports. I was on the phone, being hectored by a man who wanted somebody to move a car illegally parked in a residents-only spot, when Bernie came in. I waved him to a seat, but he ignored me and went straight through to the washroom. I heard its door open and close. When I hung up my phone, Bernie was sitting in front of me, one leg crossed over the other, prodding a BlackBerry.

I said, "Playing Frogger?"

"Very funny," he scowled, giving me a heavy-lidded look and shoving the BlackBerry into his pocket. "Frogger went out 30 years ago. You need to move with the times."

"I'm just finishing up here. Feel like grabbing some food?"

"Nah," he replied listlessly.

"Feel like ending it all? Sticking your head in a gas oven?"

"Not right now. Thanks for asking."

Bernie's thoughts were elsewhere, but he listened when I told him about Isaac's memorial service, my conversation with Nimrod and my subsequent investigations in the library.

A sudden gust of wind outside shook my window in its frame. A nor'easter was bringing in another cold front from the Arctic. The wind would be howling across Saanich potato fields, swirling around Mount Douglas, lifting roof tiles, roaring down Old Town's frigid back alleys. "Weather like this, I feel sorry for street kids," I said. "If they don't get inside, they'll freeze tonight."

"I feel sorry for them too," Bernie said, roused from his brooding thoughts. "For some kids more than others, to be honest. Get right down to it, street life usually starts out as self indulgence."

"And before they know it they have very heavy problems. They've indulged themselves into a boneyard."

"Yeah, I know. Cynicism's getting to be a habit with me. Maybe it's my age." Bernie sighed and added, "I drove past the Warrior Reserve earlier. Noticed lots of activity near your longhouse. Something going on?"

"Winter Ceremonial."

"Native magic!" he said, wide awake at last. "You told me you'd explain it to me sometime."

"Did I?"

"Yes. Should I shut off my bullshit detector before you start?"

I leaned back in my chair.

"You don't actually believe in magic," Bernie prodded.

"I don't?"

"Don't go all Masonic on me. Everybody's intrigued by the occult," Bernie said. "A physicist was talking about time and space on TV the other night. It was mostly over my head. Interesting, though. She got into some weird and wonderful stuff about string theory. How the universe contains several dimensions. Ten at last count. Maybe more. It's been proved mathematically."

"If it was on TV it must be true. Our shamans have been

describing extra dimensions to my people since about 8000 BC. Now you're telling me it's mathematics."

"So, Silas. Reading between the lines, you *do* believe in magic?"

"What *is* magic?"

Bernie put both index fingers to his temples and pretended to gaze into my mind. "Magic is when things happen that have no natural explanation," he said. "I mean, things caused by witchcraft, angels, creatures from other worlds. I'm talking about the real thing, not stage magic. Sleight-of-hand, conjuring, card tricks, smoke and mirrors, rabbits jumping out of hats … that stuff doesn't count."

"Natives do plenty with smoke and mirrors," I told him. "Longhouse ceremonies evolved a long, long time ago, and there's lots of staged stuff involving hidden trap doors, moveable black screens and boxes. Dancers fool the audience with wooden masks. White folks witnessing longhouse ceremonies for the first time are usually disappointed. They've seen David Copperfield in Las Vegas. Native rituals don't compare. Real Native magic takes place offstage."

"Where?"

"In another dimension."

Bernie leaned forward. "Go on, keep talking."

I shrugged my shoulders, and Bernie said, "What? You don't like talking about it?"

I hesitated, wondering how to answer. The thing about Native spirituality is, it's hard to explain and easily misunderstood. I got to thinking about shamanism, and the next thing I knew, Bernie was kicking my foot. "Earth to Seaweed."

"I was thinking."

"Wait a minute. Do Natives believe in a supreme being?"

"Some believe there's a supernatural old man, Creator of the

World—but he isn't all-powerful. And there's none of this good-versus-evil stuff you find in most religions. Some of our elders try to influence spirits."

"So you admit it? You *do* believe in spirits?"

"I ought to. Until a century ago, when the missionaries showed up and did their number on us, the Coast Salish people shared their entire world with supernatural beings. Guardian spirits and demi-gods surrounded us. Shape changers and ghosts. Miracles were part of everyday life."

"Pity they're not part of my everyday life. We'd have this Isaac Schwartz case nailed down in a jiffy," Bernie said, laying his hands down on the table and contemplating them.

I noticed a black half-moon under his right index fingernail. It must have been caused by tamping his pipe.

"Tell me what you know about whaling shrines," he said.

"You asked me before and I told you—not much. What's up?"

"We picked up a kid selling crack a few days ago. Brent Laker. Said he'd tell us about some big robbery being set up if we'd go easy on him."

"And?"

"Laker didn't actually *know* anything worthwhile. Just that there's some street buzz about whaling shrines."

"I'd like to talk to Laker."

"You can't," Bernie said, standing up. "We charged him with trafficking, but Judge Mildred released him on his own recognizance. He's long gone."

I HAD BEEN struggling with my hostility toward DCI Bulloch all day. About nine p.m., my paperwork and takeaway pizza finished, I succumbed to a disloyal impulse. I locked up and went over to police headquarters, determined to stir things up. Unlike many

Native ways, the Coast Salish way does not counsel against extreme measures. Sometimes it even encourages them.

A duty sergeant informed me that Bulloch had left for the day. So far, so good. I took the elevator to Bulloch's floor and entered his private office. This was a definite no-no, but I knew it was worth the risk when I discovered that the box containing Isaac Schwartz's papers was still in the bottom drawer of Bulloch's desk. This was significant. In my considered opinion, that box should have been in Bernie Tapp's possession, as key evidence in an active investigation.

I sat down in Bulloch's rolling swivel chair to have a closer look at the box's contents. The most intriguing item was the sales catalogue from Tuttle's auction house. It described 200 lots of paintings, Old Master drawings and antique furniture that had been sold in Victoria in July 2002. About 50 lots had been drawings. A few of the entries were illustrated. Most of the Old Master drawings had been executed in pen and ink, about a quarter of which were colour-washed. There were reclining nudes, river gods, *Pietà*'s and architectural studies. Intriguingly, someone had circled half a dozen of these lots with black ink and noted their selling prices.

The first lot circled was a drawing of Daphne and Apollo by Alessandro Allori. It had sold for $38,000. There were two drawings by Marcantonio Franceschini—one of a draped woman, another of a seated philosopher. Each had sold for about $28,000. The fourth drawing was by Baccio Bandinelli, of a man leading a trained bear. It had fetched $64,000. The last drawing circled was by Giacomo Cavedone. It showed Jupiter in the clouds, hurling thunderbolts. This had brought $16,000. All of these fragile, beautiful drawings were hundreds of years old.

Another find was an expensively bound book entitled *The Prowdes of Peeling*, published privately in 1952. It was a history of the Prowde family, tracing its roots to a certain Alfred Prowde, a freeman who settled in the Lancashire Fylde in 1153. Since 1682, the family seat had been Prowde Hall, near the village of Peeling. Half of the book was taken up with photographs, which were only slightly more enlivening than the prose.

I yawned through the tiresome pages without encountering anything of note—except that some of the pages had been ripped out. I wondered how Isaac had come by this particular book, and why he had kept it among his personal papers.

I put the box back in the drawer and used my cell to call Bernie at home.

"You again?" he grumbled when he came on the line.

"Meet me at Lou's for breakfast. We need to talk."

OUR SERVER BROUGHT us coffee and cinnamon rolls hot from the oven. I sliced my roll and covered it with a thick layer of butter. Bernie ignored his roll and chewed the stem of his unlit pipe instead.

I bit into my roll. "I don't care how many units of cholesterol are in a scoop of butter, Bernie, I'm not giving it up for anybody."

"That's right," said Bernie. "Enjoy yourself while you can. Bad times are coming."

"For all of us?"

"Nope, just for you, buddy," Bernie said, scowling. The scowl wasn't directed at me. He was probably thinking about DCI Bulloch.

"What's the latest on Sammy Lofthouse?" I asked.

"Nothing. The last I saw of Lofthouse was at the city morgue, identifying Mrs. Tranter. Since then he's skipped out of sight—but that's allowed under our democratic system."

"And you have no views on the matter?"

"Sure, only I'm not getting my shorts into a knot about it.

Maybe Lofthouse thinks his life's in danger until Richard Hendrix is put away."

"Lofthouse is a busy lawyer, Bernie. It's not like he can take days off when he feels like it. You know that as well as I do."

Bernie didn't respond, so I kept pushing. "How did Sammy act at the morgue?"

"Act?"

"How did he look? What was his demeanour?"

"He'd been drinking. His stomach might have been upset. When they rolled Mrs. Tranter out of a cold drawer, he took one look, went white and vomited."

"I didn't think Sammy was squeamish."

"Me neither, but I guess seeing that naked old body stretched out shook him."

I finished my cinnamon roll and wiped icing sugar from my fingers with a napkin, turning it into a sticky ball. I said, "If I was Bulloch and I wanted to find Sammy, I'd search tax assessments. See whether he owned any secret real estate, some place he could use as a bolt hole."

Bernie was paying attention, so I added, "If Lofthouse owns real property, he pays school taxes. In the school rolls there'll be records of his telephone numbers, even unlisted ones. If he owns real estate there'll be records of his occupation, how many children he's fathered, how much livestock he owns."

"Wonderful," Bernie said, giving me a sideways look. "You know how to obtain unlisted telephone numbers—you're beginning to sound like a detective." He smiled and added, "Except Bulloch wouldn't do any of those things. He'd get me to do them."

"And?"

"We've been making the odd inquiry."

I waited.

"Lofthouse owns half a dozen condos," Bernie said. "Four in Victoria and a couple in Parksville. They're all rented to long-term tenants. They're tax shelters, not safe houses."

"Sammy was under lots of pressure," I said. "And not only because of Hendrix. There was a guy in Swans parking lot a coupla days ago shoving him around. A big Native wearing a toque and a navy pea jacket." Bernie's cinnamon roll was untouched. "Aren't you going to eat that?" I hinted.

Bernie pushed his plate at me. "You're a hungry young man. Take it." He looked at his watch. "I gotta get going soon. What did you want to talk about?"

"Does Bulloch still think Isaac was killed by a Native?" I asked.

"I don't know. Native or not, if Bulloch can get away with it he'll lumber Richard Hendrix with everything outstanding on his desk. Bulloch hates loose ends."

"If Hendrix killed Mrs. Tranter, what does Bulloch think the motive was?"

"Revenge," Bernie said, with a straight face. He pushed himself up from the table. "I'll see Bulloch today. Let him know Isaac left big money to McNaught's mission. I doubt it'll change his thinking."

"The biggest change needed around here is a new DCI," I said.

Bernie studied me thoughtfully, neck tendons jutting as he bit down on his pipe. "You watch your ass around Bulloch, Silas, or he'll have you off the force. He'd like nothing better." And with that he headed out the door.

Lou refilled my coffee. He had a morose air. "Somebody was asking for you earlier. A pretty lady," he said.

For a wildly optimistic moment I thought it might have been Felicity Exeter. My hopes were cruelly dashed when Lou added, "Little woman about 30, dark hair, spoke with an accent."

"Canadian, Irish, French? What?"

"Gimme a break. I'm Yugoslavian. Everybody's got an accent, except me."

MRS. TRANTER'S DEATH was, in Bulloch's words, none of my goddam business. But out of curiosity, I detoured by the Tranter house on my way home that day and circled the block, looking for parked police cars, marked or unmarked. There weren't any. The stakeout was over.

Two empty garbage cans stood beside Mrs. Tranter's garden gate. I hadn't noticed them on my last visit. I climbed the front steps to the house, twisted the old-fashioned bell switch and heard tinny peals inside. Nobody answered. I banged on the door once more, then circled the veranda. The back door was a flimsy hollow-core affair with a cheap lock. I opened it in two minutes using my Swiss army knife.

The house was damp and cold. It stank of cooking and of tobacco smoked by people long dead. I opened curtains and looked around the ground-floor rooms. Upstairs were two large unfurnished dormer rooms with dusty bare floors.

Mrs. Tranter's archaic wood-burning stove was largely responsible for the house's spectacular filthiness. The kitchen cabinets hadn't been cleaned in years. Dust lay on counters and grease coated the stovetop. But everything was stowed neatly—plates, saucers and knives were where they were supposed to be. If you were blind, you could live with dirt, but you couldn't live without order. Things improperly stowed would be lost.

In the living room, I looked again at the chair by the fireplace where Mrs. Tranter had sat the night she changed her will—where she must have often sat, alone, friendless, nourishing bitter thoughts about her feckless nephew.

My hands got dirty from opening drawers and moving things

around on shelves. Looking for what? I didn't know. Forensics had already searched the place thoroughly. I roamed from room to room, feeling uneasy. Something was wrong, out of kilter.

Puzzled, I went outside. The grounds seemed as before: overgrown, neglected. Beyond Hendrix's former shed stood a small greenhouse with many broken panes. Near it, a 50-gallon drum incinerator was dissolving to rust, flakes of red oxide leaching into the muddy earth. Inside the drum was a soggy mass of half-burned kitchen debris and newspapers.

Haunted by the vague sense that I had overlooked something important, I went back inside the house. Then I saw it. Propped against the wall near the fireplace was Mrs. Tranter's white cane. Why hadn't she taken it with her when she left for the Red Barn Hotel? Without it she must have been nearly helpless.

CHAPTER TEN

I measured half a cup of Quaker oats into a saucepan, added one and a half cups of water and a sprinkle of salt, and left it to simmer on my wood stove while I shaved and half listened to CFAX radio news. By the time I realized I'd heard Richard Hendrix's name mentioned, the story was over. I flipped to another station and heard the same news item. The RCMP had picked up Hendrix. A logger, only too happy to blow the whistle on the detested activist, had spotted him on northern Vancouver Island.

My porridge was perfect. I'd timed it just right, lifting the pan from the stove at that critical moment when the oats start to congeal in the bottom of the saucepan. A few seconds too long and it burns, becoming inedible to all but Yorkshire terriers and a few hardy Scots.

It wasn't yet dawn, but people were stirring all over the Warrior Reserve. There must have been 500 visitors camped in tents and trailers in the parking lot. Smoke rose from barbecues and campfires where people were preparing bannock, bacon and eggs, and coffee. The ancient winter feast and the magic that my Coast Salish cousins had come to witness awaited us.

I followed the porridge with half a grapefruit, thinking about

Hendrix. By now he'd be locked up tight inside the Campbell River jail. Would he be savvy enough to keep his mouth shut until he'd consulted a lawyer? Probably—over the years he must have acquired some prison smarts. He'd survived more than one skirmish with the law, but in all likelihood he'd soon be blabbing about his stay at Felicity Exeter's cottage.

I had been thinking about Felicity a lot, wondering whether there was a man in her life. Maybe she would enjoy hugging a Native policeman for a change, instead of a tree.

I dialled her number. A recorded message informed me that the phone was not in service. Then I remembered—Hendrix had cut her line. Should I drive out and speak to her in person, discuss Hendrix's arrest? Any excuse to see her would suffice.

The weather report called for snow systems moving south. Up-island, north of the Malahat, there were 10 centimetres of new snow on the roads; highway travel without chains was impossible.

I wondered how my MG would handle in that much snow. I'd bought my sporty little head-turner with virtually no rust with insurance money when my previous vehicle—an '82 Chevrolet—crashed and burned. My favourite mechanic, Ted, a cockney cynic, had been uncomplimentary when I drove my new acquisition into his garage, complaining about its defective headlights.

"Those are Lucas lamps," he'd smirked, wiping greasy hands on his sleeves before rolling himself a cigarette. "You'll never be happy with 'em. Joe Lucas invented darkness. People say he did it as revenge against America."

"What did America do to Joe Lucas?"

"Nothing, personally. But us Brits have long memories. We haven't forgotten our beloved George the Third."

Five hundred dollars later, Ted had replaced the MG's original twin-6 batteries with a single 12-volt system. He renewed yards of wiring, fixed the windshield wipers and the clutch. With a bit of fine-tuning, Ted told me, the engine would be all right, but he doubted whether the steering would last much longer without a major overhaul.

"How much?"

"You can't economize on steering gear, Silas."

"Cut your cockney blarney. I'm not turning you loose on this thing without an estimate."

"For you, Silas, I'll do it for $900. Plus tax. I'll make the new bushes myself, using oil-impregnated neoprene. The car will steer better than new."

"How much to make the bushes out of ordinary neoprene? Don't forget I'm already into this bomb for two and a half grand!"

"You buy a champagne car, you gotta pay champagne prices," Ted shrugged.

"What have you got against old MGs?"

"Nothing, I love 'em. Every time I get one in the shop, I admire the beautiful design, those nifty little rust patches on the sills, those cute red carpets rotting on the floorpan. All the bits falling off are of genuine British manufacture."

But after Ted's ministrations, the MG was running like a thoroughbred.

Thinking of things British reminded me of the Bainestons. I had a sudden idea and phoned the British Consul General's office in Vancouver. After identifying myself and explaining what I wanted, I was connected to a secretary named Joan Wilson. "I'm involved in a criminal investigation," I told her, "and I'm seeking information about pre-war Germany. Is there any possible way of determining if there's anybody still alive who was employed at the British Embassy in Germany between about 1937 and the outbreak of war?"

"You want to ask them questions, is that right?"

"Exactly."

"I expect there are, but they'll be long in the tooth by now, of course. And their memories may no longer be reliable," Joan replied, with a lovely English accent. "But I'll see what I can for you and call you back. Don't hold your breath, though. It'll take me a while I think."

I gave Mrs. Wilson my cellphone number, thanked her and hung up.

BEFORE HE DISAPPEARED, Sammy Lofthouse had told me that Ellen Lemieux worked as a checkout clerk in an organic garden shop near Elk Lake. Elk Lake is miles out of Victoria, but I drove there anyway. The shop was a converted roadside barn surrounded by fields in winter fallow. In addition to fruits and vegetables, the shop sold vitamins, dried foods, free-range eggs and fireweed honey. A bored teenaged girl was tending the checkout, glancing through a magazine instead of polishing apples or taking an interest in me, her lone customer. I roamed the aisles with a shopping basket, selected a head of romaine lettuce, a bunch of spring onions, five pounds of potatoes and some apples, and lugged them to the checkout. "Is Ellen Lemieux around today?" I asked casually.

The clerk frowned. "No. Ellen phoned in sick. I'm filling in."

"That's too bad," I said, sliding a 20-dollar bill across the counter. "I expected to see her here."

"Ellen might be in tomorrow. I hope so," she added, with a touch of impatience. "She's been missing a lot of time lately. This is supposed to be my day off." She eyed my uniform as she handed me my change. "Is anything wrong?"

"Oh, no," I said. "It's personal. I'm an old friend of the family. I just heard she was working here. I've lost track of where she's living. I think she moved from that old place on McKenzie."

"I didn't know she'd lived on McKenzie," the clerk said. "Far as I know, Ellen's always lived on Gladstone Avenue."

I ALWAYS CARRY a Victoria phone book in my car. There was only one E. Lemieux listed on Gladstone Avenue. I drove over there and cruised slowly along until I spotted the address. The house was a small 1940s frame bungalow located about two blocks from the Belfry Theatre, in Victoria's Fernwood district.

I parked a hundred yards down the street. I was considering my next move when a woman I assumed was Ellen came out the front door and walked down the driveway to a Monte Carlo, carrying an overnight bag. Hurriedly I pulled out my digital camera and managed to get a few telescopic shots. I was surprised to discover that she was Native. She stood a little over five feet tall and was, to my eyes at least, extremely attractive.

She put the overnight bag in the back seat, then got in and started the engine. But instead of driving off, she waited in the car. After a couple of minutes she gave the horn a couple of impatient toots, whereupon the front door of her house swung open. A man came out, lugging a heavy canvas bag—it was Lennie Jim. I took some more shots of Lennie putting his bag into the trunk and climbing into the passenger seat. They drove off.

It was time to take stock, think things through. But I had the excitement born of hunting down a dangerous quarry. The excitement my ancestors must have felt while harpooning massive whales with wooden spears. Well, if my hunch was right, Ellen Lemieux was a worthy adversary. I cautioned myself not to tailor facts to fit the wild theories growing in my mind.

I parked around the corner, walked back to Ellen's house and rang the doorbell. There was no reply. Lace curtains parted in the window of the house next door. An unshaven, bald man was watching me.

At the back of the house was a small yard with a couple of apple trees, a patch of frozen lawn and a vegetable garden with several glass-covered cold frames. A black plastic compost bin stood beside a galvanized steel garbage can. I peeked into Ellen's basement through slats in the window blinds and saw a big white freezer and neatly stacked patio furniture.

A male voice said, "Ellen ain't home, officer. Can I help you?"

It was the neighbour, standing in his back doorway. He was about 60 and was wearing jeans and a heavy bomber jacket zipped up to his chin.

"I'm here about the bylaws," I said officiously.

"She never mentioned bylaws to me," Baldy said in an aggrieved tone.

"Why should she?" I snapped. "What's it got to do with you?"

I turned my back on him before he could answer and studied Lemieux's back door. It was a cheap invitation to burglary. Two minutes with a Swiss army knife, and anyone could be in the house.

At the bottom of the yard was a shed with a half-opened door. Baldy watched me go inside it. The building had a recently raked dirt floor. Garden tools were arranged on shelves and hanging from hooks. There was a tidy workbench with special containers and jars for storing nails and screws. A wheelbarrow stood next to a new-looking trail bike with a high-tech helmet dangling from its handle-bars. There was also one of those heavy two-wheeled dollies used by movers. The dolly and the wheelbarrow were stencilled with the name of the garden shop where Ellen worked.

Baldy had gone back inside his house, leaving his door ajar. A woman with curlers in her hair, wearing a grey apron, was watching me from the doorway now. She was clutching a small fluffy black and white dog to her bosom and seemed half asleep.

This must be a low-crime neighbourhood, I reflected, if Ellen could leave valuable garden tools in an unlocked shed. She could thank neighbours like Baldy for that. Well, I'd learned one thing—Ellen Lemieux was neat.

Her garbage can was half full of household waste and papers. I lifted the bag out of the container and slung it over my shoulder. Baldy was shouting something, but I didn't look back.

Snow had started to descend from fast-travelling clouds, sprinkling large, soft flakes on Gladstone Avenue and on a lone man plodding wearily toward Fernwood's homeless shelter.

BACK AT THE office, I covered my desk with newspapers and dumped Ellen Lemieux's garbage onto it. Wearing latex gloves, I picked my way through the labyrinth of her private life.

Ellen liked McCain's frozen vegetables, TV dinners, Ernest and Julio Gallo's burgundy wine and Weston's arrowroot cookies. She dined at Chinese restaurants and bought her underwear from Victoria's Secret. When it came to jeans, she preferred the Bay. To my surprise, I found a discarded early Christmas card sent to her by a George Purdy on Adanac Street. Ellen's last telephone bill was $43. Her house was owned and managed by Buntins Properties. Rent was a surprisingly low $850 per month.

I phoned Buntins Properties and asked for the rentals manager.

A man came on and said, "Jacques here. How may I help you?"

"Mr. Jacques, this is Jim Tucker of Ace Housing in Kelowna," I lied. "One of your tenants named your agency as a reference. I'm just checking."

"Don't blame you. Some people don't deserve a home, but once they're in, you're dead—can't move them out with a crowbar. Who are we talking about?"

"A woman called Ellen Lemieux. Can you confirm that she's a good tenant?"

"I'm pretty busy," Jacques grumbled in a tone of long-suffering impatience. I thought I'd lost him, but he said, "Hang on a minute." There was a pause, then Jacques came back on, "Yes," he said. "We've had no complaints. She's okay so far; looks after the house, pays her rent on time."

"How about Ms. Lemieux's previous rentals, or personal references?"

"Lemme see. Yes. She had a reference from a personal friend on Adanac Street. They said she was okay. I don't see any problem."

"Thanks, Mr. Jacques."

"What did you say your name was?" he asked.

I hung up quickly and noted the return address on the Christmas card from George Purdy.

I was writing up my log when my phone rang. It was Lou, reminding me about his daily special—today it was Hungarian goulash in a secret sauce. He wanted to know whether he should send some over.

"Don't bother. I'll be right there."

As I locked the door and started down the street, a man who had been loitering near my doorway suddenly turned and hurried away. I was so preoccupied thinking about Ellen Lemieux that I hardly noticed. I was halfway into Lou's café before it penetrated my consciousness that the loiterer was a Native man wearing a black toque and a navy pea jacket.

I looked back. He had crossed the street to a bus stop and was glaring at me, his dark features bulging with malice. It was Lennie Jim. A line of traffic and a double-decker bus prevented me from crossing the street. By the time I did, Lennie was nowhere to be seen.

THE GOULASH WAS delicious. Lou served it personally and with a flourish, a red-and-white-checked napkin over his arm. The chef's special came with focaccia from Ottavio's Bakery. Lou sat across the table, watching me eat and waiting for compliments.

I said, "If you put any more red wine in this sauce, buddy, you'd need a licence from the liquor board."

Lou—artistically sensitive to critical nuances—bridled. His eyebrows shot up and he snapped, "What? Is not good enough for you?"

"It's wonderful," I said sincerely. "I'm crazy about it. All I'm saying, Lou, is if you served this gravy in a glass, a pint would put most people under the table."

Lou interpreted this as praise. He said proudly, "I make the wine myself. Is Alicante. I buy my grapes from a Portuguese guy. He brings 'em up from California in a reefer truck."

"I know," I said. "One August I helped you make the stuff, remember? Me, Don Gain and Richard Marshall went with you to a yard somewhere near Hillside, picked up 10 flats of grapes. We took 'em to your house, pulled the stems."

"That's right. The three of us got pissed." Lou sighed with satisfaction, remembering. "Alicante is always good."

"I like your Chardonnay too."

"Chardonnay is okay for oak-barrel snobs," said Lou, with undisguised scorn. "Me, I prefer Alicante."

Bernie Tapp came in and sat down with us. He ordered goulash too, and when Lou had gone to fetch it, he said, "Heard the latest on Richard Hendrix?"

I nodded. "CFAX says he was nabbed up-island. Has he made a statement?"

"A statement, not a confession. He says he heard about the Tranter killing on the radio, panicked and ran away."

"What do the Mounties think?"

"They say he's acting crazy. Think he's capable of anything."

Lou brought Bernie's dinner. As he ate, Bernie mused, "It's funny, the things people get up to in this town."

"That right?" I asked. "Funnier than politics, or funnier than Laurel and Hardy?"

"Well, I'll tell you and you can decide." He frowned. "A concerned citizen phoned the station earlier. Complained about a cop driving a red car. Might be a Jaguar, or a Triumph, he said. It could even be an MG coupe. Apparently, this cop is going around Fernwood, collecting people's garbage."

"Oh," I said. "I was going to tell you about that."

"Tell me now."

I detailed what I'd found in Ellen's garbage. Listening, Bernie tore a piece of focaccia bread in half, dipped it in Lou's sauce and ate without commenting on either the sauce or my story.

I changed the subject. "Did you identify any interesting prints from Mrs. Tranter's hotel room?" I asked.

He shook his head. "Nothing significant. Hotel staff, mostly."

"But none of Hendrix's?"

"Correct," he sighed. "So why did Hendrix do a runner?"

I had no answer for that one. Maybe he *had* just panicked, like he had told Felicity and the police in Campbell River.

"Look," Bernie said. "Hendrix, Lofthouse and Lofthouse's secretary were the only people who knew Mrs. Tranter was staying at the Red Barn that night. Lofthouse has an alibi. His secretary has no motive. That leaves Hendrix."

"Not necessarily," I countered. "All we know is *somebody* phoned Lofthouse's office to ask for his whereabouts that night. It wasn't necessarily Hendrix."

"At the moment, my money's on Hendrix," Bernie said. "One way or another, we'll find out."

CHAPTER ELEVEN

I got up at seven and confronted the day's first major decision: whether to wear my uniform or not. I ended up wearing a green Gore-Tex jacket over a plaid wool shirt, Dockers and waterproof boots. After breakfast and two cups of black coffee, I went outside. Snow-removal gangs had been out all night, and the streets were passable. I drove into town without difficulty, parked in the View Street parkade and walked around the corner to Sammy Lofthouse's office on Douglas Street.

The young woman at the reception desk was slim and cheerful, and when I entered she flashed beautiful white teeth.

"I'm Sergeant Seaweed. Ms. Sleight is expecting me."

A door with an opaque glass panel swung open at my words. Grace Sleight waved to me to come through, and we shook hands.

Grace's office had hardwood floors accented with Persian rugs. Fenwick Lansdowne originals hung on walls covered with Chinese paper. Potted palms flanked two green suede wing chairs near the window. She motioned for me to sit, but she remained standing, biting her lips and nervously crossing and recrossing her arms. She looked like a woman in mourning. Her black dress emphasized her pale face and the dark crescents under her eyes.

I said, "Thou shalt not worry. It's one commandment we should all obey."

"It's nervousness, that's all. I'm glad to see you, but things are a mess around here, and getting worse. If Sam doesn't show up in a day or two, this whole menagerie will come tumbling down. That's the trouble with one-man law firms. I'm supposed to be Sammy's chief clerk, but even I don't know what he's doing half the time. He runs this office out of a briefcase, mostly."

"Does Derek Battle know about Mrs. Tranter's will yet?"

She hesitated. "What the hell," she said, wincing. "I guess it makes no difference. The answer is no. Mr. Battle doesn't know anything yet. When he does find out, he'll be furious."

"Well, he must know Mrs. Tranter's been murdered. He's probably taking steps to probate the old will."

"I know," she said. "It's going to be a real mess."

"What's to stop you from phoning Battle yourself?"

"I'm scared."

"He'll find out eventually if he doesn't know already."

"I just hope he finds out from Sam, instead of me."

"It follows, from what you've said, that Ellen Lemieux doesn't know about her windfall yet?"

"I haven't told her, if that's what you're asking."

Grace's chin quivered and her body began to sag. She sat at her desk and cradled her head in her arms. I got up and put a hand on her shoulder as grief overcame her. In a voice muffled by her sleeves she sobbed, "Sammy thinks he's such a hotshot, you know, shooting his mouth off all the time, badmouthing everybody, playing the big-time lawyer. But it's all an act. He's never gotten over Serena walking out on him and taking the kids with her."

Grace's mascara had run. Patches of face powder smudged her black sleeves. She dabbed her eyes with a tissue, then her hand came up and closed over mine. "I'll tell you the truth, Silas," she said, her voice catching. "I think Sammy's dead." And with that she excused herself to freshen up in the ladies' room.

I went over to the window. Outside, Douglas Street was crowded. Shoppers were admiring Christmas displays in the Bay Centre's big windows. A Salvation Army soldier stood with his collection kettle at the mall's main entrance, ringing his bell. In the adjacent block, pedestrians skirted a gang of curb kids congregated near McDonald's. Somebody driving a rusty pickup truck was trying to make an illegal left turn up View Street.

Grace returned and we stood shoulder to shoulder, looking out the window in silence. I wondered if Sammy and Grace had ever been lovers. Probably not. Sammy liked flashy women—20 years younger than himself. Grace was middle-aged. Plain. Honest. With a pang, I saw Grace's tragedy. It was not that she had loved Sammy and lost. He had never even noticed her.

"Sammy gave me some cash, asked me to buy Christmas toys for his kids again. He always said he had no taste for shopping, but really he hadn't the patience. I generally buy his little boy a game. Game Boy is still big. What do you think?"

"I think Sammy's kid would love Game Boy."

Grace thought for a moment, then said, "Sammy's got enemies all over, Silas. Tough guys with no brains who think he owes them."

I nodded. Sammy had been a prosecutor once. Enemies went with the job.

Grace's tears had dried up, but an aura of misery hung about her; she was twisting her watchband distractedly. "As soon as Sammy figured out how the system worked, he changed sides," she said. "The big money is in *defending* crooks, not prosecuting them. A lot of his clients took a walk, but sometimes, the way Sam worked, somebody else would feel the heat instead. He used informers, set people up, coached witnesses."

"Do you see any connection between Mrs. Tranter's death and Sammy's disappearance?"

She shook her head uncertainly. "I did at first, but after I got to thinking about it, I don't see how it's possible. When Mrs. Tranter was killed, Sammy was miles away."

"Can you think of anybody in particular who might be down on Sammy just now?"

"Nobody in particular. There are 20 people in the joint who would knife Sammy if they could. Another 50 are walking the streets down there. Take your pick—the town has its share of angry cons."

It was time for me to get out of there. "Keep your chin up, Grace," I said, and gave her a quick hug. "Maybe we're worrying unnecessarily. Sammy will probably haul his sorry ass in here tomorrow, ask us what all this fuss was about."

"That would be quite a Christmas present, all right."

I paused at the door, my hand on the doorknob. "Does the name Isaac Schwartz mean anything to you?"

She thought for a moment. "The old gentleman they found murdered?"

"That's the one."

"I saw his name in the paper, but that's all."

I left Grace standing by her window.

The receptionist's red fingernails buzzed like hummingbirds over her keyboard in the outer office. I tried to call Felicity Exeter, but my cell wouldn't work, even when I shook it and muttered vicious threats. The receptionist smiled, pointed to a telephone in the waiting area and said, "Better use that one, sir, before you bust a gut."

I tried again and got the same recorded message—Felicity's line was still out of service. The receptionist was staring at her computer monitor, but it was obvious she'd been ready to listen in on my side of the call. I was sorry to disappoint her.

A stack of glossy brochures lay on a low table. They summarized Lofthouse's areas of expertise (criminal law, accident claims), described in glowing terms his education and experience, and outlined B.C. Law Society rates for standard services. There was a flattering picture of him on the back fold. I took a brochure with me when I left.

Out on the street, a backpacker who probably hadn't showered since puberty was eyeing a parked black Targa-style Porsche. I tagged him as a manic-depressive in the manic stage. When he touched the Porsche's door handle, I asked, "What kind of gas mileage do you get with that thing?"

The man cleared off in a hurry. That's when I noticed Joe McNaught approaching. I ducked behind the Porsche before he spotted me, and watched him go past. Then I trailed him as he waddled into the Regal Trust Company building. Panting breathlessly, McNaught crossed the lobby to the mortgage department, where he leaned on a polished marble counter and spoke to the receptionist. I idled just inside the doors as she called somebody on the phone. Moments later, the pastor was greeted by a buttoned-down managerial type who escorted him into a private office. When the office door closed behind them I moved forward and read the name on the frosted-glass door. McNaught was closeted with Arnold Bekin, the trust company's assistant senior loans manager.

I sat behind a Corinthian column in the waiting area and made myself comfortable with a copy of the *Times Colonist*. Twenty minutes passed before McNaught came out of Bekin's office. I hid my face behind the newspaper as the pastor, looking pleased with himself, went out.

Five minutes later, I tried using my cell to call Regal Trust. It worked this time, but a moment later I thought better of it. Trust companies probably used call-display phones. I went outside and used a pay phone instead. I asked for Arnold Bekin, and when he came on I said brusquely, "Hello, Arnold, this is Franklin at headquarters. We've been reviewing the Joseph McNaught file and need a fresh report."

There was a longish pause. "Yes, I see." Bekin cleared his throat. "Are you talking about the Good Shepherd mortgage, sir?"

"Yes, of course," I said briskly. "We want to know what you think of it. Will this deal fly or not?"

"I'm sorry, sir," he said suspiciously. "What did you say your name was?"

"Jim Franklin. Head office."

"I'm sorry, Mr. Franklin. If you'll just give me your extension number, I'll check the file and call you right back."

I got the message and replaced the receiver. So much for that. Any information concerning Joe McNaught would have to come from a primary source.

I'D EXPECTED TO find Joe in his office, but his door was locked. The mission seemed deserted. I went into the kitchen, where an elderly dishwasher with rolled-up sleeves was sweating over the stainless-steel sinks. The old man was engrossed in his work and didn't see me come in. Tattoos covered his arms—crosses and naked women and hearts with superimposed scrolls. Old tattoos, done by a professional, depicted tigers and mermaids and sailing ships; they were so faded that they resembled his ancient veins. The newer ones—ugly swastikas and guns and knives—had likely been hacked into his flesh by the dishwasher himself, during long, lonely stretches in the joint. From such hieroglyphics, sociologists might decipher the history of a life.

"Is Pastor McNaught around?" I asked.

The dishwasher turned quickly. He had a gnome-like face and washed-out eyes—blue irises floating in red-veined yellow pools.

At the inside corner of one of his eyes I saw a mark like a blue mole; it was a tattooed teardrop. When he smiled, it vanished into a wrinkle. "Pastor's gone out of town. You just missed him," he said. "Business."

"How about Nimrod?"

"You're out of luck, mister. Nimrod went with him. That's why I'm here. Up to my ying-yang in Palmolive." The old con rubbed his nose with a soapy finger. "Who should I say was calling?"

"It's not important."

"Whatever you say. Hallelujah, brother!" He turned back to his dishes, whistling "Onward Christian Soldiers."

Outside, a crane with a wrecking ball was demolishing what was left of the Jamieson Foundry. One last section of the foundry's corrugated iron roof remained, balanced precariously on masonry pillars. The swinging ball nibbled at the bricks. A crowd of onlookers gave a ragged cheer when the roof collapsed. Clouds of descending brick dust coated the snow like blood.

On Johnson Street, two shabby women were examining abandoned treasures in a hock-shop window. When I stopped beside them they hurriedly departed. I saw a miniature black totem pole in the window, displayed amidst cheap bric-a-brac. The pole looked real, as if it were hand-carved argillite, the sort of treasure you'd expect to find inside a glass case at Gottlieb's Trading Post. But I'd seen identical miniature poles many times before, and knew they were made of plastic.

Sometimes, when ideas entice me away from downtown Victoria, I feel a little guilty. But the way I look at it, any policeman's business has investigative functions. That, in any case, is what I told myself as I got into my car and started driving.

TWO MILES AWAY from McNaught's mission, Beach Drive winds

through some of Canada's highest-priced residential real estate—the Uplands of Oak Bay. I reached Brian Gottlieb's house just after noon. A cold wind blew across his snow-covered front lawns, bending skeletal trees and quivering thickets of delicate bamboo. The wrought-iron gates were open, and when I drove between them an unseen dog started barking. I parked near granite steps leading to a front door big enough for a cathedral. I put my thumb on the buzzer and kept it there. After a minute I went back down the steps and gazed around.

An elderly woman was standing at an upstairs window, shaking her fist at me. The dog kept barking. Undeterred, I meandered around to the back. More extensive grounds and paved terraces ran down a long slope that overlooked Cadboro Bay and the Royal Victoria Yacht Club. Brian Gottlieb, a short, thickset man wearing an old baseball cap, tattered coveralls and rubber boots, was wrapping burlap around a tender young shrub. The wind and the sea drowned out my footsteps. Engrossed in his task, the retired art and antiques dealer didn't hear me until I was almost upon him. I don't know how he recognized me, because the eyeglasses on the tip of his nose were scratched and smudged with fingerprints to the verge of opacity. But his eyes twinkled when he saw who I was, and his handshake was firm. "Let's get out of this wind," he said, leading me into a little marble-and-glass conservatory.

Gottlieb picked up a thermos jug from a tray and said, "What would you say to a cup of coffee?"

"Hello coffee," I said.

"Cops!" Gottlieb laughed, pouring me a cup. "I hope you take it black."

"Sorry to see you this way, Gottlieb," I said, gazing at the mini-12 sailboat tacking around in the water below us. "I heard your finances were on life support, but I didn't think they'd be this bad."

"Yeah, things haven't improved much since I was a ragged-ass kid."

"How much land do you have?"

"Two acres. I picked it up as raw waterfront for $12,000 in 1960." Gottlieb grinned. "The widow who sold it was sure she'd ripped me off." He pointed to a house across the water and added, "See that place? It's on the market for $25 million."

I shook my head, not in contradiction, but in astonishment.

As an antiques dealer, Gottlieb had specialized in Native artifacts and had an international clientele. He was a recognized authority in the field. I'd gotten to know him well over the years. "Lovely as this is," I said, "I'm here on business. Ready for questions?"

"Try me and we'll see."

"What do you know about whaling shrines?"

Gottlieb took off his baseball cap, scratched his head and put the cap back on again. He didn't say anything.

"I dropped by Gottlieb's Trading Post the other day," I prompted.

"I'm retired. It's not mine anymore. My kids weren't interested in taking it over, and this fellow from Vancouver made me an offer I didn't refuse."

"Yes. The staff is sorry you've gone."

"Yeah, I'm sorry too, in a way," Gottlieb said. "The business has gone sideways and some people blame me because my name's still on the place."

"Is it okay to talk about whaling shrines now?"

Gottlieb took the glasses off his nose and wiped them with a rag from his pocket. "I had a few inquiries about whaling shrines over the years," he said slowly. "There's one in a museum, in New York. If another whaling shrine exists, and it came up for sale offshore, it would be worth a fortune. It's the sort of thing the British Museum and the Smithsonian would probably bid on."

"How do you mean, offshore?"

"If one was found in B.C. and somebody tried to sell it, our government would step in. Classify it as a cultural artifact and prevent its sale or removal from Canada."

"But if somebody stole it and moved it to, let's say, California, he could do as he pleased with it?"

"Maybe. Probably. Native American artifacts fascinate people. The argument would be made that it's better to have them stored in collections, where they're taken care of, than rotting in unvisited wilderness."

Gottlieb held his glasses up to the light. They looked dirtier than before he'd wiped them.

I could almost hear the thud of earth striking the coffin of my hopes when Gottlieb said, "I heard something about a whaling shrine a week ago. One of my old employees heard a rumour and passed it on. I can't vouch for it, but something *might* be happening. Where, what or why, my employee didn't know, and I haven't followed up on it."

"One last question. Ever do business with Sammy Lofthouse?"

Gottlieb scowled. "That shyster? No, because straightforward he isn't. Lofthouse's only route between two points is a spiral."

ON FRIDAY NIGHT we played poker at the gym. Moran was the big winner, cleaning up big time in the last two hands. He won a Lowball game with a bicycle and followed that with five aces in a game of Deuces Wild. My mind, such as it is, was preoccupied with whaling shrines, Mrs. Tranter and Sammy Lofthouse. Bernie, sitting beside me at Moran's octagonal table, kept being interrupted by phone calls. When we cashed our chips, Moran was up 15 dollars, Tony was up a dollar-fifty, and I was down five bucks. Two gamblers had gone home, and Bernie was answering his phone yet again. At the end of the call he had a long face as he turned to me. "You're not driving?" It was more of a statement than a question.

"After all that booze? No chance. I'm calling a cab." I started picking up empties.

Yawning, Moran said, "Leave it, Silas. The new cleaning guy'll get it in the morning. Why don't you bums all go home? We'll see you next Friday."

"I'll see you before then," I said, straightening up and flexing my spine, stiff from sitting. "I need to get back in shape."

Everybody said goodnight. I followed Bernie downstairs, and we stood on the sidewalk under Moran's sagging canvas awning.

"That last phone call of mine. You ready?" Bernie said gloomily.

"What's up?"

"They've found Sammy Lofthouse."

I knew instantly that the lawyer was dead. "Tell me about it."

"A grader operator ploughing the highway up near Campbell River snagged Sam's body with the tip of his blade. The RCMP think Sammy's been buried in snow for a while."

"How did he die?"

"They don't know. He was frozen stiff. First thing they've gotta do is thaw him out."

"This isn't going to make life any easier for Hendrix."

"What do you mean?"

"Isn't it obvious, with Hendrix and Lofthouse *both* turning up near Campbell River? Don't tell me you think it's a coincidence."

"Whatever. All I know is, this development isn't gonna make life easier for *me*. There'll be jurisdictional hassles now. The RCMP will want to deal with Lofthouse themselves. What a pain in the ass," Bernie said, exasperated. "If Hendrix had any consideration, he'd have killed them both in Alberta and then we wouldn't have to bother with it."

CHAPTER TWELVE

After a restless night I boiled a couple of eggs for breakfast and washed them down with two cups of coffee. At nine o'clock I phoned a man I knew at B.C.'s land registry office.

After the usual formalities, mutual health inquiries and meteorological observations, I asked him if he could tell me who owned the Jamieson Foundry property, and when they'd acquired it.

"I *could*, sure, but what'll you do for me?" he answered.

"How about a couple of tickets for the fights next week?"

He called me back in 10 minutes. "The owner is a numbered company: GS2005. They acquired the property six months ago."

An idea hit me like an uppercut. I laughed and said, "GS2005. As in Good Shepherd two zero zero five?"

"That's right. Good Shepherd or Green Sausages. Your guess is as good as mine."

I stood at my window and watched more fat snowflakes descend from a white sky. Totem poles a hundred yards beyond my cabin receded into ghostlike imperceptibility. According to CFAX, the power was out in many parts of the city. Crews had been working all night, trying to cope with fallen trees and power poles.

Despite this, more Coast Salish brethren, drawn to our great

Winter Ceremonial and anxious to share its wonders and rituals, had reached the Warrior Reserve overnight. Elderly visitors kept warm in the longhouse, others hid from the weather in campers and heated tents. I looked at the snow for a while, trying not to think about the ghost-wolf that had disturbed my slumbers. Today was my day off. What my constitution demanded now was vigorous exercise. I put on a thick anorak, waterproof overpants and hiking boots, and set off.

I was striding past the band office when Maureen, Chief Alphonse's secretary, called out to me. "Silas, come on in for a minute. Chief Alphonse left something for you. I've got it here somewhere."

She poked around the chaos on her desk and eventually handed me a heavy 10-by-12 envelope. "It's a book. The chief says take care of it because it's valuable."

I forgot about my hike, went home and started reading. The book was *The Kwakiutl: 1910–1914*, by Edward Sheriff Curtis. Illustrated with magnificent—and sometimes gruesome—photographs, the book is a work of art. Curtis's camera was a Reversible Back Premo—an enormous mahogany, brass and leather contraption introduced in the late 1800s. It had a Victor rapid rectilinear lens and a shutter speed of ⅟₂₅ of a second, with rack and pinion focussing. Curtis took more than 40,000 pictures with his Premo, documenting the way of life of many North American Native tribes at a crucial point in history.

Outside my cabin, angry surf crashed against the shore. Thick ropes of kelp, tangled by inrushing waves, writhed and slid on the beach's glossy pebbles. I was contemplating the picture of a Kwakiutl shaman holding up two recently severed human heads when Chief Alphonse knocked on my door and came inside.

After hanging up his wet-weather gear, he glanced at the book and said, "See that? Curtis called us Indians. Some of our people don't like that word anymore. I don't know why." Smiling broadly, he settled down in an armchair beside my wood stove.

I added fresh wedges of alder to the fire and put the kettle on for tea. "Some of Curtis's exploits stretch believability to the limit," I said. "Except he photographed everything."

Chief Alphonse nodded. "Back in the '20s, I guess it was, Curtis had a studio in Seattle. He visited Victoria a few times, taking pictures. Curtis made one of Canada's earliest movies. *In the Land of the War Canoes* it was called."

"Any good?"

"I thought so. Maybe it's because I grew up watching black-and-white movies. Moving pictures we called 'em. Those were the days. Greta Garbo looked sexier in a black-and-white robe than Paris Hilton does full-colour naked."

The chief pondered for a while. "Edward Curtis spent a lot of time up Fort Rupert way, trying to photograph a Kwakiutl whale hunt."

"Curtis seems larger than life. Ever meet him?"

"I never met Curtis, but I knew George Hunt. Hunt was Curtis's Kwakiutl interpreter. One time, Curtis needed a mummy. George helped him find one."

"A human mummy?"

"Right."

"Where'd they find it? Wal-Mart?"

The chief eyed me soberly. "It was where you'd expect it to be—in a coffin. Curtis dug that mummy out of the ground. George used to say that Curtis was the only white man he ever met who understood the Great Mystery."

"He understood more than most of us, if he did."

The trees around my cabin creaked and swayed. Horizontal sleet now lashed windows and walls. We were warm and dry inside, though, and the weary chief's eyelids started to get heavy. The sudden whistle of steam from my kettle temporarily drowned out the outside noise. I made the tea strong, put a mug on the table beside his chair and went back to my book.

After dozing for maybe 10 minutes the chief stirred. Sipping tea beside the blazing stove, he said, "There was more to whaling than grabbing a sharp stick and heading out to sea. There was pre-whaling ritual as well. And something most people don't know about. Kwakiutl whalers always carried skulls and mummies aboard their canoes."

"*Human* skulls? Mummified *humans?*"

"People in the land of the dead have power over whales. Whalers who show themselves worthy in life come back as killer whales. Whalers took corpses and skulls from burial sites and carried 'em to sea for good luck. Killed slaves and hung their heads across their gunnels. They built secret shrines ashore. Edward Curtis heard about these things and checked it out."

Chief Alphonse laughed without amusement. "Like I said. Curtis had an interpreter, George Hunt. Hunt's dad was a white man who'd been a trader with the Hudson's Bay Company. Hunt's mother was full-blooded Kwakiutl, a chief's daughter. So George had plenty of clout and he managed to talk Kwakiutl whalers into letting Curtis tag along on their next trip. The whalers agreed, on one condition."

Here it comes, I thought.

"The condition was, Curtis first had to provide the whalers with a complete human mummy and 11 human skulls. To their surprise, Curtis took them up on their offer."

I shook my head, amazed.

The chief went on. "One night, along with W.E. Myers, his right-hand man, Curtis paddled to a cemetery island up near Fort

Rupert. Grave robbing is a big no-no—people have been hanged for it. Curtis and Myers had to keep things secret. When they reached the cemetery they found plenty of coffins and skeletons, but no mummies—the climate in those parts is too cold, too damp. Corpses up there rarely mummify. The skulls Curtis *did* find were still connected to backbones. Curtis had *some* respect for the dead. He was leery about chopping skulls from their skeletons. After a long scary search, Curtis and Myers collected only two loose skulls before daylight, when they called things off.

"But the next night, they were back at it. They were poking around in a grave underneath a big cedar when a wind blew up. According to Curtis, he and Myers were suddenly showered with skeletons and coffins, falling down from the branches above their heads. Like magic, they had all the skulls they needed. But still no mummy." Chief Alphonse took a sip of his now-cold tea, grimaced and set it back down.

"Myers had done all the cemetery searching he could stomach by then, but Curtis was determined to go whaling and wouldn't quit. After some doings, Curtis was introduced to George Hunt's wife. A woman named Loon. Loon told Curtis she knew of a mummy on an island about 30 miles from Alert Bay.

"Curtis, Myers and Loon paddled a dugout canoe across Queen Charlotte Strait to this island, taking trouble not to be seen. When they got there, Myers stayed back to mind the canoe. Curtis and Loon went ashore together. They opened up several coffins until they found what Curtis described as"—Chief Alphonse paused to recollect the exact description—"'a beautiful mummy of the female species.' Curtis never knew if it was Loon's relative, but it might have been. Loon called the mummy by name and had a long one-sided conversation with it. Loon also told the mummy about the honour it was going to receive."

My mouth was dry. I'd seen some of Curtis's mummy pictures, and "beautiful" is not the word I'd use to describe ancient desiccated corpses bent double with knees drawn up to their chins.

I dumped out the chief's cold tea, took the pot from the stove and refilled our cups. Chief Alphonse was slumped down in his chair, gazing at the ceiling. He cleared his throat and continued, "Curtis delivered a mummified female body and 11 human skulls to the whale hunters. The Kwakiutls were amazed. Still, Curtis had kept his part of the bargain, so they were honour-bound to keep theirs. Curtis got to participate in a Kwakiutl whaling ritual, as well as an actual hunt."

The chief stared at me, nibbling his lip, then added, "Kwakiutl pre-whaling ritual is a heavy secret. All that's known is, it included mummy-eating."

Air escaped my lips in a long, unbidden sigh.

"The rituals took place and Curtis photographed bits of it. He was a full party to everything that happened. For the rest of his days, Curtis refused to answer people who asked him if he'd tasted mummy himself. All Curtis ever said was that cannibalism had been outlawed by the British. Mummy-eating was cannibalism, and the penalties were harsh."

Embers settled inside my stove with a soft thud. The chief rose slowly and ponderously from his seat and went to the door. I picked up our cups and placed them by the sink. The chief put on his hat and coat. "Your next step is to see Chief Numcamais. He's expecting you."

FREDDY ALBERT HAD given up commercial fishing because of some visions he'd experienced during a sweat-lodge session. He was starting to see white people as witches who used magic to sow illness and malevolence among the First Nations. Now, instead of trolling for salmon in the fresh air, Freddy spent most of his time in sweat lodges or Internet chat rooms. He'd joined the American Indian Movement, was studying Coast Salish mythology and telling anyone who'd listen that soon North America's Native peoples would rise up and smite the white man, hip and thigh. They would sweep palefaces from the earth, along with alcohol, drugs, telephones and SUVs. In Freddy's coming new age, giant firs and cedars would replenish sacred forests. Immense herds of buffalo and elk would repopulate the Great Plains, trample the whites' palaces and slums, bars and jails. In other words, Freddy had become a tiresome crank. But I needed a favour.

I found him on the Warrior beach, chanting ancient songs and wearing a Thunderbird mask decorated with eagle feathers. He was utterly engrossed in ritual and it took a while before I got his attention. I asked if I could borrow his troller for a couple of days. "Go ahead," he said. "Just don't forget to fill her tanks when you're done."

AFTER BEING DELIVERED to the brink of extinction by nineteenth-century hunters, British Columbia's sea otters are staging a slow comeback. Three of the sleek endangered animals were resting on the floats when I went down to the Warrior Reserve wharf that afternoon. Its wooden planks were slippery with slush and otter shit. The friendly creatures, big as harbour seals, waited until I got within about 10 feet of them, then lazily flipped themselves into the water with a sinuous twisting motion that left their whiskers dry and their heads facing me.

I boarded Freddy's troller and checked its bilges, fuel tanks, engine oil and coolant levels. They were okay, but Freddy's radar wasn't working. He didn't have a GPS either—I'd have to navigate the old-fashioned way. The troller's diesel started easily. I kept an eye on the oil and battery and temperature gauges until they stabilized. When the engine had warmed to 210 degrees, I unhitched the mooring lines and headed out. The curious otters followed me for a while. Beyond the harbour's stone breakwater I encountered six-foot waves. The troller bucked a bit till I throttled back to about four knots; then she rode nicely. Fisgard Lighthouse fell astern. Waterfront houses nestled at the foot of tree-covered slopes.

A fishing boat dragged its lines off William Head. I could see a man in a yellow slicker cleaning fish in the stern. Seagulls surrounded his boat, in a circling halo of wings, ready to dive for discarded scraps. Bald eagles soared high above, patrolling the frigid waters between two rocky headlands.

Victoria faded behind me as I headed northwest. As I put distance between civilization and myself, I stopped thinking about mummies and tried to put the facts that I'd learned about Isaac Schwartz and Mrs. Tranter into some sort of pattern. I didn't get very far. If there was a pattern, it wasn't obvious to me at that time.

My mind slipped into irrational mode—I thought about spirit whales, and witches. Sixteen years of formal education and a degree in anthropology has not completely eradicated my Coast Salish belief system, so perhaps it *was* First Woman who moderated the ocean winds for my benefit. Seas were almost calm when I cleared Race Rocks an hour later, eased inshore and sighted the flashing navigation beacon I was looking for. Six years had passed since I had last visited this place. I sailed parallel with the coast until I spotted a familiar pyramid-shaped rock marking the entrance to a sheltered bay. With about two feet of water between my keel and the bottom, I crossed a sandbar into a safe anchorage.

Freddy's winch was jammed; I lowered the hook by hand. When it bottomed I let out another 10 fathoms of heavy chain. After another struggle I manhandled the dory over the side, rowed it ashore and dragged it up the beach. A trail up to Chief Numcamais's place seemed narrower and steeper this time. It was late afternoon when I scrambled uphill, feeling my way across tree roots, deadfalls and rocks. In the fading light, an owl hooted. I heard something else and stopped in a clearing to listen and look. Fifty feet away, a pair of wide-set eyes was watching me. The eyes disappeared as the animal turned its head. I saw another pair of eyes, then they too disappeared. I shivered, hearing twigs and fallen leaves crunching beneath broad footpads as the wolves moved unhurriedly away.

The cabin I sought stood alone among the trees. Built of split-cedar boards that had silvered with age, it blended into the landscape as naturally as trees and rocks and green moss. Dim lamplight shone from the small four-paned windows. After hailing the house, I let my echoes die and listened, but there was no answer. I pushed the cabin door open.

Numcamais, a chief of five names, was working at a table lit by an oil lamp. Entering, I heard the swift flutter of feathers. A raven with one trailing wing perched in the shadows above one window. The raven fixed me with one eye, turned its glossy head to look at me with the other, and then opened its heavy bill and made a few strangled cries.

Chief Numcamais had not moved or acknowledged my presence. I settled myself on a chair near the stove and waited.

The old chief was carving a coffin lid with a curved, steel carving knife, its razor-sharp blade resembling a spoon with sharpened edges. He was incising the shape of an eagle's head. The lid was nearly finished. Below the eagle were bear, raven, frog and killer whale—the carver's family tree. Mine, too.

The raven hopped down from its perch, alighted on Chief Numcamais's shoulder and stretched its bill inside the chief's breast pocket. Smiling, the chief took seeds from the pocket and scattered them on the table. The bird pecked away, clearing wood shavings with its feet as it ate.

Still without looking at me, the old man spoke. English wasn't his first language, or even his second, and his greeting was in Coast Salish—words of welcome in a tongue slowly dying on this coast.

Switching to English, he said, "Raven came here in the late snow, a long time ago. He's got one broken wing so he can't find himself any more lady loves. Raven and me, we're growing old together. Sometimes I tell him stories, and he listens. Sometimes he tells me stories."

The chief had seen nearly a hundred winters. Now he was almost blind—he was carving that coffin lid more by feel than sight. Long ago, he had slept in a longhouse with famous hunters. Numcamais had sailed in 80-foot war canoes. Once, he'd paddled from the Queen Charlotte Islands to Victoria wearing nothing but a cedar-bark cloak and a woven hat.

Chief Numcamais called me Silas, pronouncing my name in the old way. I'd recently inherited a new name, and I expected him to ask if I was wealthy enough to spring for a potlatch, but he didn't.

"This is bad weather for Spirit Quest," Chief Numcamais said. "Let's hope nobody gets frostbite. It's hard, dancing without toes."

He reached for a round tobacco tin, took out a handful of sweet-grass, placed it in a skillet and lit it with a sliver of wood from the stove. In a minute, the sweetgrass was smoking nicely. The chief did some hand medicine over the pan and wafted smoke over his head and face and shoulders. I did the same.

"Maybe this year's spirit questers won't find their tamahnous the first time out," the chief said. "I didn't. My first time out, all I got was dirty. Next time I went looking for tamahnous it was the year's oldest moon. Bitter cold. My uncles had told me I should go without food for three days first, so that's what I did. Went three whole days without anything except water before I set out. Three days after that I'm sitting on a beach, calling for tamahnous to come to me. I'm starving and miserable. I was ready to quit again when Spirit told me to eat raw octopus, build my strength up.

"What I did, Silas, I got a long stick and went into the sea near some rocks. Octopus love crabs and clams. Any time you see a pile of empty clamshells underwater, you're probably near an octopus burrow. What you do is, you poke around with your stick, trying to get Mrs. Octopus mad at you. If she gets mad enough she'll come out of her burrow and move someplace else. That time I'm talking about, I found some empty shells, poked for a bit, then waited. After a while I saw the tip of an octopus tentacle come out from a little cave. Then a bit more. What you do is, when you think you're ready, you reach down, grab a tentacle and throw Mrs. Octopus onto the beach. But you've got to do it right. It takes a bit of practice to be a good octopus catcher. That time I reached down into the water, grabbed a tentacle and tried to throw her ashore. But Mrs. Octopus's other arms were wrapped around some rocks. I couldn't budge her. Next thing I know she's all over me, pecking away at my chest with her sharp beak. Those tentacles were like strong rubber ropes. I was helpless. She's pulling me under, cold seawater is breaking over my head. I thought: *It's all over, I might as well stop struggling.*"

The old chief was really caught up in his story now.

"I went right under but I couldn't see a thing because Mrs. Octopus shot black ink in the water. I guess we went half a mile before she let go of me. I was in the underwater spirit world by then. It's not as cold as you might think. I didn't see many fish. No wrecks. I got used to being down there.

"Well, I still had my tamahnous to find so I climbed into a land of ice where I met Raven. He give me bannock soaked in oolichan oil. When Raven asked me what I was doing there, I told him. 'I'm looking for my tamahnous,' I said.

"Raven said, 'Seeking your tamahnous? Where?'

"I pointed uphill to the highest peak.

"Raven said, 'Don't go near it. *Baxbakwalanuxsiwae* lives there. Man-Eater-at-the-North-End-of-the-World lives there.'

"Raven took his wings off and laid them on the ground. Dark fog spread over the mountains. Raven just wanted to stop me going up there, that's all, but by then I'd earned a bit of tamahnous and I got rid of Raven darkness with fire from my medicine bag. I was pretending to be brave, but I was scared when I wandered into that strange part of the spirit world.

"I stepped over the skeletons of otters and wolves as I came to Stone House. Red birds with beaks like knives flapped all around. Inside Stone House, magic crystals were raised up on a platform. Some crystals were white, others blue. They made loud humming noises and they moved in circles like dancers. When crystals touched each other, sparks flew like bolts of lightning. Then I saw Man-Eater."

Chief Numcamais was suddenly quiet.

I'd grown up listening to Man-Eater stories. Man-Eater the shaman king, a creature with an immense dog-like body covered with gnashing mouths. I knew about Man-Eater's horrifying wife and her female slaves who hunt constantly to feed Man-Eater's insatiable appetite. Every Salish kid knows about Man-Eater's corpse-littered domain, about the giant cranes and ravens ranging up and down outside his mountain cave, feasting on men's eyes.

Chief Numcamais said, "Man-Eater touched my hands and it put me asleep. Tamahnous came to me in a dream and gave me Thunderbird Song. In my dream I picked four quartz crystals, put them in my medicine bag, then I went straight to the longhouse and did my first hamatsa dance."

I spent the night in Chief Numcamais's house. The next

morning after breakfast, we took some supplies and went for a ride together in Freddy's boat.

THE HIDDEN COVE was half an hour from Chief Numcamais's place. We anchored in the lee of a densely treed island and launched Freddy's dory. The chief navigated, and I manned the oars. It was low tide and heavy surf pounded the shore. Flotsam whirled in a savage riptide. Finally we rounded a spit and came upon a strip of sheltered beach about 50 feet across. A slightly higher tide would have submerged the beach entirely. As it was, our dory grounded on sand about 20 feet offshore. We got a bit damp pulling the dory high and dry. The chief was a tough old bird and seemed none the worse from his wetting. I think he was actually enjoying himself. He eyed little jets of water spurting intermittently from holes in the sand and said, "This always was a good clamming place." Then he pointed.

A steep, unscalable cliff faced us, its bottom 10 feet coated with barnacles and mussels and the rest of it rising another 30 or 40 feet to forested overhang. I followed a movement with my eyes and saw a mink scamper behind a driftwood log. A bald eagle coasted overhead, accompanied by her chick. But at that moment Numcamais wasn't interested in wildlife. He kept pointing ahead. I couldn't see what he wanted me to see, and told him so.

"Good," he said. "The secret is still safe."

We'd brought dry kindling and a small tent—one of those hemispherical units stiffened by flexible rods—with no floor to it. While the chief dug clams, I lit a fire on a nearby shelf of rock. When the fire was burning nicely, I built it up with driftwood and added some stones collected from the beach. After a while the fire burned to embers and the stones were very hot. We positioned the tent above the heated stones and had an instant sauna. We went inside and warmed up.

"A long time ago, a young Coast Salish warrior was on this beach, seeking his tamahnous," the chief said. "That young warrior ended up in the sea. Somehow or other, he got tangled up with a big octopus. She yanked him underwater, but she was kind-hearted, not cruel. Instead of drowning him, she dragged him along an underwater passage into a dry cave."

He put clams on the fire, then led me outside the tent. The beach was now totally submerged on a rising tide. He pointed to a crack in the cliff face and said, "The entrance to that underwater cave is across the beach, right there." Grinning mightily, he added, "If you want to have a look inside it, you better take your clothes off."

I got undressed and waded across to the cliff. I took a deep breath and dived in before I could change my mind.

The chief had directed me to an underwater tunnel about 10 feet long. I emerged in a domed limestone cave, roughly 70 feet in diameter, with a dry sandy floor. Diffused light emanated from above, providing just enough light for me to see about 50 carved wooden figures, approximately life-sized, arranged in a circle 20 feet across. At the foot of each figure lay human skulls. Other skulls were impaled on stakes. Dozens of whale ribs were propped upright against the walls, like Gothic arches. Water, dripping from stalactites, fell onto a little cedar house at the back of the cave before draining away around the cave's circumference. A dozen carved and painted cedar coffins lay here and there on the sand.

I spent only a few minutes in the cave, maybe 5 or 10, before swimming out. I was half-paralyzed with cold, speechless almost, when I got inside the tent. The chief, eating roasted clams, waited until I'd soaked up some heat before asking me how I'd liked the cave.

"I liked Disney World better."

"That's too bad," he said, "because you've got at least one more visit ahead of you."

"Not today, I hope."

"Not today, Silas," he said, handing me a nice fat clam on the half-shell, "but soon."

Rain hammered the roof of the tent. We were in no hurry to leave. I spent some time telling Chief Numcamais about finding Isaac Schwartz, and the curious marks I'd seen on his body. He asked me to describe the marks in detail. I did the best I could. After thinking for a while, he said, "They're not Coast Salish designs. But I've seen Nimpkish petroglyph markings up the coast that looked a bit like that."

CHAPTER THIRTEEN

Tuttle's Antique Auctions was located on Wharf Street, close to the Seattle ferry terminal. Twenty small Canadian flags dangled limply from short poles above the display windows. Wednesday auctions had been held continuously at Tuttle's for more than a hundred years. Most of Victoria's early settlers emigrated from the British Isles, bringing family treasures with them. Four times annually, Tuttle's held special auctions attracting bidders from Los Angeles, New York and London. Prices sometimes matched those obtained at Christie's or Sotheby's.

When I got there, the staff was arranging lots for the next sale. Viewing areas had been roped off. At the back of the salesroom was an office with windows overlooking the auction floor. A fresh-looking woman who wouldn't qualify as an antique for a long time was doing paperwork behind a mahogany counter straight out of a Dickens novel. I told her my business and she directed me upstairs to Mary Jung's office.

I found Ms. Jung inside what might qualify as the city's untidi-est office—apart from my own. Papers and photographs cluttered her desk. In and out baskets overflowed, and a printer was spew-ing more paper into a tray. Dozens of pictures in heavy gilt frames leaned against the walls. *Objets d'art* bearing numbered tags stood on shelves or on the floor. When I entered, Ms. Jung was speaking into one of two telephones. She waved me to a seat, and I stepped carefully towards her desk.

Ms. Jung had one of those serene faces that give otherwise ordinary-looking women an exotic kind of beauty. She had black, shoulder-length hair and wore a black silk jacket over a white cotton shirt unbuttoned far enough to excite a eunuch. She finished her conversation, but before we could speak her second phone rang. She answered it, then asked the clerk to hold all her calls. She eyed my uniform and asked, "How may I help you, officer?"

I told her I was trying to unravel a 50-year-old mystery.

"Really," she said, sounding intrigued. "Tell me more."

"An art-collector friend of mine passed away recently. Years ago, he divested himself of some Old Master drawings. After he died, an auction catalogue for one of the Tuttle's sales was found among his effects."

My words triggered something. She crossed to a filing cabinet, removed an accordion folder and brought it back to her desk. She untied the red string holding down the flap and pulled out a hand-written note. She read it, then put it back in the folder. "If you want information about past sales, there isn't much I'm willing to tell you. People who entrust their business to us expect us to keep it private."

Her fingers were beating a little tattoo on the edge of her desk as she added briskly, "What, exactly, do you want?"

I studied her. She was like stainless steel—smooth and probably bulletproof. I said, "A couple of things. First, I'd appreciate it if you could tell me a little bit about the trade in Old Master drawings."

"Exploring even a fraction of that business would take all day, and I don't have all day." She examined the polish on her long finger-nails. "You'll find reference books in any decent library."

I thought that was it, but after a second she looked at me again and relented. "This will have to be brief," she said, "but here goes." She settled back in her chair.

"Painters like Michelangelo, Rembrandt, Rubens, and of course lesser artists, made hundreds of sketches—little compositions on paper before they got started on their oil paintings. Paper isn't a very durable material. Old inks fade. Things get lost, or thrown away. Only a fraction of the drawings still survive. Even so, until fairly recently it was possible to buy good Old Master drawings for relatively little. Today, even works by third-rate artists can fetch enormous sums. When wealthy Japanese buyers came into the market, prices went stratospheric, the market went crazy. Now German and Italian buyers are bidding up good work as well. We expect this trend to continue."

She gazed thoughtfully at me as she considered her next words. "Tuttle's is a relatively small auction house, but a lot of fairly high-end Old Master drawings are consigned to us. Internationally, there are four or five important sales every year at Christie's, Sotheby's and Swann's. Those sales attract buyers with very deep pockets indeed. But buying drawings can be risky. It's a specialized field, and there are plenty of fakes floating around." Her bright eyes were unblinking as she added, "It's contradictory. Beautiful art attracts some rather ugly people."

"In the catalogue we found, somebody had highlighted certain lots, all of them drawings. What I'd like to know is, who consigned those drawings here? Who bought them?"

The phone rang again. Ms. Jung leaned forward and picked it up, listened for a moment, then replaced it without speaking. She said, "You see how it is? The phone rings even when I ask them to hold my calls. I'm pretty busy, so I won't waste words. Consignors' and purchasers' names are confidential. I won't divulge any names without a court order."

My hopes were fading along with Mary Jung's smile, but I said, "There's one thing you *can* tell me without betraying a confidence ..." I broke off as somebody rapped on the office door. A man appeared and said nervously, "I'm sorry to interrupt, Ms. Jung, but Mr. Palfrey's downstairs again. He says it can't wait."

She nodded calmly. She returned the accordion folder to the cabinet, excused herself and left the room.

I went to the cabinet immediately, took out the folder and opened it. Many of the drawings had been consigned by Isaac Schwartz—the rest by a Mrs. Dorothy Baineston. I returned the folder to the drawer and left the office quickly, almost colliding with Ms Jung.

"You're right, Ms. Jung," I told her. "My request for information is unreasonable. I won't waste any more of your time. Thanks."

She gave me a surprised look and was about to speak, but I was already walking away.

Back on the street, outside Tuttle's, it occurred to me that some of my actions were verging on the furtive and shabby. But I'd promised Moran I'd find Isaac. And I'd promised myself that after finding him, I'd find his killer. I rationalized all the way to the public library.

My police uniform attracted curious glances as I dug books from the racks. The one that particularly interested me was the pre-war German memoir by Angela Knoeffler. I made myself comfortable in a quiet carrel and turned to the section about the dinner party in Berlin-Dahlem—the party hosted by Sir Hugh Baineston, the diplomat art collector. It seemed obvious now—Baineston was the man to whom Isaac Schwartz had entrusted his drawings before being arrested by the Nazis.

Then I checked copies of *Debrett's Peerage*, *Burke's Landed Gentry* and *Who's Who* for the years between 1937 and 1950. Sir Hugh Baineston made the lists for the years 1937, 1938 and 1939. After that he vanished.

Born near Hoylake, Cheshire, in 1909, the only son of an English baronet, Baineston had been educated at Rossall School and at Cambridge. Afterwards he joined the British diplomatic service. Baineston succeeded to the baronetcy upon the death of his father, in 1938. He married Dorothy Jane Booth, of Fleetwood, Lancashire. Before the Second World War, Baineston had been second secretary at the Berlin embassy. Had he been killed during the war? If he was still alive, Sir Hugh would now be in his 90s.

I went back to my office, took out my Isaac Schwartz file and for the fourth time studied the *Prowdes of Peeling* book. This time I concentrated on photographs. There were pictures of tennis parties, garden parties, church fetes and bazaars, gymkhanas, yachting weekends. Young men in striped blazers and straw boaters and ladies in long dresses and beautiful hats evoked the sense of an elegant vanished age. Many pictures showed the Prowde family gathered on the steps of the house, flanked by maids, chauffeurs, housekeepers and butlers.

MASON'S HEALTH CARE Services was located in a refurbished Georgian house on Superior Street. I parked my MG on a yellow line and went inside.

A passing truck brought the house perceptibly alive, ruffling the leaves of a potted ficus. A middle-aged nurse in a white uniform sat behind a desk. A lapel badge identified her as Tilly Muir, RN. It's strange, but I now have difficulty remembering exactly what she looked like. Her face was somehow two-dimensional, her natural expression severe. My instincts told me that extracting useful information from Nurse Muir would take effort and tact. But I was wrong. She loved to talk, and she wasn't the least bit intimidated by a man in uniform.

"Hello," she said, smiling up at me. "You look healthy enough. Sure you're in the right place?"

"Sergeant Seaweed. I'm inquiring about someone who used to work here."

"Seaweed!" she laughed. "You don't look like a Bladderwort, so you must be related to the Kelps, of Wreck Beach."

I chuckled at her joke, but quickly moved on.

"I'm checking up on a woman named Ellen Lemieux," I told her. "I believe Ellen was with your agency at one time."

"My agency!" she echoed. "I wish it was. I'd be rich. But I'm just a wage slave for Doc Mason, the old fart. I could make twice as much working in a hospital, except I hate shift work."

"Me too. Graveyard especially."

Her severe look returned. "What do you want to know about Ellen Lemieux?"

"Can you confirm that she was a former employee?"

"Sure. But we haven't seen her in a while. She's not in trouble or anything, is she?"

"It's just routine."

"It's none of my business, but Ellen always seemed kind of lost to me," Tilly confided.

"Lost?"

"Out of the loop. Loner. You'd try communicating, but she'd be staring into space. You knew she wasn't listening. Tell the truth, I felt sorry for her."

"Was she a good employee?"

"Hard to say, to be honest. The thing is, after a bit of initial training, our workers get very little supervision. We send them out and they're on their own, unless they get into trouble. If there's an emergency they either phone me or call 911. Ellen seemed to be capable. Never caused any trouble for the agency. Clients never complained."

"Was Ellen a trained nurse?"

"Are you kidding? This is a bedpans-and-diapers service. We

provide caretakers for the elderly, not trained nurses. Don't quote me on that, though," she added hastily.

"Did you know Ellen socially, or just professionally?"

"Both, at first. You know Ellen has Indian blood?"

"I've always assumed so."

"Before landing in Victoria, she lived her whole life on northern reserves. Didn't know a soul here. She was lonely, so I took her to an Outdoor Club dance once. Introduced her to a few people. Ellen wasn't into dancing; she was just crazy to meet men, anybody in trousers. With her looks, she didn't need to work hard."

Tilly produced a strained smile. "Ellen invited me to her house one night. Two guys were there, drinking and carrying on. Proper wolves. It wasn't my scene, so I left in a hurry. One guy came outside, wanted to walk me home. I got rid of him, but after that it was strictly business with me and Ellen."

I played a wild card. "These guys. Did one of them happen to be a big, long-haired Native?"

Her eyes widened, and I knew I'd hit the mark. "That's right," she said. "He's the one tried to tag along home with me."

"Remember his name?"

"Morley, I think? Maybe Maurice? I'm not sure. It's a while ago. Is he in trouble?"

"This is an ongoing inquiry. You never know what's relevant, what isn't."

"It's probably a good thing Ellen isn't with us anymore. People like her can drag an agency's name into the mud, I've seen it happen."

"You say there were no complaints from clients."

"Ellen only had two clients while she was with us. They've both passed away since."

Tilly consulted the Rolodex on her desk. "Ellen's first assignment was Mr. Terrel. That job lasted two weeks. After that, she had Mrs. Micklethwaite, in that lovely old house on Adanac Street. When Mrs. Micklethwaite passed away, Ellen left the agency."

"Was she dismissed?"

"Heavens, no. But Doctor Mason only pays minimum wage; it's hard enough to *get* people, let alone keep 'em."

A little bell rang in my head. *Adanac Street.* Then I remembered. George Purdy—the man who had sent Ellen Lemieux a Christmas card—also lived on Adanac.

I thanked Tilly for her assistance and went out onto Superior Street. A female commissionaire had just shoved a ticket under my wiper. Another 30 bucks down the drain. Audibly cursing the iniquities of fate, I got into my car and started the engine. The commissionaire, glancing my way, saw that I was in uniform and came back.

"Sorry about the ticket. I didn't realize this was a cop's car," she said. "How come you didn't hang a police tag on your rear-view mirror?"

"I forgot."

"You know there isn't a thing I can do now," she said, showing me her little hand-held computer. "Your ticket's in the system already."

"You realize, I hope, that a single ticket infraction could permanently ruin my chances of promotion?"

Her face fell.

"Just kidding," I said, putting the MG into gear. "I've already been promoted above my ability."

MY NEXT STOP was Adanac Street, in the Fairfield neighbourhood of Victoria, near the Cook Street village. Some of Victoria's early lumber barons built their mansions here, on acreages overlooking the Strait of Juan de Fuca and the Olympic Mountains. Over subsequent decades, old-money families had retreated to the Uplands and Oak

Bay. Grand homes still remained, but many had been converted into apartments, their acreages subdivided into smaller lots.

In one of Adanac Street's well-tended yards, an old man was stringing Christmas lights across some low hedges that lined his front walk. He had an unlit pipe clenched between his teeth. If I had remembered the house number correctly, this was George Purdy. I stopped beside his gate and said hello. The old-timer seemed more than happy to stop work and chat awhile. He dropped an orange extension cord on the ground and in a gruff but not unfriendly voice asked, "Something I can do for you, officer?"

I pointed to the small house next door. "Isn't that the Micklethwaites' old place?"

"Sure. The Micklethwaites were my neighbours for 30 years." Purdy sighed. "The Tans own the place now, but they're always working so I never see 'em." He grinned. "The Chinese don't seem that sociable. Not like the English."

"The Micklethwaites were English?"

"Born and bred," Purdy answered readily. "Jim and his missus came out from the Old Country in the '50s. Jim worked in Eaton's furniture department till the day he died. Jim's wife and mine were great pals." Purdy shook his head. "They're all gone now. I'm the only one left."

"You've seen some changes," I said, to draw him out.

"Changes, but not necessarily for the better. When we bought this house, you could still see the strait from the upstairs windows. Now they've built that apartment building over there so my view's gone. In the old days, Mary and me would stroll down to the park at the bottom of the street. Sit on a bench and watch the boats sail by."

Purdy stopped talking to light his pipe.

"So the Micklethwaites were English?" I repeated.

"Both of 'em. Loved his garden, Jim did. Used to talk about the lovely gardens over in the Old Country. Must have been really something, those places—all lawns and statues and ornamental ponds. Jim used to show me pictures of this big house he worked at before he came to Canada."

"Was Micklethwaite a gardener there?"

The old man laughed and shook his head. "Over home he was a *butler*. Employed by some English toff. Jim's father and grandfather had been servants for the same family. But then the war came and Jim did five years in the British army. Saw a bit of life. When the war ended the world had changed, and so had Jim. Opening doors for people who thought they were above him? He couldn't do it anymore."

"Did the Micklethwaites have children?"

For the first time, the old man looked wary. Instead of answering, he scratched the tip of his chin with the bowl of his pipe, bright eyes glittering. "Something wrong?" he asked. "This a criminal matter?"

"Probably not. Just routine."

The old man shrugged. "Well, I guess your questions can't hurt the Micklethwaites now, can they? They're both dead and buried. And to answer your question, the Micklethwaites were childless. They had no relations in the whole world, as far as I know. When Mrs. Micklethwaite was widowed and taken with her last illness, a nurse came to look after her. Lived in the house permanent like, till Mrs. Micklethwaite passed away. Very sudden, it was."

"That nurse was Ellen Lemieux, I suppose?"

"That's right. Ellen. A nice girl, beautiful. But very quiet. Kept to herself. I liked her, though. When she cooked for Mrs. M. she'd sometimes bring me over some." He thought for a moment. "I haven't seen Ellen since Mrs. Micklethwaite died, but she did telephone me a couple of times."

"You wouldn't remember the name of the family that Micklethwaite worked for in the Old Country?"

"It happens that I do," said the old man, "The Prowdes. Jim used to say that they were Prowde by name and proud by nature."

The air seemed suddenly colder. I thanked Mr. Purdy for his help. We shook hands and I took my leave.

CHAPTER FOURTEEN

Driving away from Adanac Street, I felt the guilt that comes from neglecting one's ordinary duties. As everybody knows, a uniformed cop's ordinary duty is to pound a beat—make his presence known to as many rascals as possible. So I drove back downtown, parked on Fisgard Street and set out on foot. During the next hour I persuaded six University of Victoria students protesting Canada's role in Afghanistan to rethink their idea of building a tent city on Pandora Street. I also called Buster's Towing on my cellphone and had them haul away a '73 Mazda abandoned near St. John the Divine Church.

The next thing I knew, it was raining hard. I happened to be outside the Good Shepherd Mission, so I went inside. This time I found Joe McNaught in his office, bent over his desk, holding a pen in his fat fist as he worked on the mission's accounts. The black-robed pastor rocked back in his steel chair and gave me a strained smile.

"Where's Nimrod?" I asked without ceremony,

McNaught scratched his bald head with the pen. "I can't say, brother. He comes and he goes."

"Nimrod lives here. He's supposed to be your strong right arm in the kitchen."

"He's my strong right arm in the kitchen when he's not drunk or face down in a gutter."

"The last I heard, Nimrod had sworn off the booze."

"Well, see, Nimrod has this problem," McNaught replied, sounding for all the world like a patient schoolmaster addressing a simpleton. "There's some kind of bomb inside his head. Every once in a while the bomb explodes and Nimrod's brains go down the toilet. That's when he runs down to the nearest liquor store, picks up a jug and finds himself a nice quiet back alley."

McNaught's right wrist bent upward and he stared at the silver rings on his fat fingers. I waited.

"The last time I saw Nimrod was several days ago," McNaught finally said. "We had some business in Chemainus. When we got back to Victoria, the car needed gas and I made the mistake of giving him cash to pay for it. If you need him real bad, I'll put the word out, but I have to tell you this: Nimrod won't be much use to anybody until he's run his devil into the ground again."

"How long do his binges usually last?"

"Depends. He's getting old, running out of steam. In his heyday they lasted for months, years." McNaught admired the rings on his other hand. He gave me a sly look and said, "The word on the street is you had your wrist slapped by Bulloch."

"I'll survive. What bothers me are guys like you, who think *my* brains are in the toilet, like Nimrod's."

"Well, I always knew you were sensitive," McNaught said, smirking. "Beats me how you ever became a cop in the first place. You should have been a social worker."

"Or a pastor in a downtown mission."

McNaught shook his head. "You have the wrong idea, Silas. Being a pastor down here, you've got to be tougher than the competition. Tougher than hell."

"All right, tough guy," I said, showing him my teeth. "Tell me who torched the Jamieson Foundry."

McNaught's grin faded, but he recovered quickly. "That's what I like," he said, easing a finger into his ecclesiastical collar. "Teasers. Guys who talk in riddles. Think they can blow smoke in my eyes."

"That's good, coming from you. Your whole act is smoke and mirrors."

"Away you go, Silas," said McNaught, trying to brazen it out and waving me toward the door. "Just run along. You can't stampede me."

But McNaught was anxious, I could tell. In a lengthening silence I became aware of the sweet smell of incense that overlaid the sour mission odours of cooking oil, unwashed bodies and Lysol. I heard laughter in the corridor outside, and a banging door.

"Tell you what I think," I said sharply. "I think *you* burned it down."

"The Jamieson Foundry? Me? Why would I do a thing like that?"

"Oh, maybe to save yourself a little money when you come to build on the property."

There was a brief silence, then McNaught said, "Keep talking."

"Well I'm glad you're not arguing with me, Joe, because I know that you own the Jamieson property. What I don't know is how you raised enough money to buy it."

"You should know, because I already told you. I got the money from Isaac Schwartz, remember?"

"You told me Isaac left $50,000. With Victoria real-estate prices the way they are, there's no way you could have swung the deal with that."

McNaught's black eyes were unreadable. I thought he'd clammed up, but he surprised me. "You've done okay, Silas. I thought Isaac and me did a pretty good job of covering it up. How'd you find out?"

I ignored his question and said instead, "I know, among other things, that you've been dealing with the Regal Trust Company. What I'm thinking is, maybe you're planning a big new church on the old Jamieson property."

"Okay, fine. I won't deny it—it'll be public knowledge before long anyway. You're right. This church is too small; we need to expand." McNaught made a fan with his hand, his fingers splayed in a farewell wave. "Now, off you go, Silas," he said in a quieter voice. "I'm busy, and you're making me nervous."

"What's the matter, Joe? Conscience bothering you?"

My last remark struck a nerve. The pastor lumbered to his feet, helping himself up by pushing against the chair's arm rests. Standing, he thrust his hands into the folds of his robe and gazed at me for a long minute. Shaking his head, he walked over to the window and stared out at a single ray of sunlight slanting through a gap in the clouds. It was the kind of sky favoured by painters for religious compositions involving heavenly messengers. If McNaught had any guiding angels up there, they were invisible to me. He was on his own.

"Now that we're being so upfront about everything, what did you want to see Nimrod about?" McNaught finally said.

"Nimrod was the only man who spent any time talking with Isaac Schwartz. And I don't think Nimrod knew that Isaac was rich."

"So what?"

"Funny thing, secrets. There are some secrets people take to their graves. Other secrets, they just won't stay put—they're busting to be told."

McNaught's expression was blank. He had recovered his composure and was the tough no-nonsense street pastor again. I needed to shock him. "After Isaac's service, Nimrod was sure that Isaac died broke. It got me thinking. I wondered why Isaac never told *Nimrod* he had money, but he told *you*."

I gave McNaught a chance to speak, but he kept quiet. I took another gamble and said forcefully, "Isaac's money was earned in a shameful way. My guess is, he had to tell somebody. So he told you instead of Nimrod."

McNaught said innocently, "I was his pastor—he could trust me. Isaac told me he was getting back something of his own. An investment that paid off big."

"Did he tell you that it was an investment in blood money?"

That was too much for McNaught. His shoulders slumped. Speaking in a softer voice he said, "I'm no Judas. Isaac's money wasn't for me. It was for my flock."

McNaught lifted his arms, then let them fall again to his sides. "For years, Isaac Schwartz donated to the Good Shepherd Mission," he said. "He'd come in with a cheque. Sometimes for $10,000, sometimes for $50,000. It was money he got from selling art." McNaught caught my eye and added, "God gives and God takes away. He takes life. Sometime he takes hope, and only He knows why. Mine are little people, Silas; they've got nobody but me. I give them food and bring them to Jesus. They've been robbed of everything. They've lost their jobs, their families, their self-respect. All they've got is me."

"Spare me the warmed-over guff," I said. "If all they've got is you, they haven't got much."

Those words didn't faze McNaught. He had withdrawn into his head. He wasn't listening to anything except his own thoughts. He outlined an imaginary building with his hands and said, "I have this dream. I want to build a big new church—a combination church and clinic for street people. A place where addicts and people with AIDS can get treatment. We'll have beds for the homeless. We'll have classrooms. We'll have a Native friendship centre. Teach your people fresh off reserves how to survive the city.

"It hardly seems fair, sometimes, those fat cats in their fancy offices out there. Those businessmen, stockbrokers, rich property developers—how come they've got so much and my people have to sleep under bridges?" He held his arms out now in a helpless gesture.

"If you do end up building a new church, you'd better build it with fireproof materials," I said. "Install plenty of sprinklers, because you might have one helluva time buying fire insurance."

Talking about his dreams had strengthened McNaught. "Ah, go on," he said. "You've got what you came for, Silas. Now quit hassling me."

His normal composure was back. It would be a waste of time to grill him further. His guard was up now—he was boxing clever.

I was at the door before I asked, "Remember the old lady who sat at the back of the chapel when you did Isaac's service? The woman who left early?"

"Yeah, you mentioned her before. Lady in a fur coat?"

"You said you'd never seen her before. Seen her since?"

The preacher shook his head. "No, I haven't. I'll keep my eyes peeled. She was probably some old widow who just likes funerals."

I went outside and stood on the front steps. Panhandlers, runaways and just plain crazies, attracted to the mission like iron filings to a magnet, stamped their feet in the cold. Across the street, a posse of teenaged Chinese girls sashayed by, freezing in their low-slung pants and navel-revealing short jackets.

I called Bernie on my cellphone, but the police dispatcher told me he had booked off sick. I called him at home. His wife answered.

"Hello, Marie. Can I talk to Bernie? It's important."

"Aw Silas, give the guy a break. He's laid up in bed, weak as a kitten, coughing and sneezing."

"Not pneumonia?"

"The doctor says it's just a bad chest cold. He's run down from working too many hours. He never gets enough sleep."

"Well, tell him I called and give him lots of TLC," I was saying when Bernie came on the line.

"What's up?" he croaked.

"Nothing, go back to bed."

"I'm *in* bed. Is this to do with Isaac Schwartz?"

"Yeah."

"All right, come on over. Wear a face mask in case I sneeze in your face."

Marie was protesting strenuously, but I pretended not to hear and hung up.

MARIE WAS WAITING for me at the door. Bernie must have lectured her, because instead of arguing she kissed my cheek and led me straight upstairs to the master bedroom. Bernie was propped up against the pillows, looking feverish. His red eyes were streaming, and he had Kleenex in one hand and a glass of hot orange juice in the other.

"Got plenty of rum in that glass, Bernie?"

"Sure. You want one?" Bernie sniffled, pointing to a vacuum flask on the bedside table. "Help yourself."

It was like stealing from orphans, but I poured myself a glass anyway and sat down in a Morris chair with a leather cushion. Bernie's eyes seemed to have sunk deeper in his head. I thought his hair looked thinner too, but it must have been my imagination—it was only two days since I'd last seen him.

"I just spoke with Joe McNaught," I said. "I'm pretty sure he torched the Jamieson Foundry. If he didn't do it himself, someone acting for him likely did."

Bernie was overtaken by a coughing fit. Rocket-propelled influenza droplets filled the air and left him breathless. I got up to leave, but he waved me back to my seat. "Okay," I said. "Five minutes, then I'm outta here. Let me do all the talking; you just take it easy."

He nodded in agreement and I continued. "Isaac Schwartz, to all appearances a penniless Holocaust survivor, is murdered. Except he wasn't so penniless—before he died, he gave a million dollars or more to the Good Shepherd Mission. McNaught told me that Isaac got this money from selling art. Now, a few facts. Before the war, back in the late '30s, Isaac was swindled out of some Old Master drawings by a wealthy Englishman, a man called Baineston. Isaac and his family ended up in German concentration camps.

"Baineston was a bigwig. His full name was Sir Hugh Baineston, and his wife was Lady Dorothy Baineston. The Bainestons went missing in Europe during the war and were assumed dead. But maybe they're *not* dead, because somebody calling herself Dorothy Baineston has been consigning valuable Old Master drawings to auctioneers."

Bernie's cough began again, but this time he kept a Kleenex to his mouth. I waited until he stopped.

"I think Isaac found out about those consignments and discovered that the drawings had originally belonged to him. He did some ferreting, and that's what got him killed."

Bernie was staring at the ceiling. He said thoughtfully, "Okay, but the important question is, how did *Isaac* end up with the money?"

"I don't know yet. Anything I say would be guessing."

"Go see Savage and Bulloch," Bernie advised. "Now. Lay your cards on the table."

"Waste of time. Savage will tell me that Isaac's murder is Bulloch's business. Bulloch will tell me it's none of *my* fucking business. This is a complex case, I prefer we wait till you can handle it personally."

I WAS STILL thinking about Isaac Schwartz when I got back to the reserve and picked up my mail. My cabin was freezing inside—I used most of the mail to light my stove. The only genuine piece of correspondence had arrived in a heavily embossed envelope; it was an invitation to a Christmas party at Felicity Exeter's house. Casual. RSVP.

Should I phone? What I really wanted was to find some quiet place where I could hold Felicity's hands while gazing deeply into her sexy green eyes. Enchant her with Coast Salish legends, charm the pants off her. The holding hands part would be nice, too ... Reality intervened. A woman like her, rich and beautiful? She had her pick of men. Who was I kidding?

On the other hand, many powerful women have trouble getting suitable dates. Maureen Dowd—*The Times'* ace butt-kicker—had complained about that very thing on *Larry King Live*. I derailed that train of thought too, switched back to the real world and decided to just phone. This time my cellphone worked, and so did Felicity's line. A hoarse male voice answered, "Exeter residence. Porteous speaking."

"My name is Silas Seaweed. May I speak to Ms. Exeter?"

"I am sorry, sir. Ms. Exeter is not at home. Do you wish to leave a message?" Porteous' voice was businesslike, curt.

"Will you tell her that I received her invitation? I'm phoning to accept."

Porteous coughed. "What did you say your name was?"

"Seaweed. Silas Seaweed."

"Fine, I'll tell her."

I replaced the receiver thoughtfully. Who the hell was Porteous? How come the hoarse voice? Smoked too many expensive Havanas? Not very smart—couldn't remember my name for two seconds. Porteous was probably Felicity's rich lover. With their kind of money, you didn't need brains—what you needed were clever accountants. Well, it had been a nice dream.

I looked out my window. Winter's storms were temporarily abated; in the fading afternoon daylight, the sea outside my house was still. White swans cruised majestically near the wharf, contrasting nicely with a flock of high-flying crows, flapping to their night roosts on Victoria's offshore islands. A mile beyond the Fisgard Lighthouse, the horizon was barely visible where black sea joined blacker sky.

I was opening a box of Kraft Dinner when my phone rang. It was Felicity.

"I'm sorry to disturb you at home, Mr. Seaweed. I did call your office, but all I got was the answering machine."

"Funny you should call. I just telephoned *you* to accept your invitation. Mr. Porteous answered."

"Lovely, I'm pleased," she said. "Look, sorry if this is a bit abrupt, but I'm in a quandary. I need advice and don't know who to ask."

"Fire away."

"It's a bit complicated, actually. I'm not sure where to begin."

"Maybe we could meet, talk face to face. May I ask where you're calling from?"

"The Laurel Point Inn."

"I can be there in a few minutes. If you haven't eaten, maybe we can have a bowl of chili or something at Lou's."

"Chili at Lou's sounds perfectly wonderful, but I'm afraid I can't. Not tonight."

"Take pity on me, Ms. Exeter. I was just about to make macaroni and cheese. Sharing dinner would be a Christian act, your good deed for the day."

She laughed, then added in a serious voice, "Look. Richard Hendrix phoned me from the Campbell River jail. He says he's being framed, set up. He insists he knows nothing about any murders, and I believe him."

"Did he explain how he and Lofthouse both wound up in Campbell River?"

"He can't explain it, didn't even try. Richard thinks whoever killed Lofthouse dumped his body up there to bolster the circumstantial case against him."

"Against whom?"

"Against Richard."

"That's a bit far-fetched."

She didn't say anything for a minute, and I wondered if I'd offended her. She suddenly asked, "Are you interested in art?"

"Oddly enough, I am, especially Old Master drawings."

"There's an opening tonight at the Moss Street Gallery. Seven o'clock. It's avant-garde work by the artist known as Tototo."

"Tototo?"

"Yes. I'm one of the sponsors, so I have to make an appearance."

"See you there," I said.

I was feeling good all over. I'm a sucker for beautiful rich women with dorky English names. I wolfed down my macaroni and cheese and then dozed by the stove for an hour. When I woke up, I washed and shaved and stared into my closet. What was the right thing to wear to an art-show opening? More important, what would increase my chances of getting Felicity Exeter into bed that night? I owned a pair of silk underwear, still in their box. Pink. A gift from a smartass friend. I thought about it. Would they bring me luck, or finish me off? I suspected the latter and left the underwear in their box, although I was sure that Mr. Porteous wore silk underwear all the time.

I finally chose what I hoped was trendy but casual. I decided to forego a necktie and leave my top shirt button undone—perhaps the top two, so that Felicity would see I wasn't the kind of smarmy asshole who wears a gold chain around his neck. Okay, so I wasn't smarmy. But I *was* an asshole. Why was I going to this shindig anyway? I could go to Moran's instead. Play cards and have fun with my buddies instead of hanging out with Victoria's socially superior art clique with a stupid grin on my face, listening to millionaires discussing the Dow Jones and yachts.

But for all of that, I was feeling good—and good as new, despite the eventful day—when I put on my raincoat and went out to my car.

HALF AN HOUR later I found myself in a noisy, crowded room with subdued lighting. I don't know what I was expecting from the avant-garde, but it wasn't bare walls. Waiters bearing trays of Chateau Unknown circulated among well-coiffed matrons in black silk and pearls, bearded potters in sweaters and jeans, and an assortment of stockbrokers and developers. A black-tied waiter approached. I was reaching for the last glass of wine on his silver tray when a cowboy reached beneath my arm and beat me to the draw. The gunslinger was an elderly man wearing a Mexican poncho over a green corduroy suit.

"Learned that trick in the desert," he said briskly, pouring half the contents of the glass down his throat. "Hydrate whenever possible. On the Western Front one's very survival often depended upon it."

"Of course it did. When does the show start?"

"It's already started—this is it."

He introduced himself as Norman and we shook hands.

"Don't worry, Silas," he said. "This is one of Felicity's parties. She doesn't stint. There'll be more drinks coming our way presently."

"So is this what's meant by the avant-garde?" I asked. "Odd people gazing at blank spaces?"

Norman seized my elbow, tugged me through the crowd to one

white-painted wall and pointed. There, in the wall's exact centre, was a large square of blue velvet pierced by a huge, slowly rotating stainless-steel bolt. "Behold," Norman said. "The artist known as Tototo's latest masterwork. He calls it *Empyrean Night Watch*. Feast your eyes on it, my boy. We're seldom treated to profound performative homiletics in this town. Struggle! Interpret! Don't let apparent simplicities deceive you."

"Norman, I'm underwhelmed," I said, as he deftly snatched two glasses of wine from a passing tray and handed one to me.

"It's superb, but where's the meaning?" Norman asked. "Does the artist inhabit aesthetic dimensions beyond our ken?"

I took another look. Several people were gazing at the work in apparent wonderment and awe.

"It's a joke," I said to Norman. "A bolt from the blue."

"A hit! A palpable hit!" Norman shouted with delight. "I purchased a similar work once. It was called *Wind up your Watch*. Still, as somebody once said, meanings are not things inherent in objects; they're supplied by those interpreting them."

"Is Tototo rewarded for producing stuff like this?"

"God yes. The Tate paid thousands for Tototo's *Soliloquy in Res*. It's stored in the Tate's permanent collection alongside Piero Manzoni's canned excrement."

"Sorry, Norman, something's just gone wrong with my hearing. It sounded like you said—"

"Piero Manzoni, Italian artist. Produced an edition of 30 cans of his personal excrement. Took the art world by storm. Nothing to match it since Marcel Duchamp exhibited a bicycle wheel, a grooming comb and a urinal."

"You're making this up," I said.

"No, he isn't," said a familiar female voice behind me.

It was Felicity Exeter. She was wearing gold-coloured shoes and a short sage party dress held up by the thinnest of straps. She smiled at Norman, who kissed her cheek. I followed his lead.

"You two know each other?"

"We just met," Norman said. "But I'm here to tell you that Silas is a man of rare discernment."

Felicity was standing close. Smiling into my eyes, she leaned even closer and asked, "What do you think of the show?"

I was trying to think of something to say when Norman spoke up. "There are a few artists who, through general viciousness or contempt for the public—"

His critique was interrupted by someone squeezing in between Felicity and me. It was a tall, lean and athletic-looking man wearing an Armani suit and crisp white shirt. He had the chiselled, swarthy good looks of a Bollywood matinee idol, his thick black hair swept back from his forehead. When he looked at me, I saw a long scar running across his left cheek.

We eyed each other. "I know you," he said, his mind obviously working to make the connection. I said nothing; I was having trouble believing he was who I thought he was. He'd either undergone a complete head and body transplant or he was Mo Dillon's clone.

"Christ," Dillon finally exclaimed. "It's Silas Seaweed!"

I was still trying to reconcile this presentable, tastefully clad yuppie with the overweight, greasy, pimply, total asswipe who had briefly shared my school life.

"I grew up with this guy!" Dillon said, turning to Felicity.

"Right. How ya been, Mo?" I said.

"No time to catch up now, Seaweed," he said dismissively, without taking his eyes off Felicity. "Honey, we're needed onstage. It's presentation time."

Felicity gave me a helpless shrug, mouthed the words *See you later* and was led away.

"I used to know him a long, long time ago," I said to Norman.

"That upstart?" Norman snorted, gazing after the retreating figures. "Well, I hope he's not a *friend* of yours, because he's an asshole through and through. Hear what he said? 'We're needed on stage!' I'm on the gallery's finance committee. I happen to know that Felicity donated $5,000 toward this show. Dillon talks about how much he's *going* to give us, but so far he's actually *given* sweet bugger all. Arrives in Victoria out of nowhere, takes credit where none is due. I, for one, have had enough of him."

Norman had made no attempt to lower his voice, and a few people were staring. Their eyes followed him as he strode off and disappeared into the crowd.

Dillon and Felicity had mounted a dais at the end of the room. He tapped the microphone, grinned at the audience and said, "Everybody hear me all right?" A hundred heads turned toward him, and there was a flutter of movement as the crowd repositioned itself for a better view.

At that moment I spotted Ellen Lemieux, standing near the lobby exit. She was an extraordinarily pretty woman, and I was forcibly struck by how well dressed she was; she stood out even in this crowd of expensively clad women. I cautioned myself to be on my guard as I moved gradually toward her.

"Hello, Ellen."

She looked at me blankly and offered no rejoinder.

"Remember me? We met at that party a while back," I lied. "Nice to see you here."

If she was surprised by my words, she didn't show it. She didn't react at all, except to turn and walk away.

I hesitated, then followed. I admired her golden skin, slightly raised cheekbones and almond-shaped eyes from a distance as she collected a black lambswool coat from the cloakroom, swung it across her shoulders and crossed over to the glass exit doors.

She glanced outside. Rain dripped from the trees and from the sculptures in the gallery's courtyard. A lone taxi was just departing. She turned around and saw me watching. "Who *are* you?" she asked, irritated.

I wondered digressively if Sammy Lofthouse had lied to me about this woman. She gave me a hostile look, then hurried over to the gallery gift shop, where she switched on a slightly muddled smile and asked the woman behind the counter to call her a taxi.

Watching her, I had a strong feeling of déjà vu. Curiosity overcame prudence. "I've a car outside," I said. "I'd be happy to give you a lift."

"What are you, Haida?" she asked, not looking at me directly.

"Coast Salish."

"I'm Nimpkish, but I guess you already knew that, didn't you?"

"Did I?"

"We've met before—you said so yourself," she hissed. "Now fuck off and leave me alone."

She exited through the main doors and stood alone outside, beneath the awning. Moments later she got into a taxi and was whisked away.

I went over to the cloakroom and collected my raincoat. As I was putting it on, a slightly inebriated woman began to raise her voice. "What do you mean, you can't find my bloody coat?" she yelled at the attendant. "It's *black*, damn you, *black*!"

I went back into the gallery. Felicity had finished speaking. Mo Dillon offered her his arm and helped her down from the dais. She glanced toward me briefly as well wishers surrounded her. People were drifting back into the lobby.

Norman reappeared and asked, "What was that row in the lobby about?"

"Somebody walked off with a valuable lambswool coat," I said.

Felicity caught my eye again, but this time she shook her head and raised her shoulders helplessly.

"Popular woman, Felicity, and generous to a fault," Norman said. "Known her long?"

"Not long," I said, as she was borne off by friends to a far corner.

I wished Norman goodnight and went out. Driving home, I felt as disappointed as a jilted teenager.

CHAPTER FIFTEEN

It was Saturday, and I was enjoying sleeping in until a loud noise, as sharp and clear as a rifle shot, sounded outside. I got up and opened the curtains. A nearby oak, overladen with wet snow, had lost one of its branches. I was starting to get dressed to go out there when Bernie phoned. He'd barely said hello before he started coughing.

"You should still be in bed," I told him.

"I *am* in bed," he said breathlessly. "That doesn't stop people from bugging me."

"Hey, *you* called *me*," I reminded him. "Why don't you call me back tomorrow?"

"For you, Silas, the way things look, there may not be a tomorrow."

"Sounds serious," I said, shouldering the receiver while I pulled on my jeans.

"Tell me something. How long since you read the police code?"

"Years."

"Let me refresh your memory. It's your job to *prevent* crime, not promote it."

Bernie was upset. I kept quiet and listened as I put on heavy socks and a pair of boots.

"If you want to hang onto your job, listen up," he went on. "When Derek Battle heard that Mrs. Tranter had been murdered, he started to probate her will. That's when he discovered that Sammy Lofthouse had prepared a new one. Battle got hold of a copy of the new will and saw your signature on it."

"There are too many attorneys in this town, Bernie. I suppose Battle is annoyed because Lofthouse nicked a paying customer."

"*Annoyed* is putting it mildly. Last night, Battle told the chief of police that you're criminally implicated in a conspiracy to defraud the late Mrs. Tranter's estate. That's not all. Jail softened up Richard Hendrix. He panicked when he suddenly realized that he might be facing 25 years in the joint."

"I know one thing," I said. "Hendrix didn't admit to any killings."

"Correct. Hendrix is accusing *you* of killing Mrs. Tranter. *And* Lofthouse."

I thought that over as Bernie continued. "You told me that Mrs. Tranter changed her will voluntarily. That there was no coercion?"

"Correct. She was acting of her own independent judgement. She didn't want Hendrix to inherit anything because she was tired of his laziness and thieving. She wanted Ellen Lemieux to get everything."

"You're still in a jam, buddy," Bernie muttered.

"Sammy was a devious little bastard, but in the Tranter matter I think he was on the up-and-up," I said. "The only strange thing about the will was that she wanted Lemieux's inheritance to come as a surprise." Bernie said nothing so I added, "I should know, Bernie, because I was there in Mrs. Tranter's house when the will was signed. There was no conspiracy. Mrs. Tranter was acting without coercion."

"So where does that leave us?" Bernie was thinking aloud now. "One: Ellen Lemieux didn't know about the will, so she had no motive to kill Mrs. Tranter. Two: Lofthouse couldn't have killed

Mrs. Tranter in the Red Barn because he was miles away, had a cast-iron alibi. Three: Richard Hendrix didn't kill her because, according to you, he didn't have time. And there's no physical evidence Hendrix was ever there. No fingerprints. No DNA."

"All right. Now what?"

"Chief Mallory has always been a big fan of yours, Silas, don't ask me why. But this has shaken his faith. I expect you'll be hearing from him directly. Wouldn't surprise me a bit if Mallory suspended you, pal."

I DROVE STRAIGHT to my office. The roads were probably slippery, but I was on autopilot and couldn't remember a single thing about the journey. I went to my computer, found a site for locating out-of-print and second-hand books and typed in *Prowdes of Peeling*. I got exactly one hit, but one was all I needed, and it was close to home.

Blackthorne's Books was on Fort Street. The shop was tiny—a single room crammed with dusty bookshelves reaching to 12-foot ceilings. Under a lamp by the desk, a young man was turning the pages of an old *Strand* magazine. In one aisle, a bearded local novelist was peering myopically at titles. The bookseller was an elderly woman wearing a summery cotton dress totally inadequate for the chilly premises. When I entered, she glanced up, squinting at me through spectacles with bottle-glass lenses.

"Hello," she said cheerily. "Anything I can help you with?"

"I'm the person who called you earlier, about that English family history."

The bookseller climbed out of her chair awkwardly, twisting her body sideways as she eased herself to a standing position. One of her legs was in a metal brace and was thinner than her other leg. It swung stiffly as she reached up to a shelf behind her desk and pulled out a slim volume.

My eyes shied away from her infirmity. "A bit of luck, your having exactly the book I needed."

"Lucky for both of us," she said. "This was a special order. A customer requested it some years ago. I have a book-finding service and can get most things, given enough time. But this order was difficult to fill because the book was published privately. Only a hundred copies were printed. I finally got it from a dealer in Lancaster. He had two copies of the book, as it happened. For some absurd reason he wouldn't sell them separately. When the books got here I figured I'd never get rid of the second copy. You can have it for the price I paid. Ten guineas, plus postage."

"What's that in real money?"

"Let's say 30 dollars."

I gave her my credit card and opened the book while she rang up the sale. The pages that had been ripped out of Isaac Schwartz's copy were intact in this one and consisted of more photographs. I resisted the temptation to examine the pictures then and there and asked, "Can you tell me the name of the customer who ordered the book originally?"

"I remember *him* quite well, but I don't think I can remember his name now," she said. "It might come back to me. He was an old European gentleman. I used to see him wandering the streets, but I haven't noticed him lately."

"Maybe Isaac Schwartz? He died recently."

"That's him, Isaac Schwartz!" The woman's lips curved downwards and she sighed. "Dead, you say? Ah, well. It's God's will. I wonder what Mr. Schwartz wanted with a book about a family in England? I did ask him, but he wouldn't say."

"It's a mystery," I said, as I signed my credit-card slip.

The young man with the *Strand* magazine drifted toward us. "How much for this, Mrs. Wilde?"

The bookseller glanced at it. Smiling indulgently she said, "For you, Charles, it'll be three dollars."

I said goodbye, but Mrs. Wilde was already engrossed in a conversation about Malcolm Muggeridge.

I saw Lennie Jim as soon as I came out of the bookshop. He was across the street, loitering in a doorway, his hands deep in the pockets of his pea jacket and his dark toque pulled down to his eyebrows. He allowed me a short lead, then followed, staying on his own side of the street. My stride quickened as I turned up Government Street. I caught Lennie's reflection in a shop window. He was 10 yards behind me now, catching up. I was ready to face him when fate intervened.

JoAnne, a hooker, suddenly stepped out of a doorway. She was so high she didn't recognize me in my plain clothes. She grabbed my hand, and this changed whatever plan was in Lennie's mind. He hurried off, his head down and something swinging from his hand—a bottle, maybe. By the time I had shaken off JoAnne, he had disappeared.

I hurried to my office, eager to examine the pages that had been missing from Isaac's copy of the book. The first showed a photograph of four young men. The two in the foreground wore striped jackets and white pants, open-necked shirts and the funny little caps worn by English schoolboys back then. In the rear were two men about the same age, wearing tweedy working-class suits, cloth caps and collarless shirts. The caption read: *BEST OF FRIENDS! Peter Prowde and Hugh Baineston, down from college. August Bank Holiday, 1933. Rear: James Micklethwaite and Eric Tranter.*

I pushed the book away and leaned back, one leg hooked over my chair arm. Things were beginning to add up. Jim Micklethwaite had been Peter Prowde's servant, and Eric Tranter had been Sir Hugh Baineston's. According to the caption, they'd been best of friends. If so, when Micklethwaite finally quit his job with the Prowde family and immigrated to Canada, did he keep in touch with his old pal Eric?

I wondered if Eric had been in Baineston's employ during the entire time the diplomat was amassing his collection of Old Master drawings. Probably. In time, obviously, Sir Hugh had died, as had Jim Micklethwaite and Eric Tranter.

I turned pages and found a photograph of Sir Hugh and Lady Baineston posed with Eric and Mavis Tranter. That's when I noticed something peculiar—Hugh Baineston was well over six feet tall. His wife was close to six feet tall herself. The Tranters, both of them, were shorter than average.

I phoned Sammy Lofthouse's office and got the answering machine. It was Saturday, I realized. I remembered Grace telling me that she lived in James Bay. I found her address and number in the phone book, but I got the answering machine at her place too. I decided to drive over. Maybe she'd be home and we could clear up a few things. I glanced outside; shadows moved in a doorway. Maybe it was Lennie Jim. Maybe it was JoAnne, sheltering from the cold. Hell, it was even cold inside my office. I watched as a john cruised by in a Mercury. He stopped when JoAnne emerged from her doorway. After a quick conversation she got into the Mercury and it pulled away.

I went onto the street. Cars streamed across the Johnson Street Bridge. Hands in my pockets, I walked to my car in its spot behind Swans. I was thinking about Mrs. Tranter and unlocking my car door when I heard footsteps behind me. I sidestepped too late. A blackjack missed my head and hammered my left collarbone. A lightning bolt of pain radiated down my left arm and spread through my chest. My conscious mental functions were temporarily paralyzed, but I automatically brought my arms up to protect my head. The attacker kept swinging. I rolled wildly and ended up with my back against the MG's front fender. My left hand and arm were numb, but my upper body throbbed with pain.

Somebody was kicking me now. I wrapped an arm around one of his legs and held on as he hopped backwards, trying to free himself. He finally lost his balance and fell, losing the blackjack under a car. We got to our feet at the same time. It was Lennie Jim, a black nylon scarf concealing the lower part of his face. He backed away, still dangerous, but without the advantage of a weapon.

A couple of women came around a corner and saw us. Lennie turned and ran in the direction of Chinatown's back alleys. The women—who probably thought I was drunk—watched me stagger across the parking lot. I made it around the corner and into Swans pub.

It was noisy. A Saturday lunch crowd stood three deep at the bar and every table was full. A server I knew drew me a pint of Swans dark without my asking, and said, "How's things, Silas?"

I must look normal, I realized, despite the bashing I'd just taken. I was trembling and had to cup my drink in both hands to keep from spilling it. I forced a smile at the server and turned away without speaking, looking for a place to sit. Two people were leaving a small table. I sank clumsily into one of the vacated chairs, rocking the table and disturbing the empty glasses on it. One glass smashed to the floor.

Somebody said, "Hey, man. You okay?"

"I'll be fine, don't worry about it," I said, without looking up.

"Hey, I'm not worried, but I don't think you should drive when you leave here, man."

There was laughter in the room. I didn't care very much. The people at the next table resumed their conversation. I heard every word. They were talking about Diogenes syndrome. Diogenes was an ancient Athenian philosopher who'd lived in a barrel to show his contempt for the material world. He'd wandered the streets, looking in vain for an honest man. Diogenes syndrome signalled the tipping point between eccentricity and dementia.

I SAT IN the bar for nearly an hour, hardly touching my pint. Every once in a while I checked my cellphone and saw another call-waiting message from Chief Mallory's secretary. I ignored them all—at that point I wasn't ready for a confrontation with the chief. When I finally felt a bit better I left Swans, drove to Montreal Street and parked outside Grace's house. I guess I was looking for an honest woman.

Her house was a modest fixer-upper, circa 1935, with cement stairs going up to the front door. When I banged on the front door, it opened right up, and I started to get a bad feeling about things. Cautiously, I went inside. The living room was to the left, and it wasn't impressive. There were two loveseats with faded damask covers, a tired rug weighted down by a glass-topped coffee table, a 50-dollar electric piano. A cabinet held a few ceramic figurines. The curtains were plastic lace look-alikes. If Grace were to ship the whole room to an auctioneer, she'd be lucky to cover moving expenses. It made me wonder what Sammy had been paying her.

I moved slowly down the hall, calling Grace's name and getting no answer. All the lights were on. I got to the kitchen, and there she was. She was lying on the floor on her stomach, her legs splayed and a black nylon scarf knotted around her throat.

I used Grace's phone to call 911 and spent a few minutes removing my fingerprints. I needed a place to lie low for a few hours, so I went to Moran's gym. I had a massage, followed by a very hot shower. I spent the next couple of hours under a blanket on a sofa, trying not to think about Grace.

My aches and pains were nearly gone and I was digging into a hamburger and chips at the lunch counter when Moran came over and said, "Just a reminder, Silas. It's fight night tonight. You coming?"

"No thanks," I said. "At the moment, my appetite for pain and violence is a bit diminished."

"If you change your mind, I've got tickets," Moran said. "And by the way, you look like shit. You been on a bender?"

"No. But speaking of benders, when's the last time you saw Nimrod?"

Moran cupped his chin with one hand and pondered. "The last time I set eyes on Nimrod was at the fights. Drunk or sober, he seldom misses."

I went back to the sofa and lay down again, pulling the blanket over me. After a short doze, I phoned the coroner's office, identified myself and asked the attendant to check something in Mavis Tranter's autopsy report. Five long minutes dragged by. Then the attendant came back on the line. "Sergeant Seaweed? Mrs. Tranter's height was measured at 1.89 metres."

I did a rapid mental calculation. "That's about six feet, right?"

"Almost exactly."

That made me feel better. When Chief Mallory caught up with me, I'd have ammunition with which to defend myself. Now, if I could just find Nimrod and clean up a few loose ends …

CHAPTER SIXTEEN

We were in the arena and the crowd was on its feet, screaming. Two prizefighters were slugging it out, toe to toe in the boxing ring, swapping punch for punch and giving everything they had. Moran, beside me at ringside, was going crazy, his eyes alight as the two boxers fell into a clinch. The referee stepped in to separate them. The cheers and whistles of the crowd almost drowned out the bell when it sounded to end the third round. The boxers went to their corners. Moran sank into his seat—the old fight manager was sweating as much as his boy up there in the ring.

Moran's hopeful was a featherweight called Pallin. His white silk trunks were stained with his own blood. A cut-man was stuffing cotton wool up Pallin's nostrils, trying to staunch the bleeding. Pallin sprawled back, two arms laid across the corner ropes, his eyes closed, tendrils of damp dark hair plastered across his brow like a crown of thorns.

"I hope you haven't bet the ranch on that kid, Moran," I said.

"No problem," said Moran cockily, chomping his unlit cigar. "We're coming to the fourth round. This is where Pallin wins."

"You *hope*," I said. "If he loses any more blood he'll need a transfusion."

"Yeah," Moran admitted reluctantly. "He's got a glass beak I didn't know about. We'll hafta work on that."

"What are you gonna do? Fill his nose with cement?"

I had been carefully scanning the crowd, but Nimrod didn't appear to be there.

A corner man wrung a water-soaked sponge over Pallin's head. The seconds got out of the ring and the two boxers faced each other again. Pallin's opponent had blood lust in his eyes now. Grinning, he galloped across the ring, coming in for the kill. Pallin neatly side-stepped, and the other boxer bounced against the ropes.

Moran's kid was inches taller than his opponent. He had the classic boxer's stance—right arm up to protect his chin, left arm extended to keep his opponent at a distance. Pallin's opponent was more experienced. Ring smart, he knew that Pallin's strength was fading fast. He wanted to mix it up in the centre of the ring and kept coming in like a bull, shoulders wide and head down.

Pallin kept weaving defensively, but took a smashing left hook that jarred his mouth guard out. The referee kicked the guard clear and then moved in to take Pallin's arm and lead him to a neutral corner. The crowd exploded, thinking that the referee was going to call the match on a technical KO. Moran came out of his chair and shoved his head under the ropes. He was screaming at the referee, calling him an idiot, an ignoramus and a fraud. I grabbed his arm and manhandled him back to his seat.

Ignoring the racket, the referee studied Pallin's nose and looked deep into his eyes. The other fighter was resting in the corner with one foot hooked carelessly over the bottom rope, grinning and rais-ing both arms to the crowd in anticipation of victory. The referee glanced at Pallin's corner man, who calmly signalled a thumbs-up. The referee waved the boxers on and the fight resumed.

Pallin was fast. He trapped his opponent in a corner and swung an underarm right to the belly that took the grin from his face and most of the air from his body. Pallin stepped back. The other boxer walked into a straight left to his chest and a right uppercut to his chin. His head snapped back. Moran, screaming with delight, watched the boxer's knees buckle. He was down for the count. Pallin had cold-cocked him.

Moran grabbed my hand and shook it, saying something that was lost in the uproar, then triumphantly disappeared into the crowd, looking for his bookie and his winnings. I waited for the tumult to subside and watched the duty doctor work on the prostrate fighter. A full minute passed before he was hauled to his feet and helped to a stool.

The next event was a scheduled 10-round massacre between two western heavyweights—a Vancouver slugger on his way to oblivion and a Seattle killer on his way up. Moran predicted the fight would last three rounds, but I had seen enough blood for one night and there was still no sign of Nimrod.

I collected my MG from the arena lot and drove south along Blanshard. I turned up Humboldt Street, almost deserted at this hour, and parked alongside a chest-high brick wall outside the grounds of St. Barbara's Academy.

The immense five-storey academy, long unoccupied, stood silhouetted against the lights of downtown Victoria. Its main gate was padlocked. Taking my flashlight but not turning it on, I clambered over the academy's encircling wall, lowered myself into an ancient sunken orchard and walked between rows of fruit trees, snow crunching beneath my feet.

The Sisters of St. Barbara had relinquished the building 30 years earlier, after deeding it to the city. City council had let the beautiful structure fall into ruin, and the place had been targeted by vandals and squatters. Dark clouds parted to reveal a three-quarter moon.

The academy's high spire, topped by a gilded cross, posed dramatically against a backdrop of stars. Scores of black windows reflected the glare of headlights as a taxi on Humboldt Street went by. I waited till clouds covered the moon again before crossing the open court fronting the academy. Hugging shadows, I walked around the building, looking for a way inside.

Most of the ground-floor windows were boarded up. Around back there was an ell, formed by the main building and a chapel wall. Nearby was a rusty fire escape. I climbed it cautiously. Somebody had forced a window on the second floor. I swung my legs over the sill and entered, listening intently. Icy draughts chased each other along the corridor, whistling across broken panes and wrecked mouldings. I moved forward, my flashlight illuminating piles of debris. I stopped to listen and heard faint scuttling sounds. Bats or mice or rats were in here with me. I moved 50 yards down the corridor, switched off my light and listened again, hearing nothing except the wind and the stirrings of wings or tiny feet. Ahead, to my left, a faint light gleamed dully beneath a closed door.

I pushed the door open slowly and quietly and peered into what appeared to be a chapel. A figure in a long grey cape with a raised hood was kneeling where the altar had once stood. To his left, a candle burned in a tall brass candlestick. There was no furniture in the room—no crucifixes, pipe organ or statues. The cowled figure turned its head, but I saw no face, just a black shadowy outline. I backed out of the chapel, closed the door and continued along the corridor. I stopped again to listen. This time I heard voices.

I followed the sound to a room where six men were huddled around the weak flame of an old oil lamp. The high-ceilinged room stank of urine and unwashed bodies. Wine bottles and filth littered the floor. When I entered, gaunt faces stared up at me and a hoarse voice said, "Shut the door, man, we're freezing."

I shone my light around the room and saw more men sprawled in corners. Some had sleeping bags, but others slept beneath bits of canvas or shivered in their clothes. "I'm looking for Nimrod," I said. "Nimrod's one of the volunteers at the Good Shepherd."

A man muttered, "Nimrod's took the cure, he don't hang out no more."

Another voice disagreed, saying, "Nah, he's fell off the wagon. I seen Nimrod couple days ago, tits-up in Beacon Hill Park."

I left the men in their squalor and followed my flashlight's yellow beam along other corridors, looking for more squatters and finding none. Before I left the building, I stopped again outside the chapel. This time there was no light beneath the door. I looked in anyway, but the kneeling figure had gone. Dust covered the area where the caped figure had knelt and where the candlestick had stood. I shone my light over broken panels, graffiti and filth. It was silent in there, and very cold.

It was after nine o'clock when I reached Beacon Hill Park and inspected a hobo jungle hidden in some bushes near the bandstand. It was miserably cold and deserted. I was still feeling the effects of my bludgeoning and was ready to call off my search, but I forced myself to continue on to a thick grove of wind-sculpted trees off Dallas Road. Four men were sleeping on crushed cardboard boxes in an old squat. Two were kids, no older than 15, filthy. They were with two older men beneath a piece of blue frost-covered tarpaulin. Nimrod was there too—curled on the bare ground alone, an empty bottle of Chinese cooking wine by his out-flung arm. Nimrod's hand was ice-cold; his skin felt brittle. I hoisted him upright, put one of his arms across my shoulder and dragged him out of the jungle, hoping his legs would start moving. His feet left parallel tracks in the snow; he seemed either dead or close to it. I got him into the MG, cranked up the heater and ran traffic lights on Cook and Fort streets. I peeled up to the Jubilee Hospital's emergency entrance and turned what was left of Nimrod over to the medics.

The night wasn't over. Driving down Bay Street and away from the hospital, I started thinking about Ellen Lemieux. I'd had good hunting all day. Was the time ripe for flushing more game from cover? I detoured through Fernwood.

The temperature was freezing, and I was loitering in an unlit driveway, behind a high cedar hedge. Across the street, Ellen's house stood dark and empty. Next door at Baldy's, lights were on and a TV's blue glow backlit the front curtains. I watched for 15 minutes, then decided it was time to move things along. I put on the horn-rimmed glasses I sometimes use for reading small print, crossed the street and knocked on Baldy's front door. A dog began to yap inside, and there was more commotion before the door opened a crack. Baldy's face appeared; he didn't seem to recognize me. In a loud, not-quite-friendly voice I said, "Police. Good evening, sir. We're investigating recent break-ins in the neighbourhood. We hope you might be able to help us with our inquiries."

A woman's voice called out, "Who is it, Jacko?"

The man ignored her and stared at me uncertainly. I sensed his wariness and smiled.

"Shut the door, you're causing a draft," the woman grumbled.

"What did you say your name was?" enquired Baldy.

"Constable Richard Bird. Special Squad."

"Just a minute." Baldy closed the door while he unfastened the security chain, then reopened it and motioned me inside. I stepped into a tiny hall. A little black and white dog came forward to sniff my heel. Baldy aimed a kick, which just missed its head. It retreated into the living room. Baldy's wife had muted the TV with her remote, but the big screen still glowed. Tobacco and cooking odours were heavy in the air; the untidy remains of their last meal lay on a Masonite table with chromium legs.

The woman sagged in a recliner with a cigarette in her mouth. "Who is it, Jacko?" she asked again, reaching beneath her chair to comfort the dog.

A spasm of irritation twisted Baldy's mouth. He took a threatening half-step toward the animal, and it fled the room. His wife flinched, but when she saw that Baldy was keeping his distance she muttered something inaudible and clicked the TV volume back on.

"You know what fucking time it is?" he said. "What the fuck's going on?"

I produced Sammy Lofthouse's brochure and showed Baldy the lawyer's picture. "Do you recognize this man, sir? Ever seen him in this area?"

Baldy's eyes seemed out of focus. His movements were peculiar. A sloping left shoulder and a lazy left eye suggested a recent stroke. He stared at Sammy's picture and shook his head. "You're certain this man's face is unfamiliar?" I asked again. "Never seen him at the house next door, for example? Take your time. Have a good long look."

Baldy shrugged. His wife increased the TV's volume—canned laughter resounded from a sitcom.

Raising my voice I said, "Well, thanks for your time. There are many dangerous people on the streets. Without the help of citizens like yourself the fight against crime would be hopeless."

I said good night. I could feel his eyes on me as I left his house.

I went back to my car, but instead of driving away I started the engine and let the heater keep me warm for a few minutes. A car crunched by, its headlights boring yellow cones into the light, whirling snow. I decided to risk a look inside Ellen's house.

I tried my pass keys, found one that opened the back door and entered. With my flashlight aimed at the floor, I moved through the house and into the living room. When I raised my flashlight, myriad tiny reflections suddenly shone in my eyes and glittered across walls and floor and ceiling. The effect was unnerving, until I saw that the reflections emanated from a collection of natural quartz crystals on the mantel.

The tiny five-room house, like the garden shed, was neat and clean. The bedroom reminded me that Ellen had worked as a nurse: the sheets on her bed were stretched as tight as—as tight as the blankets that had covered Isaac Schwartz's bed!

Excitement flooded through me. I moved around, opening and closing drawers, taking things out and putting them back the way I'd found them. I looked inside Ellen's bedroom closet, jam-packed with elegant and expensive clothing, including a black lambswool coat. I saw a large metal deed box on a high shelf and lifted it down. It contained about 20 manila folders filed alphabetically. The file marked "T" was stiff, tied with a red ribbon. I was about to glance through it when I heard a car pull in to Ellen's driveway.

I stashed the deed box, hurried out the back door with the file tucked under my arm and hid behind the cedar hedge. The Monte Carlo was parked in the driveway. I watched as Ellen moved through the house, turning on lights.

Even sooner than I'd expected, Baldy was banging on her front door. I stayed out of sight around the corner, but I could hear him giving her the lowdown on the visit from Constable Bird. I crept forward for a look. She was wearing flat-heeled shoes and looked even tinier than before. She didn't invite him in, and after their brief conversation Baldy returned to his own place. Well, I'd got what I wanted. Now Ellen knew for sure that Nosey Bird was closing in on her.

My feet felt like blocks of ice by the time I got back to my car. I needed to talk to someone—someone I could trust.

"You're crazy," Bernie said.

We were in his kitchen with two snifters of brandy before us. It was after midnight, too late for coffee. Bernie's wife had not looked happy when she'd said goodnight and headed up to bed.

"I'll try to keep it simple," I told him. "When Lofthouse asked me to get involved with Mrs. Tranter, I balked. I didn't trust him. Against my better judgement, I let him take me to her house. While I was there, Lofthouse asked Grace Sleight and me to witness the new will.

"I didn't see anything wrong with that. It seemed above board. But Lofthouse wanted me to evict Richard Hendrix as well. I refused because I felt I was being manipulated. Next morning Lofthouse went to Savage, complaining I wasn't doing my job properly, so Savage ordered me to co-operate. After that, several things happened. Mrs. Tranter was murdered. Sammy Lofthouse was murdered. Grace Sleight was murdered. I was attacked in Swans parking lot—"

"Wait a minute," Bernie said. "How'd you know Grace was murdered? We only just found her body."

"A little bird told me."

Bernie shook his head. "I don't want to know."

"You *need* to know," I said. I pushed the "T" file across Bernie's table. He opened it and took a good long look at the Old Master drawing it contained.

"I found that in Ellen Lemieux's house tonight," I said. "If we include the Isaac Schwartz killing, we're talking about four actual murders, plus one attack. The thing these crimes have in common is, what?"

"Ellen Lemieux," Bernie said without missing a beat.

"Correct. Give that detective a cigar."

"I think I'm starting to get it now," Bernie sighed.

CHAPTER SEVENTEEN

On Monday morning I finally phoned Chief Mallory. We had a long, reasonably amicable conversation and arranged a day and time to meet. But before anything else on this day I was going to visit the Gorge shell-midden project.

Over the millennia, the shells from countless clam, mussel, abalone and scallop dinners had been dumped at this site by my ancestors. The shells leach calcium carbonate and create ideal conditions for preserving organic materials. The Gorge dig was already a major stir. Fragments of woven baskets, human bones, wooden pegs, arrow and harpoon points and an almost intact cedar cape had been unearthed. In addition, archaeologists had uncovered the floor of a house and hearth. Carbon dating had proved that this particular site had been intermittently occupied for more than two thousand years.

Bad weather had slowed but not stopped the progress. Keep-out signs were posted everywhere, but I had a reason for visiting, and entered the site.

The site was being mapped and surveyed in two-metre squares marked by taut yellow strings. Squares had been dug to various depths through layer upon layer of compacted shell. Shovels, trowels, wheelbarrows and measuring instruments were everywhere. University of

SEAWEED ON ICE   179

Victoria students and others were dumping loads of earth onto sifter screens, shaking out loose dirt, tossing aside detritus and carefully preserving everything of possible significance. When the diggers saw an Aboriginal approaching, they stopped working. A bearded student flapped his wrist and told me to clear off. I switched on a disarming smile. Evidently not disarming enough. The bearded man ran ahead of me to a construction trailer parked onsite and hammered on its door. Dr. Tweed emerged.

Doc Tweed and I go back a long way. About once a year he treats me to lunch in return for speaking to his students about Coast Salish mythology and art and trying to answer their questions. When Tweed recognized me, he relaxed visibly. We shook hands. The student apologized and returned to his work.

Inside the trailer was a meagre display of mussel knives, stone chips, fragments of carved wood and bone, and other small artifacts. So far, the prize discovery was an eight-foot house pole in the form of a human holding a paddle to his chin. The pole lay on the floor in the centre of the trailer, taking up most of the area. I was astonished by it and opened my mouth to say something, then thought better of it.

"Take your time," Tweed said. "I've been looking at it for a week. I still can't make it out."

I leaned against the table. Outside, diggers were crouched, patiently chipping into my people's history with trowels and dental instruments. I studied the pole some more. One thing was immediately obvious. "This pole," I said, "isn't Coast Salish."

"I agree. But if it's not Coast Salish, what is it?"

"It might be Tsimshian."

He smiled encouragingly. I said, "This is like the Whole Being poles that Dr. MacDonald dug up near Prince Rupert 40 years ago. I believe he found three of them. If memory serves, he proved that the Prince Rupert site had been continually occupied for 5,000 years, at least. My people probably settled this area less than 3,000 years ago."

Tweed's eyes widened. My words had stunned him. After a hypnotic minute he shook his head. "*Whole Being!* My God, Silas, tell me more."

"Tsimshian warriors were crossing a lake in a canoe when they saw a creature from the Unknown World," I explained. "Unknowns seldom visit our world, when they do they don't like to be noticed. This unknown tried to trick the warriors by transforming itself into a log. In doing so it lost its power. The Tsimshians pulled the log from the lake and saw their own faces reflected in the water. They took the log ashore and found a human figure carved on the base. It was Whole Being."

I added, "I told that story to a Jungian once. According to him, Whole Being symbolizes the melding of the conscious and unconscious forces that endow humans with discretion and wisdom."

Tweed leaned forward and stared at me carefully. "And what do *you* think?"

"All I know is, Whole Being is a Tsimshian crest figure. It's not Salish."

There was a knock on the trailer door. "Come in," Tweed called out.

Another digger, a young woman this time, poked her head inside. "Dr. Tweed. We think we've found an occiput in IG-13."

"I'll be right with you," he answered.

I pointed to the artifacts on Tweed's table. "The Whole Being pole is magnificent, but where're the rest of your finds?"

"At the university, under lock and key. Somebody broke into this trailer a few nights back."

"What was taken?"

"A human jawbone with teeth."

"What are you going to do with the Whole Being pole?"

"Short term, we don't know. Long term, our dream is to find the money to build an archaeology museum on campus."

We stepped out of the trailer and I headed back toward my office. I was crossing Pandora Street when my cellphone rang. It was Joan Wilson, calling me from the British Consul General's office in Vancouver.

"It's about your enquiry regarding pre-war German embassy staff," she said in her actress-like English voice. "Several such people are still hanging about here and there. But the chap I think you'd be interested in is Brigadier-General Sutcliffe. The general lives in Vancouver, as it happens."

"Is he willing to talk to me?"

"Yes, quite willing. Give him a call and set up a meeting."

She gave me the general's phone number. I thanked her and rang off.

Vancouver is only a 20-minute helicopter ride across the Georgia Strait from Victoria. The Terminal City Club is situated in the heart of Vancouver's downtown business district, a few strides from Burrard Inlet. I left my hat and overcoat at the steward's desk and went through to the Members' Lounge. Apart from a maid flicking marble busts with a feather duster, the rambling place seemed deserted. The maid directed me to a numbered door with a RESERVED sign on its handle. I gave the door a discreet rap. Somebody shouted, "Come."

Brigadier-General Sutcliffe was a tall man in his mid-80s. He was extremely thin, with a large Roman nose set in a gaunt, narrow-boned face that would have looked cadaverous were it not for his all-weather tan. He was wearing an old but beautifully tailored suit, a brown and white shirt, and a Royal Artillery necktie.

He had served at El Alamein with Montgomery. When the war ended, Sutcliffe was a brigadier. To the surprise of many, he resigned from the British army, left the land of his birth and migrated to Canada.

He was sitting in a leather lounging chair, and as I entered he raised his glass and asked, "What will you have, Seaweed?"

I sat down in a matching chair and said, "Thanks, sir. I'll have what you're having."

He poured me whisky from the bottle of Laphroaig at his elbow, pushed a water pitcher within my reach and settled into his chair to listen to my story. He did not interrupt me. When I had finished speaking, he turned his gaze toward the window and sat quietly for a minute, whisky glass in hand.

When he faced me again, his eyes were flat and confused. "I have this queer déjà vu feeling," he said. "The idea that things keep repeating themselves. It's as if I'm doomed to keep retelling this story. Not to others, but to myself, so that things remain clear in my memory."

Sutcliffe poured another large Scotch for himself—his third. He was half a world and half a lifetime away from that room.

"I have to explain some things about pre-war Berlin," he said at last. "It isn't easy to convey the atmosphere, because we've all got the benefit of hindsight. And hindsight, as we know, modifies feelings. Unless one is careful, hindsight modifies memory, too. The thing that younger generations don't seem to understand is that before the war, Hitler was the most popular man in Germany."

"And he was slaughtering thousands of Jews."

Sutcliffe's shoulders sagged slightly. "Of course," he said. "But back then, many Germans turned a blind eye. They didn't *want* to know what Hitler and his bully boys were up to. They preferred to believe that stories of atrocities to Jews and Gypsies were communist propaganda. They believed it because they *wanted* to believe it. The chief fears haunting ordinary Germans before the war were, first, communism, and second, unemployment. Hitler and his propagandists brainwashed the German people into thinking that Hitler was their only defence against rampaging socialist hordes. If you want to get a real sense of the situation, watch pre-war newsreel footage. See Hitler riding in the back of a limousine as he toured German streets, every sidewalk jammed with flag-waving true believers. In the '30s, Hitler had the status of a god."

Sutcliffe had set his glass down on the table, but now he picked it up and downed its contents. I put my own glass to my lips and discovered to my surprise that it was empty. Sutcliffe, who might have been slightly drunk by then, splashed more Laphroaig into our glasses and continued with his story.

"Before the war," he said, "I was a military attaché in Berlin. The British ambassador was Benjamin Motlow. Hugh Baineston was a secretary, fairly senior. I got to know Baineston socially, couldn't help it. Baineston had twin passions—art and parties. He was rich. Lancashire mill money. Half his income went on pictures and sculptures. Lady Dorothy was Baineston's wife. They gave marvellous balls and dinners in their house at Dahlem. But stories get about, and some of the stories about the Bainestons were pretty rum. Hitler visited the Bainestons more than once and they made no bones about their feelings. They admired Adolf. They thought it was time Jews got a comeuppance. Anyway, the stories about Baineston got worse and drifted upstairs to the ambassador. There's no doubt that Baineston conspired to have Jews interned and that he profited by it. Motlow called him onto the carpet."

The fire had burned low. Sutcliffe took pieces of wood from a basket and built the fire up while he recollected himself. Replacing the tongs, he said, "Baineston was ordered back to London. It was either July or August of '39. Things were in a panic. Britain and Germany were days away from war. Sir Hugh and Lady Baineston left Berlin in a Mercedes motorcar. Baineston's servant, a chap called Grainger, followed them along, driving a big Fiat lorry loaded with Baineston's prize possessions." Sutcliffe took another sip and continued, "The Bainestons never reached London. Perhaps they wasted too much time on the road and got jammed. Maybe they became embroiled in some nastiness, who knows? But the important thing is, the Bainestons never reached England. Presumably they got lost, either in Germany or in the Low Countries."

"What would have happened if Baineston *had* reached London?"

Sutcliffe shrugged. "Don't know. There are few precedents that I'm aware of, but, given the nature of his sins, I expect Baineston would have been drummed out in disgrace."

"Not much punishment for conspiring to eliminate Jews."

"True, but that rod would have been felt rather keenly by the Bainestons. Everyone's hand would have been against them; there'd hardly be a soul in England would sit at their table after something like that."

"Who else knows this story?"

"Very few people know it. With Baineston dead, the Foreign Office kept the lid on. No doubt there's a record of the Baineston affair in Whitehall. Since these events occurred over 50 years ago, the officials might allow access to the necessary papers, if anyone's interested."

I stood up and stared out of the window.

"There's a sequel to this story," the general said. "In the '60s I read a piece in the *Times* about Baineston. Apparently he had no kin and the baronetcy had died out. Baineston Hall was taken over by the National Trust. A sad end to what had been a fine old family."

"What happened to the batman, Grainger? The man who drove the Fiat lorry full of art?"

"I'm not sure. My guess is Grainger and his wife perished along with the Bainestons."

Then a new thought struck him. "I'm sorry, I'm getting on. Beginning to forget things. That batman's name wasn't Grainger. I remember now. It was Tranter."

I thanked Sutcliffe. When I left the room he was pouring himself another Scotch.

The Burrard and Hastings area was jammed with traffic. I looked at my watch and started walking—the next helicopter to Victoria left in an hour. After unsuccessfully flagging a dozen passing taxis, I eventually caught one driven by a dignified, turban-wearing Sikh with a courtly manner. While driving he spoke in a melodious but mournful voice of the frequent muggings he risked while working Vancouver's dangerous streets.

"Move to Victoria," I said, as he dropped me off at the heliport terminal. "We only have about one taxi-driver mugging a week over there."

CHAPTER EIGHTEEN

A middle-aged man with a grey moustache was selling *Street Newz* outside a bank on Fort Street. He had a defeated man's pallor. The last time I'd seen him, he'd been a skid-row drunk. Before that he'd managed a credit union. He waved a paper at me. I flipped him a loonie but declined the paper.

Inside the Templeton Building, I rode the elevator to the top. Battle, Battle and Armbruster occupied the entire top floor of the building. I was told that Derek Battle was extremely busy, but when I told the receptionist who I was and she checked with him, he consented to see me immediately.

I started to tell him my long, convoluted story. He left his seat and paced the floor as he listened, back and forth, hands behind his back, four strides and then a quick turn along the carpet. A tall, distinguished-looking man with white hair, vigorous in his movements. He wasn't seeing anything alive; he was seeing history.

Convincing Battle that I wasn't just an accomplished liar hadn't been difficult. Now he was thinking things over. I could almost read his mind. Battle had been practising law in Victoria for more than 40 years. For the first time in his long career he'd been made to look like a fool—and by a Native policeman at that.

Well, he wouldn't stand for it. With some effort, he calmed himself and sat back down at his desk. I watched him do some slow deep-breathing exercise—taking a deep breath in through his nose, holding the air in his lungs for a count of 10, then slowly exhaling through his mouth. He seemed to lower his shoulders an inch. He repeated this, his hands resting loosely on his lap. The technique seemed to work; he was ready to speak. He looked me over as if I were a worm in his cucumber sandwich and said, "Let me get this straight, Seaweed."

"Sure," I replied pleasantly.

With the air of a prosecutor addressing a hostile witness, he said, "You've said, Sergeant Seaweed, that on the evening in question you went to Mrs. Tranter's house with Mr. Lofthouse and witnessed the signing of Mavis Tranter's last will and testament?"

"That's correct. I watched her sign it, then I signed it myself, along with Grace Sleight."

Battle's pose of courtroom detachment vanished. "That is impossible!" he exploded. "What you are saying could not have happened, except under duress."

"There was no duress."

"I was the Tranters' lawyer for many years," he declared, addressing me as if I were hard of hearing. "During that time three wills were prepared by me, personally. The first Tranter will was made in 1950. The Tranters came to my office. They appointed one another mutual beneficiaries. Upon the death of the surviving spouse the remainder of their estate was to go to a designated charity."

I interrupted the lawyer's narrative. "Mind if I ask which charity?"

"I certainly do mind!" Battle retorted. "That's a private matter between my client and me."

"Your former client."

He slammed a fist on his desk and shouted, "Damn your bloody impertinence! I won't be spoken to like that in my own office."

His bluster sounded pretty thin. All the same, I didn't want to spend all day sparring with him to get at real facts. "Fine," I said, getting up to leave. "Tell your side of story to the Law Society. I'm sure they'll give you an attentive hearing."

Battle stood up quickly and I heard his intake of breath. He spoke more quietly. "I apologize, Seaweed. Please sit down. Our feelings are getting the better of us."

I stood near the door, watching him.

Battle swallowed, "Look, perhaps you'd like coffee? It's time for my usual cup." He shot his shirtsleeve cuff and looked at his watch—a thin gold oval with a sharkskin strap. His wife had probably given it to him on their 25th.

Suddenly I felt sorry for him. It isn't easy, being a good liar. I liked his face. There was an inherent good nature in it, laugh lines around his mouth and eyes. He was wearing a pinstriped charcoal double-breasted suit and a white linen shirt with a silk tie, a suitable outfit for an advocate nearing the end of a distinguished career. In all that time he had made only one serious professional mistake. And now he wasn't sure how to deal with it.

A clerk brought in a tray—Doulton cups and saucers, silver spoons and a sterling coffee service. Battle poured my coffee straight up. He helped himself to two heaping spoonfuls of sugar and a generous measure of thick cream and stirred the mixture for several seconds longer than necessary. He was still trying to compose himself.

The lawyer took a sip. "These four walls have heard a lot of secrets over the years, Mr. Seaweed."

"It will save us both a lot of skirmishing if I tell you right out that I know a lot about the man you call Eric Tranter," I said. "I know what his real name was, before he changed it."

I saw in his astonishment how Battle's face must have looked when he was a child, and how it would probably look when he died. His mouth opened but no words came out. In a low voice he said, "All right. Let's play it your way. Who was Eric Tranter?"

"The man who called himself Eric Tranter was born in Cheshire, England. His real name was Sir Hugh Baineston. Mrs Tranter was, in reality, Lady Baineston, the former Dorothy Jane Booth. They switched identities with their servants in Germany at the outbreak of war and fled to Canada in the 1940s."

Battle sighed. The time for subterfuge had ended. "The Bainestons didn't confide in me initially," he said. "It was a long time before I found out."

He paused, and I didn't interrupt. Battle was remembering things from a long time ago. "A man calling himself Eric Tranter came to see me in 1950 and asked me to prepare wills for himself and his wife. I thought Tranter was an ordinary workman. He looked and dressed like an artisan, rather shabby, with nicotine-stained fingers. But he was a great tall fellow with one of those clipped, officer-class British accents. I assumed he was a man who had come down in the world—clogs-to-clogs in three generations, that sort of thing. But it was none of my business. The Tranters needed wills. I did what they wanted and thought that was the end of it.

"It was 20 years before I saw Tranter again." Battle shook his head. "He looked dreadful. Pasty skin, gaunt. He was living as a recluse, hardly left his house. He asked me if I could keep a secret. Then he told me his story." Battle stopped speaking to gauge my reaction.

"Go on, please."

"Tranter told me that he had been living under an alias. He was really an English baronet, Sir Hugh Baineston. Before the war, in Berlin, he'd amassed works of art worth a fortune. He acquired some of this art from Jews dishonestly and was sacked from his job with the British

Embassy because of it. In 1939 Baineston and his wife left Berlin for England. Two servants followed them, a married couple called Tranter. Before the party reached the Dutch border, war was declared in Europe. Because of the mess he was in, Baineston had lost diplomatic immunity and couldn't cross into Holland. It was ironic, yes? Baineston was in the same boat as the Jews he'd betrayed. Europe's roads were bad, clogged with refugees. The Bainestons and the Tranters were trapped. In desperation they holed up temporarily near Mönchengladbach.

"Baineston's art collection was stored in waterproof boxes. Baineston and Tranter hid it all in a bunker they'd dug themselves. When the time was right, the four of them—the two Bainestons, the two Tranters—tried to get over the border. It was night. The Bainestons went first, across a section of cleared forest, and made it into the cover of trees on the Dutch side. The Tranters were unlucky. A dog patrol sniffed them out and they were killed by border guards—gunned down trying to climb a fence."

Derek Battle's coffee was getting cold. "Well, there was nothing the Bainestons could do about the Tranters. Eventually, they managed to reach France, and they stayed there for a bit before they made it to England. At some point they hit upon the idea of assuming the Tranters' identities and moving to Canada.

"Hugh Baineston was resourceful, and clever. He waited out the war, then returned to Mönchengladbach. How exactly he recovered his art and got it to Canada I don't know, but Sir Hugh and Lady Dorothy Baineston became Mr. and Mrs. Tranter.

"But as Baineston got older, facing his own death, his art collection began to haunt him. Every time he looked at it he saw the faces of murdered Jews. So he came to me again. Told me his idea. He wanted to ease his conscience and began to sell off his collection slowly. The money, every cent of it, went to charity. I was able to help him. By the time Sir Hugh died, he had disposed of art worth a fortune."

Battle poured himself another cup of coffee. "Lady Baineston had an eye disorder. Sir Hugh looked after her himself. Towards the end of his life, Sir Hugh also eased his conscience doing charity work. Several days a week he served meals in a soup kitchen for down-and-outers."

Battle's hands were gripping the arms of his chair. He leaned forward and said, "Baineston's art didn't go into one big sale. It was consigned slowly, so as not to depress the market. Just before Sir Hugh died, he told me that there was still about a million dollars worth of art left to dispose of. Do you know what happened to it, Sergeant?"

"I think so. Correct me if I'm wrong. The *real* Eric Tranter had a friend called Micklethwaite. Tranter and Micklethwaite were domestic servants who'd known each other since childhood. When Micklethwaite and his wife emigrated from England to Canada, they somehow found out that the Tranters were imposters."

"Correct."

"How did the Micklethwaites find that out?"

"Through the Salvation Army's Family Tracing Service. See, Eric Tranter and James Micklethwaite were related—they were married to sisters," Battle said. "The Tranters were killed at the outbreak of war—but were officially reported as missing, not dead. After the war, Mrs. Micklethwaite contacted the Salvation Army in England, hoping to find her sister. The English Sally Ann search produced ambiguous results. The Tranters appeared to have survived the war, but were untraceable. Still, the Micklethwaites never lost hope.

"In 1950, the Micklethwaites immigrated to Canada. At some point, Mrs. Micklethwaite contacted the Sally Ann's tracing service here in Canada. Bingo! They got a match. The Micklethwaites immediately looked the Tranters up. But instead of meeting a sister and a brother-in-law, the Micklethwaites met imposters!"

The lawyer smiled and went on, "Actually, there were a couple of occasions when the cat almost got out of the bag. When the Micklethwaites discovered that the Tranters were frauds, they were ready to denounce them. I talked the Micklethwaites out of it."

"*You* talked them out of it?"

"Yes, and I don't regret it," said Battle, unabashed. "When the Micklethwaites knew the full story, they agreed to keep the lid on. The second, lesser threat came when Richard Hendrix showed up—the real Mrs. Tranter's nephew, Richard. But Richard had never met his aunt before, so he was none the wiser. In time, Lady Baineston became fond of Richard, Lord knows why. But she made provision for him in her will. Do you need to hear any more?"

I stood up and stretched across the desk. I shook Battle's hand. "No," I said, "I don't need to hear any more."

But even before I reached the door, I thought of something else. "Why did Lady Baineston consign the drawings to auction under her real name, instead of Tranter?"

Battle reached in a drawer for a box of tissues, blew his nose unnecessarily and walked around the room before dropping the tissue into a wastebasket. At last he said, "Look here, Seaweed. There's a perfectly good explanation, but I ask for your word as a gentleman that if I tell you it'll go no further."

"No can do. I've a pretty good idea why, in any case."

"All right. And that reason is?"

"Tell you what," I said. "If it's the reason I think it is, you're off the hook."

"To avoid taxes," Battle said promptly. "The Bainestons figured out a way to sell their art without leaving a paper trail. The Bainestons wanted *all* of their money to fund charity, not the fraction left after that crowd in Ottawa got their share."

He'd told his story like a man, and I was proud of him.

CHAPTER NINETEEN

Maureen was backing her car away from the band office when I showed up at the Warrior Reserve. She flashed her headlights, so I went over. She wound her window down. "Chief Numcamais wants to see you. Says it's urgent."

"How come you never phoned me?"

"I did. Left you a message. Is there something wrong with your phone, or what?"

"Yeah. It's on the fritz. Sometimes it works, sometimes it doesn't. I'm getting a replacement. What's up?"

"I told you," Maureen said.

"Chief Numcamais wants to see me? That's it?"

"I think so. Except the chief sounded … I think he said something about whales?"

A group of young boys were beating drums and dancing outside the door of the longhouse. The Warrior Reserve's normal population is about 350, but today there were probably three times that number crowded on our land. I checked my cellphone while I walked down to the beach. It was dead.

A few hardy souls were partying near the water, roasting hot dogs and warming themselves at campfires as they maintained their vigil for spirit questers. Freddy Albert was absent from the reserve, and his boat was missing from the wharf.

I thought for a minute or two, then went to my cabin, put a freshly charged battery in my cellphone, installed new batteries in my flashlight, dressed warmly in woollen clothes, got into my MG and set out for Sooke.

The drive from Victoria to Sooke normally takes an hour, but I blew a Michelin at Langford. While a mechanic fixed the flat, I purchased a loaf of bread, half a dozen eggs, some bacon, a can of beef chili and one of luncheon meat and a bunch of bananas. It was after dark when I pulled into an empty parking lot near Sombrio Beach.

A Parks Canada notice said:

PARK USERS ARE ADVISED AGAINST LEAVING VALUABLES IN CARS. NO OVERNIGHT CAMPING.

I left the MG unlocked to save broken windows and followed my flashlight's beam along a seldom-used trail through cold, dark woods. By the time I'd walked to Chief Numcamais' cabin, the beam was a dim glow. Nobody replied when I hailed the house. I went in. The stove was cold and there was no sign of the chief or his pet raven. I lit the stove and made myself at home. After a dinner of chili, a banana and a cup of tea, I lay down on the chief's bed and had a good night's sleep.

I awoke at daybreak, got the stove going and looked outside. There had been no fresh snow overnight. I breakfasted on bacon and eggs, built up the chief's woodpile and left the cabin the way I'd found it. With sandwiches in a zip-loc bag, plus bananas and a bottle of water, I set out to follow the chief's tracks. His prints lay close together and showed heavy heel strikes, as befitted a very old man. He'd moved along steadily, though—I could tell by the little clumps of snow kicked up by the swing of his legs.

First Nations people have selectively logged this section of coastal forest for a thousand years or more. Many giant cedars showed signs of cultural modification by ancient bark weavers, who had used the shredded or beaten cedarbark to make clothing and mats. Undulating terrain made walking easy. Apart from isolated clumps of salal and Oregon grape, there was little undergrowth. The chief's trail ran parallel with the shore for the most part, then his footprints suddenly looped inland and ceased entirely before a dense thicket of bushes and loose rock. He had left no back trail, so obviously there was a way ahead. It took me a while to find it, though, and it involved a bit of climbing, a bit of crawling and a lot of squeezing through narrow spaces. Eventually I came out on a treed escarpment overlooking the sea.

With a telescope I might have been able to see my Coast Salish cousins and their villages, 30 miles distant on the U.S. side of the Strait of Juan de Fuca. As it was, I could just make out a couple of sailboats and a barge under tow by a slow-moving tug. Then I saw, closer in, a 16-foot aluminum runabout with three people aboard, inward bound. Immediately below me was the beach the chief and I had previously visited. I spotted a heavy knotted rope, one end tethered to an arbutus. The rope disappeared down a narrow hole. I knew where it had to lead.

The rope was old, and it looked a bit rotten. Throwing caution to the wind, I used it to lower myself to the bottom of the cave.

Chief Numcamais had lit a fire down there and was seated beside it, smoking a pipe and gazing impassively into the flames. "I've been expecting you, Silas. I need company. It's not good for a man to leave this world on his own."

The cave was reasonably warm—I imagined its inside temperature was fairly constant, year round.

"There's a boat heading this way with three people on it," I said. "They'll be able to land here if they want to."

Seemingly unperturbed, the chief took a tea kettle from the fire and filled two enamel mugs. I took one and warmed my hands on it till the liquid was cool enough to drink. I toasted a Spam sandwich on the fire and offered it to the chief, but he had a bag of dried mushrooms and said that was all he needed.

He ground some of the mushrooms to powder between his palms and dumped it into our mugs. "Drink up," he said.

The potion tasted foul, but I did as I was told. By the time I'd washed the mushrooms down with unadulterated tea, my heart was racing …

Chief Numcamais was addressing prayers to the Sun, who rewarded good behaviour, when souls emerged from the shadows and walked into the firelight from between the whale ribs. I knew they were life souls because many of them were tiny replicas of people I'd known before they died. They were wearing Chilcat blankets, which surprised me, because Coast Salish ghost people generally wear Hudson's Bay blankets on their travels. The life souls came on toward the fire in a little procession, one after the other, behind the life soul and the heart soul owned by Chief Numcamais.

I felt sorry, because after death the life souls of all but infants go to the land of the dead. Heart souls perish with the body. Chief Numcamais's time was up. He was old and ready to go. It occurred to me that those whale bones and stalactites created a nice cathedral effect. If a man had to leave this life, this quiet cave was as good a departure point as any.

Eight life souls went into the little house at the back of the cave and returned with a coffin that they placed in front of us. The chief had spent the best part of a year carving that coffin, and he'd done a first-class job. It would be completely watertight, with beautiful bentwood joints.

Numcamais had been smiling with his eyes closed. Now he

opened his eyes and said to me, "Chief Alphonse told me you've been reading about Edward Curtis."

"That's right. I've got one of his books at home."

"Well, if you know about Edward Curtis you'll know about George Hunt as well," the chief said, taking a stone tobacco pipe from his pocket and stuffing its bowl with dark shag. He was doing everything slowly, as if he had all the time in the world. The life souls were in no hurry either. They made themselves comfortable around us.

With his pipe drawing nicely, Numcamais said, "Back about a hundred years ago, an American museum was interested in getting west-coast Native stuff. George Hunt did some collecting for them—totem poles, baskets, argillite carvings, the usual. But Hunt knew about something special. It was a whaler's shrine up Mowachaht way, hidden away in the woods on an island near Nootka Sound. It wasn't in a cave like this one. It was inside a cedar lodge, but it had 50 or 60 carved wooden figures, same as ours.

"Hunt made a deal to sell the shrine to his museum pals, but local Indians got wind of this. Big trouble. Rival chieftains claimed ownership of that shrine. Hunt ended up paying the chieftains $250 each—big money back then. The Mowachahts gave up their claim and Hunt and his helpers dismantled the whole outfit and moved it off site in one night. When the shrine reached New York, every artifact went straight into storage."

"Makes you wonder why they took it in the first place," I said.

The chief's pipe had gone out and he'd stopped listening to me. His heart soul took the pipe and dropped it into the fire. A little cloud of bright sparks leapt above the flames as the chief's heart soul stood up, straightened itself out and got into its coffin.

It was very pretty, the way Chief Numcamais's heart soul laid itself nicely down and folded its arms across its chest and closed its eyes on this world. His life soul was departing for the unknown. I didn't have the courage to watch it go, so I closed my eyes. I didn't want to know what kind of creatures were coming to take it to the unknown world.

I *did* know that in the beginning of time there were beings with human and animal qualities. That age ended when the Transformer changed certain living beings into stone, others into salmon or elk or worms. Some beings became fully human and were taught how to behave properly. Some early beings became two-headed snakes and crocodiles. I was thinking of these things when an elk the size of a locomotive came crashing into the back of the cave. It had antlers like leaf-denuded oak trees. Shaking its head, it demolished the cedar house, scattered stalactites and whalebones like chaff, then turned to face me. Flames shot from the elk's nose and scorched my face ...

I WOKE UP feeling dizzy.

The chief was smiling at me. "Powerful, them mushrooms?"

"You better believe it. I was hallucinating like crazy."

Numcamais stood up slowly. I helped him across to his coffin and got him settled inside it, for real this time.

Looking up at me he said, "This whaling shrine has lasted 200 years, maybe more. Pretty soon, I guess, thieves will find it and take it away to sell to the highest bidder. It's time we hid the place permanently."

"How are we going to do that?"

"Blow it up." The chief was very tired and his voice was low now. I leaned forward. He said, "It's all set, Silas. The charge is laid. All you've got to do is start a timer, then clear out."

His eyes closed. I kissed his forehead.

The chief had laid his improvised explosive device near the cave's underwater entrance. Its main ingredients were sacks of nitrate fertilizer and buckets of diesel oil. Its detonator was wired to a five-dollar alarm clock. It was the kind of explosive we use for blasting stumps. I figured out how this one worked, then went back to the coffin.

The chief was dead. I put the coffin lid in place and sat beside it for a while.

I set the alarm to go off after 20 minutes and flicked the switch. If things went right, I'd be outside the cave and well away before the explosion.

I started to climb out of the cave and was 10 feet up the rope when it snapped. I landed awkwardly, banging my head, and felt dizzy for a minute. But I wasn't dizzy enough to forget about that timer ticking away nearby. There was no way *up*, but there was still one way out. I quickly sealed my cellphone in the zip-lock bag that had held my sandwich, put it in my pocket and, fully dressed, swam out of the cave.

When I surfaced, shivering, and hauled myself onto the beach, I saw the aluminum runabout grounded 10 feet away. Mo Dillon and two young men were poking around at the base of the cliffs with long fibreglass fishing rods. The sudden appearance of a human being, rising from the sea like a seal, had startled them. I tried to run, but they recovered fast and tackled me. It was three against one. I didn't struggle.

His small black eyes showing amusement, Dillon said, "Fuck a duck. So we meet again, Siwash. I thought we might."

Frigid blasts blew in from the sea.

Dillon said, "Remember that time I busted Barnickle's nose?"

"Yeah, Mo. I remember."

"Busted Barnickle's nose and broke the principal's arm. But that's nothing compared to what *you'll* get if you don't help me out."

"What do you want?"

"I want to know exactly where the whaling shrine is," Dillon said. "Where *exactly*."

"Over there. I just left it," I said, inclining my head. "It's inside a cave with an underwater entrance."

"Perfect," Dillon said. "So the question now is, what're we gonna do with you?"

"Whatever you do, you've got to do it someplace else. This beach is going to be—"

"Shut the fuck up," Dillon interrupted. Scowling, he reached down and picked up a smooth rock the size of a tennis ball. I watched him toss it idly from hand to hand.

"We've been expecting you to find this place," I said.

"Oh? And what makes you so fucking smart?"

"The word was all over town that somebody was looking for a whaling shrine."

Dillon stopped throwing the rock and held it in one hand.

I said hurriedly, "Look, Mo. I'm levelling with you. There's an explosive set to go off inside that cave. When it does, it'll block the entrance. Go inside, and you'll die."

"Right." Dillon swore softly beneath his breath and said, "The shrine. It's in a big cave?"

"Pretty big. Size of a large house, I guess."

"Is it dark in there?"

"There's a bit of natural light. Right now there's a small fire going."

"Good," Dillon said. "A nice fire to warm ourselves by."

"Tell me something, Mo. Now that you've found the shrine, what're you gonna do with it?"

"Sell the fucker," Dillon said. "Ship it south."

One of the young men laughed. I shot him a quick look, then turned back to face Dillon just in time to catch a glimpse of the rock in his hand before he swung it at my skull. I tried to ride with the blow. Light danced inside my head and everything outside my head blurred. I was falling to my knees when Dillon hit me again. I was probably only unconscious for a minute or two, but when I came to, I was in the boat, tied to a seat. In my wet clothes I was very, very cold. Dillon was standing on the beach, grinning, enjoying my obvious discomfort.

Teeth chattering, I tried again to reason. "Don't do it, Mo, it's rigged to blow any minute."

"Fucking idiot," he said, and he walked off toward the cliff.

I concentrated on trying to release myself. Mo Dillon dived into the water first, followed by one of his sidekicks. The remaining man was shifting his weight from foot to foot, like a child overdue for a trip to the bathroom. He came over to me. "All this shit about explosives," he said. "You're kidding, right?"

"No, I'm not," I said. "What's your name?"

"Alex."

"Didn't I see you hanging around the Gorge dig once, Alex?"

Instead of answering, he turned and walked back toward the foot of the cliff.

"Come back," I shouted, struggling to free myself from the ropes. "We're running out of time."

I was still working on the knots when I heard the explosion. Ten thousand tons of loose earth, trees and rocks started to slide down the cliff. I watched it bury Alex and roll toward me in an inexorable wave.

"How the hell did I get here?" I asked. I was lying in a hospital bed. Bernie Tapp was at the foot of the bed, watching me. He was unshaven, bleary-eyed. A nurse was in the room, examining my chart. I felt pretty good except for a mean headache.

"What do you mean, how did you get here? The coast guard rescued you from a beach up near Sombrio. They said you were raving, incoherent, " Bernie said. "You're in the General. Don't you remember *anything?*"

What I recalled was waking up on the beach some time after the explosion, half-buried in sand. When I opened my eyes the only living thing I saw was a black cormorant, standing on a massive rock drying its armpits. There was no sign of the aluminum boat, although I was still tethered to one of its wooden seats. It took me awhile to free myself. When I finally succeeded, I took off my clothes, squeezed out most of the moisture and put them back on again. I found my cellphone in my pocket and prayed that it would work this time. It did. I used it to call for help.

"What happened to the guys from that runabout?" I asked Bernie.

He and the nurse exchanged glances.

"Post-traumatic stress. It does funny things to people sometimes," she said reassuringly. "He'll be all right."

Bernie cleared his throat and said, "Sorry, pal. You're the only person the coast guard took off the beach. They never said anything about other guys to me."

"Well," I said. "I'm obviously very confused."

"They think an unexploded mine went off—one of those ones that drifted across the Pacific during the Second World War. It's happened before."

"That'd explain it," I said. "An unexploded mine fits the facts perfectly."

I was feeling better every minute.

Then Bernie asked the inevitable question. "What were you doing on that beach in the first place?"

"Can't remember," I said. "It's a complete blur."

CHAPTER TWENTY

I was resting at home the next evening when somebody outside started screaming. The noise was coming from the beach. We had been expecting those screams for days. There was no visible moon, but every light was on in the village. People were running from houses and campers and tents, forming excited lines from the water's edge to the door of our longhouse. A spirit quester—or his ghost—was arriving from the unknown world. Now our great Winter Ceremony could begin in earnest. I climbed onto the roof of my cabin for a perfect view. The beach was lit with bonfires and searchlights. Warriors in Thunderbird and Raven masks guarded the naked man designated to be the spirit quester's next meal. Old Mary Cooke was standing by to ensure that the spirit quester followed protocol.

I recognized the spirit quester as Johnny Grant, Chief Alphonse's grandson. The 20-year-old came trotting toward us along the shore, wolf skins dangling from his shoulders.

Singers chanted: "Biter-Me man fell on the leg. Biter-Me man fell on the arm."

Yelling, Johnny Grant leapt upon the naked man. Wolf men pounced upon Johnny before he bit too deeply. Half-naked girls lured Johnny inside the longhouse.

Drummers had taken up the dancers' rhythmic chant. Soon the whole village was singing.

Ba Ta Ma Fe Oh La.

Ba Ta Ma Fe Oh Aa.

Inside the longhouse, Old Mary Cooke was ministering to the Bitten Man, sucking ghosts from his soul through a hollow bone. Further ceremonies would take place after Johnny Grant had been prepared for the next stage of his hamatsa journey, a procedure that might take hours or days.

I came down from the roof and went inside to clean up. Towelling myself dry by my nice warm wood stove, I thought about Bernie. I realized I had to see him again, clear up a few more loose ends up for the record. Let Bernie take the credit. He was ambitious, and my prospects for promotion were nil, whatever I did.

I dressed warmly and went out. It was dark behind my house— kids had busted the halogen light where I parked my MG. I had those youngsters and their slingshots to thank for several sets of barked shins. I needed to talk to them about it sometime. I had one foot inside my car when I heard a familiar voice behind. "Going somewhere?"

When my eyes had adjusted to the darkness and I could see who had spoken, my heart lurched and the hair on my neck rose.

Very, very slowly I withdrew my foot from the car. The tiny, white-haired woman in a ratty fur coat and tinted glasses was aiming an automatic pistol at my face. We stared at each other, six feet apart. For a long beat I could not trust myself to speak. My mouth was dry. I figured death was moments away. I had to say the right thing, and suddenly I knew what the right thing was. "Hello, Mrs. Tranter," I whispered.

Her serious expression faded and she smiled. In a clipped English accent she said, "We'll take my car, Sergeant. You drive."

I DROVE THE Monte Carlo into the driveway of the house on Gladstone Avenue and parked. The psychopath who had shared the drive with me directed me out of the car and into the house.

I stood in the living room, seeing again those cheap area rugs and the leather recliner angled toward a big plasma-screen TV. She was leaning against the door, grinning. Intense heat radiated from the gas fireplace. I wanted to ask her if I could take my raincoat off, but I didn't trust myself to speak. She still held the pistol in one hand, her finger curled around its trigger, ready to contract—but not quite yet. With her free hand she reached up slowly and removed her white wig and dark glasses. I was looking, finally, at Ellen Lemieux.

"I fooled you, didn't I?" she laughed. "I fooled everybody!" Still laughing, she unbuttoned her fur coat and let it fall from her shoulders to the floor. She was wearing a fringed black miniskirt. I forced my glance away from her beautiful legs and away from her dark unblinking eyes.

"I did fool you, didn't I? Tell me that I fooled you." She had a plaintive tone, and the phony stage English had been replaced with her natural Nimpkish accent.

"It was brilliant," I said. "You fooled Lofthouse. You fooled everyone."

"Yes, yes," she agreed, eagerly leaning forward, "but I fooled you most of all, didn't I?"

My subservient nods fed her vanity. She slipped more deeply into her natural way of speaking. "But you knew some things, right? A few little details?"

I told her what she wanted to hear. "I was lucky. I found things out by accident."

I was lying. I blamed myself for being blind and stupid. If I'd been smarter, I might have saved my own skin, as well as Sammy's and Grace's.

But she was talking again. "Lennie Jim, the fool who tried to kill you in the parking lot. I suppose he put you wise, gave you some tip-off, right?"

"Yes. He was the one. Lennie tipped me off."

"But the disguise, the disguise I wore when I pretended to be Mrs. Tranter and signed her will, that was a good one. That was fantastic, right?"

"Yes. That fooled me completely."

"I fooled you all." Her mouth opened and her glance slid away as she relived some delicious memory. Contemptuously she said, "Me and Lennie killed Mrs. Tranter, then we took care of Isaac Schwartz. We killed them both. It was so easy for me."

"You had me fooled."

"Sure, because I'm clever, see? Always the clever one. When I found out Mrs. Tranter was worth big money, I made myself cozy with her. She told me that the old German, this Isaac Schwartz guy, was being a nuisance, blackmailing her. I killed him after I found out he had no money of his own.

"When the time was right, Lennie and me killed Mrs. Tranter too. Then I pretended to be Mrs. Tranter and tricked Sammy Lofthouse into making a new will in my favour. Nobody suspected a thing!" She began to giggle. The hand holding the pistol fell to her side.

I said, "Just to satisfy my curiosity, how did you find out that Mrs. Tranter was *really* Lady Baineston?"

"From when I was nursing old lady Micklethwaite. When she knew she was dying she started babbling, told me everything."

"And Sammy Lofthouse. What happened to him?"

"Oh that was another great idea," she said, eager to boast. "Me and Lennie. We kidnapped Mrs. Tranter and kept her here in this house for a while, until we took her to the Red Barn Hotel. Lofthouse was supposed to go there to meet her and find her body. But the cops got there first."

Ellen licked her lips and raised her gun hand again. "When the police wanted Lofthouse to identify the old woman at the morgue—that's when something went wrong. He saw that that dead woman was a lot taller than me—*too* tall. Lofthouse knew *I* wasn't dead."

She was gazing at the floor. I was wondering whether to make a snatch for the gun when she looked up. "Lofthouse was dumb, but he was smarter than you. At least he knew the difference between me and the woman in the morgue."

"The woman I saw at the hotel was face down over a bathtub. The difference in height between you two wasn't that obvious," I told her.

"It was obvious to Lofthouse. He saw the tall woman in the morgue and smelled a rat. He came to see me, trying to get things straight. Right away I killed him. Later, when we heard that Richard Hendrix was arrested in Campbell River, me and Lennie took Lofthouse's body up there and left it in a snowbank."

"You and Sammy. Were you having an affair?"

Instead of answering, she drew her head back and laughed.

Ellen's scheme was undeniably brilliant. How many deaths was she responsible for?

"I suppose Grace Sleight had to die, too," I said. "Grace was the only person left alive, except me, who could ever testify that there was a fake Mrs. Tranter."

Ellen pointed the pistol toward a door and said, "That way to the basement, mister. You and me, we're gonna take a little walk down there." She grinned crookedly. "There's something in the freezer I want you to see. Open that door and start down, real slow. No funny stuff. You've been a good boy so far."

I turned my back to her and started for the door, my whole body tingling. Little currents of electricity ran up and down my spine, as though a bullet was about to lodge itself in there. I opened the basement door and started down the narrow stairway. I could see a white-enamel freezer sitting beneath a window. I wondered what in hell she had put in it. I got to the bottom of the stairs and looked at her.

Her eyes were glazed. It was cold in the basement, and now she was shivering. She whispered, "Open the freezer. I want you to see something."

The freezer wasn't empty. Lennie Jim was in it. But there was still plenty of room for me.

The noise, when it came, startled us both. There was a rapping on the glass of the basement window. I looked up to see a white face pressed to the pane. Ellen's pistol went off. A bullet smashed the window into a thousand fragments. My fist struck Ellen's chin, hard. Her head snapped back as the pistol spoke once more, its bullet nicking the concrete floor before ricocheting to the wall. Ellen's head struck the floor as she landed on her back, her neck twisted.

Outside the window, Baldy, her neighbour, was gazing at infinity, a red bullet hole in his forehead.

I used my brand-new cellphone to call Bernie.

CHAPTER TWENTY-ONE

Twenty-four hours later, Ellen Lemieux was under sedation and police guard in Victoria General's neurosurgical unit. Baldy was in a stainless-steel drawer at the morgue. Detective Chief Inspector Bulloch—more interested in garnering credit for solving a series of murders than in harassing me—was busy with press conferences. I was at home, thinking about Felicity Exeter and the party at her place that I'd been invited to. Her invitation had said casual. Certainly not jeans, I thought. Not to a party at Felicity's. I decided on the same clothes I'd worn to the art gallery.

I had a lot to tell Felicity. She would be pleased to learn that her faith in Richard Hendrix had been justified. She'd be interested to hear the complete story of the Nimpkish waif who'd fooled clever lawyers and stupid detectives and come close to inheriting a million-dollar property. I had questions for Felicity, too. It would have taken a lot to keep me home *that* night.

Fresh snow was coming down as I drove out toward View Royal. My windows kept fogging, so I was hunched forward, wiping condensation from the windshield with paper towels. Beyond the city limits the snow was deeper. A big northbound 18-wheeler passed me, encased in clouds of whirling ice crystals. The monster vehicle, festooned with red and white lights and equipped with multiple headlights, carved a moving sphere of light that I followed for a mile before I took the View Royal off-ramp. Somewhere out there, hidden in the dark, was the north end of Esquimalt Harbour and the Six-Mile pub. Also hidden were the ugly commercial developments marring this once-beautiful country road.

The MG purred along. I slowed it to a crawl and turned onto the narrow side road leading to Felicity Exeter's farm. The snow was drier here. A few cars squeezed past me, going the opposite way in a convoy. I guessed they were Felicity's departing guests, leaving early before snow socked them in for the night. The snowflakes were smaller now, hard and dry, blanketing the fields that stretched to the limits of sight. I could see no lights, either ahead or behind. I continued to where a snow-covered finger post pointed left. I slid to a stop and got out of the car for another look. I had reached Felicity Exeter's property line. I drove across a cattle-stop and found myself in a featureless landscape. Snow obliterated the road. I switched off the headlights and saw house lights glimmering in the near distance. I left the car and trudged across a white expanse to a grove of evergreens where the snow was less deep. Beyond the trees was the grey outline of a guest cottage. I finally reached Felicity's house. Clumsy with cold, I was fumbling with the bell push when outdoor lights came on. The door opened. Felicity Exeter stood there, barefoot, wearing a black dress that ended six inches above her knees.

"Why Mr. Seaweed," she said, stepping aside to let me in, "What a lovely surprise."

THE FIRE HAD burned low. I put my empty wineglass down, reached out from my place on the long sofa and switched off a table lamp. Felicity, stretched out on the sofa with her feet on my lap, murmured contentedly. I stroked one silken foot with my fingertips. Her foot arched as my fingers ran across her heel and ankle and the lower part of her leg. Her voice was low. She said huskily, "Don't stop what you're doing, but tell me the rest of it—I'm still not clear how Isaac Schwartz fits in."

"Isaac found out that the drawings he'd lost to Baineston before the war were being sold at Tuttle's. By the time Isaac figured out who had consigned them, Sir Hugh had died of old age. Schwartz was denied revenge. I don't know what he would have done if he'd found Baineston alive, but he could, and did, put pressure on Baineston's widow. He forced her to hand over what was left of their art collection. Schwartz sold it and gave the money to Joe McNaught. By a fluke, Ellen Lemieux discovered the whole secret and devised the idea of masquerading as Mrs. Tranter. She was angry, though, because Schwartz had beaten her to the money. Ellen went to Moran's gym with Lennie, and they killed Schwartz. Ellen conned Lofthouse the same way she conned me, by kidnapping and impersonating Mrs. Tranter."

"Yes, I understand that. But how did she hoodwink Richard?"

"Richard was away in Tofino the whole time Ellen was engineering her scam. Richard never met his fake aunt. Sammy never met Derek Battle's *real* client. Ellen was amazingly clever about it all. Not to say lucky. She was also setting Richard up as a patsy. He was the prime suspect when Mrs. Tranter was murdered. The scheme nearly worked. When I discovered that Ellen had nursed Mrs. Micklethwaite, that she had prior knowledge of the Bainestons, and that the real Mrs. Tranter/Baineston was a head taller than the woman who signed the will, things fell into place."

My hand was gently stroking Felicity's knee.

She said dreamily, "Tell me about the man who strangled Grace and tried to kill you in the parking lot."

"Lennie Jim. Lennie was just a poor schmuck Ellen recruited

to do her grunt work. She assumed Isaac still possessed valuable art, and when she found out he didn't, they murdered him. Killing must have excited her, because afterwards she and Lennie had sex in Isaac's bed."

Snow had dampened all sound. I thought Felicity had fallen asleep and took my hand away from her leg. Her eyes opened. She said, "I have a canoe. Sometimes I paddle around, setting crab traps. Do you know about those mysteries too? Where crabs are?"

"There are a lot of good crabbing places around here."

"We could go out together sometime. That is, if you like exploring, and you like crab roasts."

"I'd like that. I like canoes and picnics."

After a pause she said suddenly, "Did you find Ellen attractive?"

"She was gorgeous to look at," I replied.

"You didn't answer my question."

"All right. I thought Ellen was very attractive. But that was before I spoke to her in the art gallery. Afterwards, I knew that she was a seriously flawed human being. She stole a coat that night, although I couldn't do anything about it. Not then."

"She was a monster."

"She was *crazy*," I said. "Baineston was a crook, but he had one redeeming feature. He stole art because he loved beautiful things. Those people planning to loot the whaling shrine were just greedy."

"Few of us seem to understand that we can never really *own* anything—except ideas. Memories of people, and poetry, and ideas. Things not made, but earned."

Her eyes were like little diamond points.

"I've been meaning to ask you," I said. "Who's Fred Porteous?"

She chuckled deep in her throat and stirred slightly, pushing both feet against my thigh. Smiling, she curled upright and brushed my cheek with her lips. She said, "Fred's my handyman. Keeps an eye on the place when I'm not around. Helps me with the sheep."

She got up and walked across the room, pausing for a moment to stand in the doorway of her bedroom and look back at me. Smiling, she turned away.

CHAPTER TWENTY-TWO

The entrance to the Warrior longhouse is at the gable end, facing the sea. Its doorposts are carved and painted heraldic poles. The door itself is shaped like a raven's head; a long red plank represents the raven's tongue. To enter the house, you ascend the tongue. When you reach the top the tongue pivots, like a teeter-totter, and lets you descend into the raven's belly.

The longhouse was jam-packed with Coast Salish from up and down the coast. It was dark in there, and hot. Two eagle-masked warriors showed Felicity and me to the high tiers normally reserved for women.

Chief Alphonse was standing alone in the centre of the house, near a blazing fire. He had a talking-stick in one hand and a carved wooden rattle in the other, and was magnificent in a woven cedar-bark steeple hat and a long red blanket decorated with pearl buttons. On the floor, spaced at intervals around the room, were drummers and singers wearing eagle-feather suits. We'd arrived just in time to see six shamans emerge from the underworld—a hole in the floor. The drummers had been beating a regular rhythm till then. At the shamans' arrival the drummers increased their tempo. Shamans began to dance and sing the Biter-Me song. Men and women with

SEAWEED ON ICE   **215**

rattle bracelets around their wrists and ankles came down from the tiers and joined the shamans in a circle dance. Others took up the shamans' chant. The noise became stupendous when Joey Mack, who weighed 300 pounds or more, leapt onto the floor carrying a bottle of oolichan oil. Joey downed the whole bottle in one draught, whereupon, stupefied, he fell flat on his face. It took several warriors to carry him off.

Chief Alphonse shook his rattle and pounded with his talking-stick to restore order. The audience members returned to their seats. The brief ensuing silence was broken by overhead wailing. Wails became screams when Johnny Grant appeared at a hole in the roof and dropped partway down into the longhouse. I knew what to expect because I'd seen this before, but even so it's always a shocker.

Johnny's naked body gleamed with sweat. He was suspended from four ropes—one around each bicep, the others around his ankles. Beside me, Felicity caught her breath and shivered with fright. I put my arms around her and held her close as Johnny was slowly lowered to the ground. After a moment's rest, Johnny was hoisted aloft again.

Dangling from the roof, Johnny sang his hamatsa song in Coast Salish. Translated, it was:

He went all around the unknown world to find food,
He went all around the unknown world to find human flesh,
He went all around the unknown world to find human heads,
He went all around the unknown world to find corpses.

Johnny's expression was seraphic. When his song ended, he was lowered to the ground. Chief Alphonse pounded with his talking-stick and shook his rattle again. Johnny lay inert until four big wolf-men with ropes sprang forward. Johnny tried to escape, but the wolf-men held him. Old Mary Cooke made hand medicine over his body.

Naked men emerged from the underworld. When Johnny saw them, he became enraged. Gnashing his teeth, howling, he towed his attendants to a male victim, seized an arm and appeared to bite a chunk out of it. A shaman sprang forward to examine the victim's wound.

Again, Chief Alphonse pounded the floor with his talking-stick. Singing and dancing seductively, half-naked girls enticed Johnny into a subterranean den, and we saw him no more.

WE HAD GATHERED to lay the foundation stone for Joe McNaught's new mission. Joe was standing on a dais, clutching a microphone and smiling at the small crowd. To my eyes, the pastor looked more like an all-in wrestler than a cleric, but I had to admit that he was an impressive figure. McNaught's scarlet robe, billowing in a warm summer breeze, emphasized his vast girth. In comparison, Victoria's mayor and her entourage looked drab and uninteresting. Derek Battle was there, along with a few government dignitaries and representatives of main-line religions. Nimrod fussed about, apparently healthy and certainly energetic after rehab. Detective Chief Inspector Bulloch was there in full uniform. He had been lionized by local media for capturing Ellen Lemieux and was still basking in the radiant glow of good publicity. Bulloch's name was even being bandied about as Chief Mallory's possible successor.

McNaught droned on and on. Bernie stood beside me, shaking his head and frowning. Like me, Bernie seldom took McNaught at face value. Cynics, we were always alert for hidden agendas and semi-serious skulduggery.

"Derek Battle and Joe McNaught appear to have settled their differences," I said.

Bernie nodded. "Battle had no choice. Baineston's money was supposed to go to charities in accordance with Baineston's express wishes. The Good Shepherd wasn't even on the list. But possession, as they say, is nine-tenths of the law. Isaac Schwartz diverted all of his gains to the Good Shepherd. McNaught spent the money as fast as Schwartz handed it over."

"Speaking of handing things over. How's Ellen Lemieux doing?" I asked.

"Still out of it. She'll be detained in a psych hospital during Her Majesty's pleasure. I hope it's a long time, because that woman is nuts. She had a long rap sheet up north. Her dad is supposed to have died in a hunting accident. Bella Coola RCMP think Ellen shot him, but they couldn't gather enough evidence to charge her."

McNaught was winding up an immodest personal history.

Bernie nudged me and said, "Here comes that big surprise I was telling you about."

McNaught stretched out a hand. Nimrod put a silver-plated trowel in it. At the same time, a big yellow construction crane lifted a polished-granite foundation stone into the air and swung it into position.

McNaught pointed and said, "This foundation stone is being dedicated to the glory of God and to the eternal memory of our chief benefactor and friend, the late Isaac Schwartz. We are raising a temple to feed the souls and bodies of our beloved congregation."

The mayor started clapping. Polite people joined in. The crane operator gave his air horn a few jolly toots.

McNaught, enjoying himself, added, "Isaac Schwartz was a good man, maybe a bit unorthodox. A lot of people have the wrong idea about the way that Mr. Schwartz earned his riches, for which I blame the popular press. But I say this: the Lord's work needed money, and Isaac was the guy who delivered." He continued in this vein for another 10 minutes, outlining the good works planned for the new mission.

The construction boss—visibly impatient—came forward, tugged McNaught's sleeve and pointed to his wristwatch. The pastor wanted to argue. The boss put both hands on his hips, leaned forward and jutted out his chin until McNaught backed off. By now the crowd had thinned. Casual spectators, bored and not knowing what was going on or who McNaught was, were drifting away. The pastor waddled to the edge of the dais and down two steps to the spot where the foundation stone lay. The mayor, wearing her gold chain of office, got to her feet, looking flustered, and hastened to McNaught's side. Then she and McNaught started to argue.

I said, "Let me guess. The mayor expected *her* name to be on that foundation stone, right?"

"It ought to be. That's what McNaught promised her," Bernie said, smirking. "But he put his own name on it instead. It's a ploy not unknown in politics."

"A controversial guy, McNaught. Knows how to attract publicity."

"You said it, pal." Bernie raised and dropped his shoulders in a gesture of weary resignation. "I've had enough of this. What do you say we grab a cup of coffee?"

We turned our backs on the arguing mayor and the beaming preacher and walked away. The sun was hot. Men and women strolling by had the cheerful look of summer vacationers.

Bernie said, "Missing Persons is looking for Mo Dillon."

"That right?" I said, staring straight ahead.

"His mother reported him missing around the time that Second World War mine nearly killed you."

"Amazing coincidence."

"That's what I think. How's Ms. Exeter?"

"Fine. We're going canoeing later, catch a few crabs. Later on we'll have a roast and eat 'em on the beach."

"Before you do that for her, how about doing something for me?" Bernie said, coming to a stop and looking me in the eye.

"Depends," I said. "What do you want?"

"Tell me how Isaac Schwartz's body was moved from Mowaht beach to Chief Mishtop's cabin."

I shook my head and smiled.

Bernie persisted. "Nobody's gonna tell me two normal people carried him up there that day. It was tough enough for us to *walk* in all that mud, so don't tell me Lennie Jim and Ellen Lemieux did it."

I told a lie that sounded like truth and said I didn't know how the body got there. I didn't know how could I tell Bernie, in all seriousness, that Isaac Schwartz's body had obviously been moved by *something*, and that the only suspect I could think of was a creature called Man-Eater-at-the-North-End-of-the-World.

ABOUT THE AUTHOR

STANLEY EVANS' previous novels are *Outlaw Gold*, *Snow-Coming Moon* and the five books in the Silas Seaweed series: *Seaweed on the Street*, *Seaweed on Ice*, *Seaweed under Water*, *Seaweed on the Rocks* and *Seaweed in the Soup*. Stanley and his family live in Victoria, BC.

ISBN: 978-1-894898-34-8   ISBN: 978-1-894898-51-5   ISBN: 978-1-894898-57-7

ISBN: 978-1-894898-73-7   ISBN: 978-1-894898-92-8

"Makes great use of the West Coast aboriginal mythology and religion."—*The Globe and Mail*

"The writing is wonderful native story telling. Characters are richly drawn . . . I enjoyed this so much that I'm looking for the others in the series."—*Hamilton Spectator*